WE CAN'T BE BROKEN

H.K. CHRISTIE

First edition: February 2017

ISBN: 0-9982856-0-9

ISBN-13: 978-0-9982856-0-3

For my family

CHAPTER 1

I WOKE to the sound of footsteps running down the hall and a voice yelling, "The *baby* is coming!" The baby is coming? Ohh. The baby is coming! I jumped out of bed and ran down the hall, being careful not to slip on the hardwood floors. I reached Mom and Dad's room and stood in the doorway. Mom was lying on the bed with her long curly brown hair wound up in a bun and her bright blue eyes focused on the midwife, Callie, as beads of sweat trickled down the sides of her face. Callie, an older lady with tan skin, chocolate-colored eyes and straight, waist-length brown hair, stood next to the bed speaking intently to Mom. Dad, a tall guy with silver hair and blue-gray eyes, was already dressed for the day in blue slacks and a white button-down shirt and stood at the foot of the bed in a huddle with my sister, Kelly, and my brother, Sam. Dad saw me standing in the doorway and waved me over.

I walked toward the huddle and noticed Sam was suffering from serious bed head, his straight brown hair going in all directions, and Kelly had her dark curly hair pulled back in a messy ponytail. Both were still in their pajamas. I leaned into the huddle. "What did I miss?"

Dad said, "Mom's in labor. Callie thinks the baby will be here soon. The three of you can stay in here, but you need to be extremely quiet and can't bother your Mom. Okay?"

Kelly, Sam and I agreed. Suddenly Mom started groaning and let out a loud scream. Kelly, Sam and I glanced at one another in horror. Callie attempted to comfort Mom. "You are doing great, Agatha. That was a good one. Are you ready to start pushing on the next contraction?"

Mom struggled to respond but finally said, "Okay."

Callie called out to Dad, "Jasper, I'm going to switch places with you. Come stand by Agatha and hold her hand." Dad walked quickly over to Mom.

She then approached Kelly, Sam and me. "Okay, kids, are you ready to see your new baby brother or sister? He or she will be here pretty soon! I'm going to need you to stand over there on the other side of the bed, okay?" We silently nodded.

I remembered going to Mom's prenatal visits and thinking that Callie, who was wearing her usual flowing skirt and Latin-inspired tunic, looked like she still belonged in the seventies, and that a hippie was going to be delivering my new brother or sister. Now here she was doing just that.

Callie walked to the foot of the bed and gently placed her gloved hand on Mom's knee and said, "Whenever you're ready Agatha, push." What followed was screaming from my mother while Dad and Callie assured Mom she was doing a great job. Callie stood up to make eye contact with Mom. "I can see the head, Agatha. Just one more big push!" We heard a loud grunt-like scream from Mom. Within seconds we heard the baby cry.

Kelly, Sam and I mustered up the courage to walk over and see where the crying was coming from. We saw a gooey pink baby with the umbilical cord still attached. Callie held up the baby with one arm and announced, "It's a girl!" Kelly and I cheered.

Sam's blue eyes opened wide. "A girl? Another girl?" The room quickly filled with laughter.

Callie extended her hand, which held a pair of scissors, to Dad. "Well, Dad, do you wanna cut the umbilical cord?"

"Sure." Dad smirked as he reluctantly took the scissors and cut the cord.

Callie picked up a blue washcloth and gently wiped the baby's face and handed her to Mom. We all walked over to Mom, and then Dad leaned in and kissed the baby on the forehead, gazing at her without saying a word. Kelly asked, "What are we going to name her? Did you pick out a girl name too?" Everyone had predicted the baby would be a boy and had already been calling it "Matthew" through Mom's belly.

Dad cocked his head to one side. "Hmm. No. What should we call her?" Mom glanced at Dad and chuckled. "I don't know! I was sure she'd be a boy!" I couldn't believe they hadn't even considered a girl's name. It wasn't like they had known for sure it was going to be a boy, it was just a feeling. Mom and Dad told us they would need some time to figure it out.

In all the excitement I hadn't noticed the carnage that seemed to be everywhere. While we were having our family moment, Callie had been cleaning up the blood and goop that was all over the bed. She stopped and said to me, "You know, in some cultures they eat the placenta. They make a soup and the whole family eats it." I grimaced, as did Sam and Kelly.

She beamed. "Actually, it's quite nutritious!"

I quickly learned that the icky ball of blood that came out of my Mom was the placenta. Yuck! Why would she tell that to a nine-year-old? Mom, who had overheard the conversation, was clearly amused by our reaction. She sat up and said, "Guys, what do you think, should we make placenta soup?" She giggled as she pulled the baby close and gave her a kiss on the cheek. It was unanimous. Nobody wanted placenta soup. While the adults tended to the baby and the mess, I ran into the kitchen to call everyone I knew.

Being nine, I couldn't actually call everyone I knew, since I only knew two phone numbers by heart. First I called our old neighbors, who were less than thrilled to be awoken at 5 a.m. and then called Grandma Jess. When she answered, I said without pause, "Hi, Grandma, it's me, Casey. The baby's here! It's a girl!"

Her voice, now practically a shout, exclaimed, "Oh heavens! A girl!" She told me to tell Mom and Dad that she would be over to the house in about forty-five minutes.

I thought to myself, she must be so excited to finally have a real grandchild. Us kids were technically step-grandkids that she spoiled and treated like her own, but when she had heard the news that Mom and Dad (technically my stepdad) were pregnant, she had screamed, with tears in her eyes, "Finally a grandchild!"

On my way back to Mom and Dad's room I thought back to the first time we had met Grandma Jess. It was about four years ago, when we had just moved in with Dad; I was five, Sam was six and Kelly was eight. Dad had brought us to Grandma Jess's house to introduce us. When she opened the door, I saw that she was curvy with silver curly hair and had Dad's blue-gray eyes and smooth skin. She wore gray slacks with a lavender sweater and a large sparkly necklace. As we stood in the living room, Dad had said, "Hi, Mom. You remember Agatha?"

"Yes, of course, dear. Hi, Agatha." Grandma Jess leaned in and gave Mom a hug.

"How are you, honey?"

"I'm well, thank you." Mom looked over at us kids.

"I'd like to introduce you to my children: Kelly, Sam and Casey." Grandma Jess's eyes widened, and her penciled-in eyebrows arched.

"Well, hello! I've heard so much about you! I'm so glad to finally meet you! Please feel at home and call me Grandma." She went up to each of us and gave us a hug. She led us into the kitchen and offered us cookies fresh from the bakery she worked at. The kitchen was covered in butterflies in the form of magnets, plates, figurines and wallpaper, and some were even hanging from the ceiling on strings. I stood there eating my cookie while trying to count them all. That day, Kelly, Sam and I got a new Grandma, and we loved her.

I got back to Mom and Dad's room to find that it had been cleaned up considerably. Dad was standing next to the bed holding the baby who had been wrapped up in a little green blanket. The baby was so tiny compared to Dad, who was more than six feet tall. I sat on the bed next to Mom and told her, "I just got off the phone with Grandma Jess. She's totally excited. She said she'd be here in forty-five minutes."

Mom replied, "Okay, great."

"So have you come up with a name yet?"

Dad glanced at Mom and said, "Well, we were thinking maybe Agatha, like your mother."

I shook my head. "No! They can't have the same name. What about something like it, like Ann or Anna? But certainly not Agatha."

Dad touched Mom's hand. "What do you think of the name Anna?"

She gazed at the baby in Dad's arms. "I do think she looks like an Anna." Mom reached up to put her hand on Anna's cheek.

She said, "Hi, Anna!" and the baby squirmed.

Dad laughed softly. "I think she likes it. You like that, Anna? Hi, Anna!"

Right then and there it was decided. Her name was Anna.

Anna was here, and our whole life was going to change. A baby sister! Finally, I was no longer the youngest. It was the most exciting day of my life. Despite such a monumental day, Mom and Dad said we had to go to school. School? On a day like this? Anna was here! I wanted to stay home and play with the baby, but

Mom insisted that we had to wait until after school to even hold her. We didn't argue.

I got dressed in a pair of jeans and a red sweater that displayed a friendly penguin. I brushed my teeth, washed my face and combed my straight brown hair, clipping it back with a red floppy bow. I couldn't wait to tell everyone at school about Anna. Before heading off to my school, Mountain Elementary, we had the usual breakfast of cereal and milk. I didn't think it was a very special breakfast for such a special day. We rushed through breakfast, got bundled up in our winter coats and Dad drove us to school.

At school, I ran up to my teacher and told her about Anna. Dad was with me and confirmed that indeed we had a new baby at home. Mrs. Drager congratulated us and assured me I could share the news during show-and-tell. When it was my turn to tell, I got up and walked to the front of the room. All eyes were on me. I beamed, "Today my little sister, Anna, was born!" The kids didn't seem nearly as excited as I expected. They just sat there in their desks staring at me.

During recess, I ran to the giant tires on the playground, excited to tell my best friends, Sally and Heather, about my news. Sally was quiet and funny, while Heather was loud and talked constantly. Lookswise, they were complete opposites too. Sally was tall and lanky with curly blond hair and green eyes, whereas Heather was short and doughy with straight, dark hair and big brown eyes. After I told Heather that I loved her unicorn and glittery rainbow sweatshirt, I shared my news. They seemed mildly interested at best. They were more interested in how Chuck got in trouble during class for making fart noises. These girls just didn't understand what a special day it was. I finally got a younger sibling. I'd been waiting for this my whole life! Or at least since Mom had met Dad.

WHEN MOM MET DAD, I thought to myself, I bet they'll have a baby and I won't be the youngest anymore. Is it weird that that was my first thought when meeting Dad? I remember the day like it was yesterday. We walked up to his jewelry store, passing his white Corvette in the parking lot. Mom had stopped us and said, "Look there, kids, he drives a Corvette and it has an eight track in it!" I didn't know what an eight track was, but Mom made it seem like it was pretty great. When we walked into the narrow shop filled with glittery diamonds and shiny gold, Dad was standing behind the counter. He leaned over to give Mom a kiss and then said hello to us kids. I had admired his silvery hair that matched all the jewels in the case. Although he was obviously older than Mom, she didn't mind and we thought he seemed nice.

AT LUNCH, Sally, Heather and I ate our lunches and then walked around the track. The talk about Anna had already faded, and the topic switched to who had the most pairs of Guess jeans. Apparently, Chrissy had three pairs of Guess jeans and a pair of pink Reebok sneakers. Some kids were so lucky.

Finally, the school day ended and we were going to get to go home and see Anna. Once the bell rang, I packed my things into my backpack and walked to the front of the school where Dad was going to pick us up. I approached the pickup curb and saw Kelly and Sam were already there. Kelly, always fashionable, was wearing acid-washed jeans, a white cable-knit sweater and a green beaded necklace. She always tried to wear something green because she said it brought out the green in her eyes. I walked up to them. "Hey."

Kelly, with her I'm-so-cool-because-I'm-a-sixth-grader attitude, said, "We were just talking about Anna and who gets to hold her first. I think I get to hold her first because I'm the oldest."

Sam squinted. "Well, if that's the case, then I get to hold her after Kelly. You're last!" As he laughed at me, his brown hair bounced up and down.

I rolled my eyes. "What's new? I'm always last."

Just then Dad pulled up in our new blue station wagon. Kelly sat in the front as Sam and I climbed in the back. When we got home, the three of us ran through the front door and headed straight for Mom and Dad's room. Mom instantly told us to be quiet and to wash our hands if we wanted to hold Anna.

We ran to the bathroom that was just outside the room. Kelly washed first and left the bathroom; Sam was next and then me. After I finished washing my hands, I went back into the room and sat on the edge of the bed next to Sam. Kelly sat closest to Mom, holding the baby, rocking her from side to side while trying to avoid having her long dark, curly hair hit Anna in the face. A few minutes later, Mom suggested that Kelly let Sam hold the baby. Reluctantly Kelly handed the baby to Sam, kissed her on the cheek, told Mom she'd see her later and left the room.

Sam held her tight and began talking to her. "Hi, Anna! It's me, your brother, Sam." Anna just stared at him with her wide blue eyes. Soon Anna started to fidget and make funny noises. I told Sam, "I think she's trying to tell you that she wants me to hold her."

Sam smirked at me. "I don't think that is what she's saying. I think she's trying to say, Sam is the best! Aren't you, Anna?"

Mom put her hand on Sam's arm. "Sam, why don't you go ahead and let Casey hold her. Anna needs to eat soon."

Sam carefully handed Anna to me while explaining I had to support her head and then walked out of the room, waving to Mom as he left. As I cautiously cradled Anna in my arms, I tried my best to not drop her. I sat there staring at her pink squishy face and big eyes that stared back at me. She was like a real-life Cabbage Patch Kid. Except that Cabbage Patch Kids didn't come with quite so many accessories!

Mom and Dad's room was now overflowing with piles of tiny

baby clothes, blankets and washcloths that were all stacked on top of Mom's dresser on the left side of the room. At the end of the dresser was a diaper pail with deodorizer to keep from stinking up the house as well as a giant bag of cloth diapers freshly delivered from the diaper service. I didn't understand why Anna couldn't have disposable diapers like all of the other babies. I think Mom was just being old-fashioned, like when she made the decision to have a home birth. I don't think I'd ever met anyone who wore cloth diapers and was born at home other than Anna. It was 1986, not 1886!

As I held her she continued to make funny little noises and wiggle around. When Anna started to cry, I asked, "What should I do?"

"She's probably hungry. Why don't you hand her to me."

I carefully handed Anna to Mom.

"I think we both need our rest."

"I understand. Bye, Anna! Get lots of rest!" I waved at Mom as I walked out of the room and set out to find out where everyone had gone.

I walked down the hall to the TV room and found Dad, Kelly and Sam sitting on the couch watching a show while discussing what to have for dinner. Dad decided pizza was the best and easiest option; we agreed. Over dinner, I wondered if Anna would take all the cheese and toppings off her pizza like I did. Maybe. Kelly and Sam always made fun of me and said I was weird.

After dinner we did our homework, watched The Cosby Show and then headed back to our room to put on our pj's. It was a rare night where Kelly would let me listen to my radio station in our room. I was thrilled to hear my favorite song, "Let's Hear It for the Boy." I sang as I danced around the room, blissfully unaware that just fourteen months later we would get devastating news that would change our lives forever.

CHAPTER 2

ON A LAZY SATURDAY MORNING, I sat on the living room floor watching Anna at her new play kitchen. She was decked out in rainbow-striped pants, a long-sleeve yellow shirt and a thin yellow headband that held back her shoulder-length, strawberry blonde hair. The kitchen set was pink with a fake oven and microwave that didn't open. It was given to her a few months before for her first birthday and she wasn't quite sure what to do with it. Up until now she used it mostly as a crutch to avoid falling. Her walking still needed a bit of work, as she was pretty wobbly and often dropped to her bottom or flat on her face when she tried to run.

While I tried to show her how to pretend cook on the pretend stove, Anna clutched her fake plastic sink and made a funny squinting face. I chuckled. "What are you doing, Anna?" She grinned at me and did it again. I shouted over to Sam. "Hey, Sam, you've gotta see this face Anna's making!" Sam ran over from the couch and sat in front of Anna and me.

"Oh my God, Sam. You've gotta see this face." I told Anna, "Do the face, Anna!" Anna braced herself while making the same funny scrunched-up face. Sam and I cracked up as Anna smiled, proud of herself. Kelly heard the commotion from our bedroom and walked over. She peered over at Anna. Between fits of laughter, Sam explained, "Anna is making this face. It's hilarious. You've got to see." Sam looked at Anna. "Do the face, Anna!" Anna did the face, and Kelly started cracking up too.

Anna continued to grin at us each time we laughed. Mom walked by wearing a pair of light blue jeans and a white cotton T-shirt and asked what was so funny. I told her, "It's so funny. Anna grabs onto the sink and then makes the funniest face!" I laughed just remembering it. "Come on, Anna, show Mom the face!" Anna glanced up at Mom but didn't make the face.

Mom studied Anna. "What's going on, Anna?" Anna sat down and picked up her Ernie doll. Ernie, of the famous Bert and Ernie, was her favorite toy.

Mom said, "Oh well, I guess I won't see it. I'm making lunch soon, so you guys need to wash your hands, okay?" We agreed as Mom walked into the kitchen.

A few days later, when Mom picked up Sam and me from school, she explained that Anna had a doctor's appointment and that after we picked up Kelly we were going straight there. When we got to Kelly's school, she got into the backseat of the car with Anna and me. I told her, "Anna has a doctor's appointment, so we're going there, not home."

"Why does Anna have a doctor's appointment?"

Mom replied, "Anna's not feeling well. I think she's constipated. Remember that face you said she was making? It was likely her trying to have a bowel movement."

"Oh. Is that serious? I didn't think you'd have to go to the doctor for that."

"Not usually, but it's better to be safe than sorry."

I glanced at Anna in her car seat. She was adorable with her big blue eyes and chubby cheeks. She wore a yellow dress and matching yellow headband with a large flower on top. I put my hand in front of hers, and she grabbed my fingers. I studied her for a moment. "Not feeling good?" She paid no attention to my question as she continued to pull at my fingers and then made a quick grab for my earrings. I moved my head back to avoid having my earrings pulled out.

At the doctor's office Mom went up to the receptionist to check in, while Kelly, Sam and I went over to the waiting area with Anna. The room was rectangle shaped with the reception desk on one end and little wooden chairs, books, toys and puzzles along the sides. Anna was particularly interested in a puzzle where you have to put the right shape in the right hole. She had a little trouble figuring out what to do, but she seemed determined to get it right and didn't want any help. This went on for a while until she decided she wanted to read a book instead. Sam found one of her favorites, Go, Dog. Go! by P. D. Eastman, and sat next to her on the floor to read it with her. Her chubby little fingers tried to trace the words as Sam read. When Anna's name was called, Mom picked her up and walked over to the door that led to the doctor's office. The three of us were left in the waiting room by ourselves.

It reminded me of all the years it was just Kelly, Sam and me, before Anna was born. My earliest memory was of an old apartment we used to live in before we met Dad. We would play out in front of the white building that had paint peeling off, with a couple of neighbor kids that were similar in age. Next to the building was a giant field of dirt and weeds. It wasn't exactly a great place, which was why we were so thrilled when we met Dad and got to move into a big, clean house that was situated in a housing development with manicured lawns as well as a community pool and tennis courts. It had a TV room, a living room and a formal dining room with a crystal chandelier. Kelly and I shared a room, while Sam had a room across the hall. It seemed perfect. We had a mom and a dad and a great big house.

That same summer we moved into the big house, Kelly, Sam and I joined the swim team. Kelly and Sam won lots of ribbons, while the only one I got was for placing third in backstroke against the boys, instead of girls, an accident made by the event organizers. Either way, I was excited to win something for the first time, and I think it was meant to be, since it also happened to be my sixth birthday. After the swim meet, we had a small party at the new house. Mom and Dad got me a bunch of presents, including a shiny new baton, for twirling. I was so excited, I ran to put on my favorite skirt, that also twirled when I spun around, and put on a show for them. It was as if things couldn't get any better.

I GLANCED BACK over at Sam and Kelly. Sam was acting out Go, Dog. Go!, pretending to be one of the dogs, on his hands and knees, and Kelly sat cross-legged acting out the part of the announcer. They were both laughing but were soon hushed by the receptionist, a large woman with big, curly dark hair that looked like a giant helmet and wire-rimmed glasses. Sam walked up to her and asked, in his most angelic tone, if she had pen and paper so that we could play tic-tac-toe. She begrudgingly handed him some paper and pens. Kelly and Sam played first and decided that the winner would play me. We played tic-tac-toe for what seemed like ever. By the time Mom and Anna came back out, Kelly was the reigning champ.

When Mom walked through the door, she wasn't smiling, and her eyes were red, like she'd been crying. Anna was quiet as she rested her head on Mom's shoulder, and Mom held her tight. They walked directly up to the receptionist, picked up some papers and walked over to us. "Let's go. Now." We didn't hesitate and followed Mom and Anna back to the car. When we got in the car, Kelly asked, "Is Anna gonna be okay? Did she get medicine for her constipation?" Mom didn't respond.

Kelly, speaking a little louder, asked, "Is Anna okay?"

"Anna needs to have some more tests, so we have to go to Children's Hospital in Oakland."

Kelly's voiced lowered. "What kind of tests?"

Mom glanced in the rear mirror. "Some blood tests and a CT scan to get a picture of her insides."

I sat up straight and leaned toward the front seat. "Why do they need blood tests? Why do they need to get a picture of her insides?"

The car suddenly became noisy as Kelly, Sam and I continued to ask Mom more questions about Anna's tests. Mom told us to be quiet and that we would talk about it later. We protested. She sternly said, "Not another word." And we rode the rest of the way home in silence.

When we got home, Mom told us that the testing had to be done right away and that us kids had to stay home. Mom packed up a few things, made a phone call in the kitchen and then left for the hospital with Anna.

Later that evening, when the three of us were in the living room watching TV, Dad walked through the front door carrying a pizza. Almost in unison, the three of us got up and walked into the kitchen. After Dad set the pizza onto the kitchen table, Kelly glared at him as she asked, "Where's Anna? How did the tests go? When are Mom and Anna coming home?"

His face was blank. "Mom and Anna are still in the hospital. They are going to keep her overnight until all the tests are done and they've gotten the results back."

Kelly put her hands on her hips. "What do you mean overnight? That doesn't make sense. What aren't you telling us?"

"Okay. Just calm down for a minute. Why don't we sit down at the table, eat dinner and I'll tell you what I know."

I could tell Dad was getting annoyed by all of Kelly's questions and was hoping they wouldn't start to fight. When he pulled out the chair to sit down, I noticed his hands were trembling. Once seated he began. "When Anna went to the doctor, he found a large lump in her abdomen, which made him quite concerned. So he said that we needed to have additional tests done at Children's Hospital in Oakland."

I asked, "What kind of tests?"

"She is going to have a CT scan and some blood work done. The tests will tell us if there is anything abnormal going on with her blood cells."

I didn't understand what he meant, so I asked, "What about the CT scan? What's that for?"

"The CT scan, sometimes called a 'CAT' scan, is a machine that will give us pictures of Anna's insides. It will help visualize the lump her doctor felt to get a better idea of what it is."

Kelly's eyes widened. "They're putting Anna in a machine?!"

Dad explained, "Anna will lie down on a platform that will position her in the machine. The doctor said that if she was scared, she could bring her Ernie doll. The machine won't hurt her. It doesn't even touch her, actually."

For once, Kelly, Sam and I, without being told to be quiet, were very quiet. We ate our pizza in silence. I'm not sure I'd ever seen Dad with tears in his eyes before. He no longer appeared big and intimidating, but instead he looked limp and tired.

I suddenly thought back to earlier in the day when I had remembered getting that baton for my sixth birthday. The day after my birthday, Sam was fooling around with the baton, against my protests, and bent it. I was so upset, I ran and told Dad. I had no idea he would grab the baton from my hand and confront Sam the way he did. He took Sam into his bedroom and hit him with the baton until it broke in half. Kelly and I heard the baton hit something solid and then heard Sam's screams from our bedroom across the hall. We sat on my bed and covered our ears until it stopped. When it was over, Kelly and I were too scared to leave our bedroom, so we didn't until it was time for dinner. At dinner, I sat next to Sam at the table. Each time his back touched the chair he winced. I realized that must have been where he got hit. I wanted to run to my room and cry. I couldn't figure out how our wonderful dad could go from loving father to a monster that hurt Sam, all in one day.

I returned my attention to my family who sat silently around the kitchen table. Sam had his head down, as did Dad. Kelly was starting to get up and clear her plate. She put her dish in the sink and walked out of the kitchen. After dinner, I said good night to Sam and Dad and went back to my bedroom and read the latest Sweet Valley High book until I fell asleep.

THE NEXT DAY I got up and went into Mom and Dad's room, but Dad wasn't there. I went down the hall to the kitchen and found him sitting at the table. He glanced up from the newspaper when I walked in. "Morning, Casey, how did you sleep?"

"I slept okay. Have you talked to Mom? Is Anna okay?"

"I just talked to Mom. We're still waiting to hear back on the results."

"When do we think we'll get the results?"

"We should hear later today."

"So, after school?"

"Probably by the time you are home from school."

"Who's gonna pick us up?"

"I will."

"Are you going to take us to school this morning too?"

"Yeah."

"Oh, okay." I made myself a bowl of cereal, ate it in silence and then finished getting ready for school.

Later that day, Dad picked up Sam and me from our school.

On the drive to Kelly's school, Mount Diablo Junior High, I asked Dad if he'd heard back about Anna's tests. He said he did but wanted to wait until we had picked up Kelly to talk about it. Sam peered in the back at me. I glanced up, arching my eyebrows. We drove to Kelly's school in silence. Dad pulled up to the curb, Kelly waved to her friends, who had yellow permed hair and bangs that seemed to defy gravity, and got into the backseat with me. She asked, "Why the long faces?"

I explained, "They got Anna's test results back. Dad said we had to wait to pick you up before he'd tell us anything." She sunk back in the seat.

"Oh."

I tilted forward. "Dad, now that Kelly is here. Can you tell us about Anna's tests?"

At first he didn't respond, and then he spoke softly. "I'll tell you when we get home."

When we got home, we followed Dad into the kitchen. He told us all to sit down at the kitchen table. Once we were all seated, he started to explain.

According to the tests, Anna had what was called neuroblastoma, a rare type of childhood cancer. She had a large tumor that was obstructing her bowels, causing her to be constipated.

I thought back to earlier that week when Kelly, Sam and I were laughing at Anna's funny face. We were laughing at her cancer. My insides seemed to dart inward. It was hard to breathe, and I thought I might be sick. I glanced at Kelly and Sam. Sam's head was down, and Kelly stared straight ahead with tears in her eyes. Nobody spoke. I didn't know much about cancer, but I knew that it was bad. How does a toddler get cancer? She wasn't a smoker, and she didn't work in a coal mine. I didn't understand it at all.

Dad stared at the wall. "Anna's being prepped for surgery. She is having surgery on Friday."

Kelly almost jumped out of her chair. "That's in two days!"

"The doctors feel it's important she has the surgery to remove the tumor as soon as possible. We're going to visit her in the hospital tomorrow. Are you guys okay with that?" We were.

Kelly tensed. "Do we have to go to school tomorrow?"

"No, we're going to visit her in the morning, so you'll have to miss school."

Kelly's voice got higher as she asked, "What about Friday?"

"Friday we'll also be at the hospital, all day, so that we can be there as soon as she's out of surgery."

Kelly relaxed her jaw. "Okay."

CHAPTER 3

THE NEXT MORNING, we walked single file out to the car. Kelly got in the front seat, while Sam and I buckled up in back. Dad started the car, and the radio began to play "Satisfaction" by the Rolling Stones; the Rolling Stones was one of Dad's favorite bands, so we knew it well. He loved old rock and had tons of records he used to play back when we listened to records instead of cassettes. We'd sit on the living room floor playing records while he'd tell us tales of being in Berkeley during the sixties and hanging out with Janis Joplin and Jimi Hendrix. I didn't know who either of those people were, but he made it seem like they were a big deal.

Sam started to sing along. "I can get nooo satissssfactionn." He bobbed his head up and down as he sang. I shook my head and rolled my eyes. "It's I can't get no satisfaction, not I can get no satisfaction. 'I can get no' doesn't make any sense!" Sam seemed disinterested in my correcting his song lyrics and kept singing. Before I knew it, Dad and Kelly were quietly singing along too. Knowing the words, I joined in. There we were on the way to the hospital singing along to the radio. It was so normal, so happy. The next song came on, but I didn't know it and neither did Sam and Kelly. We sat in silence the rest of the drive, which seemed to go on forever, when in reality it was only forty-five minutes from our house in Clayton to Children's Hospital in Oakland.

When we finally arrived at the hospital, we pulled up to the curb in front of the building, where there were automatic doors on the left and right as well as a lot of people out front. On the right-hand side there was a large sign that said, "Emergency." There were families, old people and young people walking around and others in wheelchairs among what appeared to be hospital staff; I saw one doctor wearing a white coat and walking with two other women in blue scrubs. We peered through the windows and saw a security guard, a large African American man with big eyes and plastic-rimmed glasses wearing a dark blue uniform with a badge that read "Security," approach and tap on Dad's window. Dad rolled down the window to hear the guard who told him we had to move and park in the parking structure across the street.

Dad found a parking spot in the garage and then we got out of the car and walked outside to the sidewalk across from the hospital. While we waited for the crosswalk light to tell us it was okay to cross, I studied the five-story building, its countless windows and all the people in front of it, as well as those going in and out in a steady stream. We were soon going to be just like those people going in and out. I began to feel scared and nervous as we walked across the street.

It felt like when I started a new school in the middle of the year and I had to walk up to the front of the class for the teacher to introduce me. The teacher would say, "Class, we have a new student today. This is Casey. Everyone say, 'hi' to Casey!" All the kids would say, "Hi, Casey," I'd find my desk and then try to make my face go from red to its normal, ivory color. The last time I had to change schools midyear was when Mom was pregnant with Anna, and we moved into the house in Clayton where Anna was born. We had to move midyear because Dad had just gotten out of prison, after being away for six months, and wanted to be closer to his store. We were excited to have Dad home and that soon we'd have a new sibling. Well, not all of us.

Sam wasn't quite as happy, since he'd quickly grown to, secretly, dislike Dad after the baton incident and all the other times he got into trouble. I used to tell him to try not to get in trouble and then it wouldn't happen anymore. I guess he couldn't help himself especially after Mom and Dad came home and told us they had eloped. He had such a fit and of course got into trouble. It was scary when it happened to Sam. I can't imagine how I'd feel if it ever happened to me.

I think the only time Sam was happy was right after Mom announced she was pregnant with Anna because at the same time she told us Dad was going away, to jail. Apparently something was wrong with how Dad was doing business and he got into trouble. Dad insisted he was innocent. I had no reason not to believe him. Whatever the reason, I remember Sam was thrilled Dad was going to be out of the house.

I glanced over at Sam and then Dad as he led us through the automatic doors on the right. The reception area was noisy with the sounds of people talking, babies crying and electronic equipment. The information desk was on the left, next to that was a play area for children and on the right was a sea of chairs. There were kids crawling around and playing at the toy station, as well as smaller children who were held close by their parents sitting in the sea of chairs with worried expressions on their faces.

Dad walked up to the information desk. "Hi, we're here to see Anna Galvin."

The young African American woman with brown eyes and dark hair pulled back into a short ponytail and wearing a light blue button-down shirt asked, "What's she here for?"

Dad responded, "She's being prepped for surgery tomorrow."

"Oh, then she'd be in the main building. This area is just for emergency. You'll need to go back outside to the other double doors. They'll be able to help you there."

Dad thanked her and headed back outside, Sam, Kelly and I followed behind. We walked through the double doors to a much smaller waiting room with about twenty chairs, a closed gift shop on the right and the information desk directly ahead. There wasn't anyone in the room other than the attendant, a large, dark-colored man without any hair on his head, also wearing a light blue button-down shirt, at the information desk. Dad led us up to the desk. "Hi. We're here to see Anna Galvin."

The attendant glanced at us kids. "Are they siblings?"

"Yes." Dad gave a polite smile.

"No problem." The man picked up the phone, talked to someone on the other end, scanned a piece of paper and hung up. "She's in room 5123. I'll need each of your names. Does anyone have a cold or not feel well today?"

"No, everyone is feeling okay, right, kids?"

We nodded. The man peered down at me. "Young lady, what's your name?"

"I'm Casey. I'm Anna's sister. We are the closest in age, but I'm a lot older."

He grinned and wrote my name on the visitors badge and then handed it to me; I stuck it on the front of my jacket. He did the same for Kelly, Sam and Dad and directed us to the elevators down the hall. Sam ran to push the button to go up. The doors opened, and we piled in. Sam asked Dad, "Does Anna have her own room? Does she have a TV?"

"I don't know. We'll have to wait and see."

"I hope she does. I hope she at least has a TV."

Kelly shook her head at Sam. "Stop being so childish. This is a hospital. Anna has cancer and is having surgery tomorrow. Who cares if there's a TV?"

"Jeez. I was just asking."

A moment later we heard the chime of the elevator telling us we were at Anna's floor. We stepped off the elevator to cold air that smelled metallic and like old medicine. I wrapped my arms around myself and followed Dad down the hall. I observed the framed artwork on the walls that were pretty good but also appeared to have been drawn by a child. The pictures were of balloons, rainbows, people and the sun. At the end of the line of pictures there was a photo of a fair-skinned girl with straight, brown hair and brown eyes, about my age. She smiled as she held a marker and a notepad in each hand. I made the logical conclusion that she was the artist. Once we got to the nurses' station, the blond-haired young nurse wearing pink scrubs and a stethoscope directed us to Anna's room. Anna's room was a few doors down; the door was open.

We followed Dad into the room. There was an empty bed on the left and a drawn curtain next to it. Behind the curtain, which acted as a room divider, was Anna's crib as well as some chairs and a bathroom and a window on the right. Mom was sitting on the chair next to Anna's crib holding Anna. Mom was wearing the same thing as the day before: light-blue jeans and a peach sweatshirt, with no makeup and her hair pulled into a ponytail. She had dark circles under her eyes. Anna wore a hospital gown that was white with small dark blue flowers on it, and a tube was running out of her arm that was attached to an IV pole.

When Mom saw us, she stood up and spoke softly in Anna's ear. "Look who's here, Anna!" Dad held out his arms to take her from Mom. Anna's eyes lit up as she squealed, "Dada!" Us kids didn't waste any time saying "Hi, Anna!" "How are you?" "We missed you!" Dad held her as we took turns giving her a kiss on the cheek. After all of the kisses and hellos, us kids took up the remaining seats in the room and watched Anna as she played with Dad.

A nurse with honey-brown hair and blue eyes walked in wearing blue scrubs with a pen on a necklace, a stethoscope and an ID badge with a sparkly balloon sticker on it. The badge read

"Janet Kane, RN." She said to us, "Anna has visitors! Are you all her brothers and sisters? And this must be Dad!"

Mom grinned. "Yes, this is my husband, Jasper, and these are my other children: Kelly, Sam and Casey."

"Wow. Anna is so lucky to have so many sisters and a brother! She's clearly quite happy to see you! I'm Janet, and I'm one of Anna's nurses. I'll be helping take care of Anna while she's here."

We took turns saying "hello" and "nice to meet you."

Nurse Janet left the room, telling us she would be right back; she must have realized we were short a chair because when she returned a few minutes later she had brought a chair with her. Mom thanked her for being so thoughtful and kind. Nurse Janet then walked over to Anna's IV pole, pushed some buttons and lifted the bag hanging from the top. Nurse Janet asked Mom, "Can I get you anything? Is there anything you need?"

"No, we're fine. Thank you so much, Janet."

Nurse Janet glanced over at us kids. "It was nice meeting all of you. Have fun visiting with Anna, but be sure to let her get lots of rest. She has a big day tomorrow."

We promised we would. After Nurse Janet left, we stared at Anna. The sunlight through the window illuminated her golden hair and made her eyes sparkle. She wore a gigantic grin as she grabbed for Dad's nose; I stood up to touch Anna's hand, and she directed her grabbing to my fingers. She was so strong, I thought she was going to pull my finger from the socket. How could she be sick when she seemed so strong? Just then a doctor walked in. He was tall with dark hair, olive skin and brown eyes and was wearing green scrubs. He went right up to Mom. "I need to examine Anna and confirm the procedure for tomorrow. How has she been feeling?"

"She seems okay. No problems so far."

"Good. I'll need you to put her down on the crib so I can examine her."

He felt around her neck and her belly. Within a minute he

was finished and proceeded to explain to Mom when the surgery would start, how long it was expected to take and how long after she could be visited. He didn't seem to take a breath in between. He asked if there were any questions; Mom fired off about twenty. He calmly answered each one as he studied Mom's and Dad's faces. "I will take good care of her. Get some rest. We'll see you tomorrow." He tilted his head toward our group and walked briskly out of the room. Kelly's face twisted. "Who was that?"

Mom walked over to Anna's crib and picked her up. "That was Dr. Trekker, Anna's surgeon. I was told he is the best there is, and we are very lucky to have him. We should all pray together for Anna."

We sat there in silence for what seemed like an eternity, praying. I think it would have gone on forever if Anna hadn't started crying. Apparently, she was hungry, so Mom began to nurse her. Dad said we should go down to the cafeteria and check out what they had for lunch.

We stopped at the nurse's station to ask where the cafeteria was. The nurse told us that it was on the second floor and pointed toward the elevators. We took the elevator down and were surprised to see that the cafeteria was already bustling with people and had a line all the way out into the hall. Dad raised his eyebrows. "How does McDonald's sound? We could go get it and bring it back for Mom too, and you know how Anna loves to nibble on the fries." It was agreed, and we left the hospital to pick up lunch.

When we came back, we had to go back through the information desk on the left, but this time we knew the drill. The same attendant checked us in and said that our lunch smelled great. He wished us a good day, and back up to Anna's room we went. When we arrived, Anna was asleep and Mom was sitting quietly along the window seat. She quickly jumped up and motioned for us to go out of the room. She walked out to the hall with us.

"Anna's asleep and I don't want her to wake up. Why don't you guys go down to the cafeteria and eat it there?"

Dad held up the bag. "We brought you some lunch and some fries for Anna. Do you want to come with us?"

Mom stared at Dad with disbelief. "I'm not leaving Anna."

"Okay. Here, take this. We'll be back soon."

Mom took the bag of food. We went back down to the cafeteria, found a table and began eating our lunch. Sam asked Dad, "Is Anna going to die?"

"No, of course not."

Sam's mouth twisted. "But cancer kills people, and she has to go into surgery right away. Could she die?

"We shouldn't think like that."

Kelly's mouth dropped open. "How are we supposed to think?"

"We have to hope and pray that she is okay."

I stopped eating my fries. "What exactly is neuroblastoma? I've never heard of that before. Is it like leukemia? How did she get it?"

"Neuroblastoma is a rare childhood cancer. It isn't the same as leukemia. Anna has a tumor—that is cancerous—in her abdomen. It's as big as a grapefruit, which is pretty big considering how little she is. The doctor said it was slow growing, which is the good kind. Since it's slow growing, we can fight it before it gets out of control."

I was still confused. "But how did she get it?"

"The doctors don't know how she got it. They think she was born with it."

I sat back in my chair. "It sounds like we can fight it and she will be okay?"

"Yes, we will fight it." Dad let out a breath and stared out the window.

We finished eating our lunch and headed back upstairs to Anna's room. When we walked back into her room, Mom motioned for us to sit down and be quiet. Dad sat down next to Mom on the window seat and put his arm around her. Us kids each took a chair. Kelly chewed at her nails, while Sam pulled at a string on his shirt. A little while later, Nurse Janet walked into the room. She went directly up to Anna's IV pole, studied it briefly and then glanced over at us. She spoke quietly to Mom and then walked back out, waving as she left.

When Anna woke up, she whined a little bit and then sat herself up. She put her arms out and said, "Mamma!" Mom jumped up from the window seat, ran up to Anna's crib and picked her up. Anna put her head on Mom's shoulder and then sat up straight. Anna put up her hand and said, "Hi!"

We all started talking to Anna at the same time. Mom told us to quiet down so that she could feed her and then walked over to Dad. They spoke quietly and both wore long faces. After Mom sat back in the chair next to the crib, Dad got up, kissed Anna on top of the head and faced us. "All right kids, let's pack up. We are going to go home so Anna can rest."

Kelly furrowed her brow. "But we are being quiet. Can't we just stay?"

"No. We need to let Anna rest. She'll want to play if we stay, but that isn't what she needs right now. She needs rest."

Kelly muttered something under her breath as we got out of our chairs and said our good-byes to Mom and Anna. We walked out of the room while Sam ran ahead to push the button at the elevator. While we waited for the doors to open, Kelly questioned Dad. "I don't get why we have to leave. She was sleeping fine when we were here. I think Mom just doesn't want us here."

Dad clenched his jaw. "That isn't true, and you know it. We need Anna to get as much rest as possible. We need to think of what is best for Anna right now. Tomorrow is a big day."

Kelly wasn't convinced we actually needed to leave. She huffed a "fine" and walked into the elevator.

I asked, "Will we get to see her before her surgery tomorrow?"

Dad shook his head. "No."

"Why not?"

"They need to prepare her for the surgery. Only Mom can be with her. We will have to wait in the waiting room."

I thought aloud, "Maybe I'll bring some books or something tomorrow—to pass the time."

Sam's face brightened. "And some paper and pens. We can play tic-tac-toe!"

"Good idea! I'll pack those too."

Dad stared at the elevator ceiling. "Yep. We'll be waiting a while."

On the car ride home we peppered Dad with questions about Anna's surgery. "How long would it take? Are they going to take out all of the tumor? How long before we can see her?" Dad, obviously annoyed with us, did his best to answer our questions. By the time we finished our drive home he seemed to be losing patience. When we had pulled into the driveway, Sam asked, "What's for dinner? Can we have pizza? And Mom's not home, so can we get Coke too?" Dad didn't answer. Sam asked again. Dad grimaced. "You call and order whatever you want." When we got home, Sam ran to the phone in the kitchen and dialed. Dad went upstairs to the bedroom and closed the door. Kelly and I went into our room. I started reading a book, while Kelly listened to music on her Walkman.

Half an hour later we heard Sam yell, "Pizza's here!" Dad, who had already changed into his pajamas, came downstairs to pay the delivery man for the pizza and bottle of Coke. We sat at the kitchen table eating dinner and making funny voices. I started with my best Yoda impression. "Sammm, Monkey face you have. Soda drinks you." Sam and Kelly laughed. Sam used his fingers to pull out his ears and moved his mouth like a monkey. "Eee-ooh, eee-ooh-ooh soda, eee-eee-ooh-ooh soda." Within minutes we were all laughing. Between the impressions and Sam's laugh, which was more of a honk, even Dad started to chuckle. All of a sudden it seemed like a normal day again. After dinner, Dad went back upstairs, and Kelly went into our room, shutting the door behind her. Without Mom there to restrict our TV viewing, Sam and I decided to watch TV until we fell asleep, which was much later that night.

CHAPTER 4

EARLY THE NEXT MORNING, I woke up to the realization that I was still on the living room floor, in front of the TV. While Sam slept soundly on the couch, I got up quietly and turned off the TV. Without the TV on, I realized there weren't any other sounds in the house; Dad and Kelly were still asleep too. I snuck back into my bedroom, curled into my bed and went back to sleep. What seemed like only seconds later, Dad was banging on our door, warning us that we had to leave for the hospital soon. I rolled over to see that Kelly had just been startled awake. I muttered, "You can have the shower first," and rolled over and went back to sleep. When she came back into the room after her shower, I forced myself out of bed and headed to the bathroom. Down the hall, I saw that Sam was still asleep on the couch in the living room; I was so jealous that he was able to sleep through just about anything. After I took my shower, I got dressed and packed my backpack with books, pens and paper.

I put my backpack on and walked to the kitchen. I saw that everyone but Sam was at the table eating cereal; I got my bowl and joined them. A few minutes later, Sam walked in with wet hair that now appeared black instead of his normal light brown color. He got his bowl, sat down and joined us. I asked, "So did you guys pack stuff to keep busy while we wait?"

Kelly said, "I'm just bringing my journal, that's all I need." And then went back to playing with her cereal.

"Oh, cool. How about you Sam? Did you pack anything?"

"I forgot. Dang. What should I bring?"

"I brought paper, pens and books. I guess I could share my paper and pens."

"Okay, thanks. I'm good, then."

Dad forced a smile. "Thanks, Casey. I forgot to remind you guys. I'm afraid it's going to be a long day. Right after you finish eating we are going to leave for the hospital."

A few minutes later we piled into the car, and Dad turned on the radio. No one sang along. Dad quickly became agitated as the traffic on the freeway started to get worse. I heard him mumble swear words under his breath that had something to do with being late and traffic being worse than normal "of all days."

When we arrived at the hospital, we went into the garage and crossed the street like the day before. We went through the automatic doors to the left and went directly to the information desk. Dad said to the same attendant as the day before, "Hi. We are here to see Anna Galvin. She's having surgery today."

The man said, "Just a moment." He picked up the phone and made a call, spoke for a few moments and then hung up.

"Anyone feeling sick today or been around any sick people?"

Dad responded, "No, we're all fine. We were here yesterday."

"Okay. Well, the surgery is on the third floor. You can take the elevator up and follow the signs to the waiting room. You can't miss it." Dad nodded.

The attendant chitchatted about the weather as he filled out our badges. I waved good-bye to him as we walked to the elevator. When we entered the elevator, Sam asked Dad what floor, pretending to be a doorman. Dad forced a grin. "Three, please."

Sam tipped an invisible hat. "Very well, sir."

After pushing the elevator button, Sam asked me, "Can I have the pen and paper now?"

"I'll give it to you when we get to the waiting room, okay?"

"Okay."

When we stepped out of the elevator, we followed the signs to the surgery waiting room. The room was smaller than the other waiting rooms: it had about ten chairs with brown cloth seats and a few fake-wood side tables. Kelly, Sam and I sat down as Dad walked up to the window and talked to the person behind the glass. It was funny, us sitting there all in a row, as if we were posing for a picture.

Once Dad was finished talking to the fair-skinned, gray-haired woman behind the window, he walked back to the chairs and sat down next to Kelly. Sam asked me, "Hey, can I get that paper and pen now?"

"Sure." I went into my backpack and pulled out a notebook and pen and handed it to him.

"You don't have one without a unicorn and a rainbow on it?"

I rolled my eyes. "Sorry, Charlie, it's all I've got."

He mumbled, "Great, thanks," and then proceeded to open the notebook and start drawing. I pulled out the latest book in the Sweet Valley High series and began reading.

About twenty minutes later, Mom bounced in wearing dark blue jeans and a yellow sweater. She had put on makeup and wore her hair down, showing off her long curly hair. Dad stood up when he saw her, walked over and gave her a hug. The three of us stood up to give her a hug and then sat back down. Still standing, she said, "Well, they just took Anna in for surgery. So now we wait."

Kelly asked, "How did she do when they came in for the prep?"

Mom chuckled. "She did great. She kept trying to pull at all of the equipment they were trying to use on her. One time she was able to pull off one of the nurse's stethoscopes. Anna cracked up! She had all the nurses laughing."

Sam snorted. "Figures!"

We all agreed, Anna was always doing something to make us laugh. Mom finally sat down next to Dad and continued to tell him that she had called Grandma Jess, Aunt Ella and Grandma Mary. Grandma Jess and Aunt Ella would be there in a few hours.

After Mom got up to talk to the woman behind the window I asked Dad, "Why does Mom have so much . . . energy? It's like she's wired. Yesterday she seemed so tired."

"It's just nervous energy. Though, it definitely helped that she finally got to take a shower and change her clothes."

"Ohhh." I went back to reading my book.

The next several hours we tried to keep busy. Sam and I read, played tic-tac-toe and drew pictures. Kelly either stared into space or wrote in her journal. Mom and Dad talked quietly or walked aimlessly around the waiting room. At lunchtime, Dad, Sam and I went to the cafeteria; Kelly and Mom said they weren't hungry.

When we got to the cafeteria, Dad said we could have whatever we wanted. Sam and I enthusiastically grabbed our trays. I got mashed potatoes with a side of mac 'n' cheese, Sam got fried chicken, mashed potatoes with corn and Dad got soup with salad. In addition to our entrees, Sam and I both made a do-it-yourself sundae with the soft-serve machine. Sam put all the possible toppings on his sundae. It looked like a pile of melted garbage. After we got through the long line to pay for our lunch, we found a table and sat down. I stared at Sam's sundae and exclaimed, "Gross!" Sam's mouth curved upward as he licked his lips and scooped a spoonful of ice cream. "Mmm, delicious." We continued to eat and goof around; Dad sat quietly watching us.

After lunch we went back to the surgery waiting room. Mom, and now Kelly too, were pacing. Dad tried to convince them to go and eat something, but they insisted they couldn't.

A few minutes later Grandma Jess arrived wearing a scarf over her curly gray hair, no makeup and a pant suit with a dark gray coat. Instead of her normal bubbly, fun self she appeared old and tired. She hugged all of us and then asked Mom how the prep went, when did she go in and if we had heard anything about Anna's surgery. Mom sat down with Grandma Jess and explained everything that happened that morning and that we still hadn't heard anything about the surgery.

About an hour later, the women behind the window called out Mom's name. "Agatha Galvin." Mom and Dad ran up to the counter. They leaned over to listen and spoke for a few seconds. They appeared a bit more relaxed as they walked back over to us. Mom gave us the update. "They told us Anna is out of surgery. Dr. Trekker, Anna's surgeon, will be out soon to talk to us."

Grandma Jess and us kids launched into question mode. Mom quickly hushed us. "She said the surgery was over. The surgeon would talk to us soon. That is all they said. It's all I know right now. We have to wait for the surgeon for any more details."

Just then the door opened, and we all stood up thinking it was the surgeon, but instead it was Aunt Ella. She had worn her long red hair in a ponytail, bright makeup and a sassy pink suit dress with high heels. Ella was Dad's much younger sister; she was definitely our "cool" aunt and still lived at home with Grandma Jess. She would always let us wear her makeup and paint our fingernails. She walked over to where we stood and gave us each a hug. Grandma Jess sat her down and filled her in on the current situation.

After talking with Grandma Jess, Ella started chitchatting with Kelly and me. "So, girls, how's school?

Kelly perked up. "Good."

"How about you, Casey?"

"Good."

"Whatcha reading?"

"Oh, this is the latest in the Sweet Valley High series. I just got this one. It's really good. Elizabeth just started volunteering at a hospital and got kidnapped! Her twin sister, Jessica, is a wreck!"

She chuckled. "Sounds good. How about you, Kelly, you reading anything?"

"Oh, no, I was just writing in my journal."

"Writing about boys in junior high? So do you have any boyfriends?" Ella teased.

Kelly's cheeks turned red. "I'll tell you later—not in front of Mom and Dad." Ella raised a brow and sat back in her chair.

Just then the door opened and we all turned to see. It was the surgeon in green scrubs and matching cap. We all stood up and rushed over to him. Mom beamed. "Dr. Trekker! How did it go, how is she?"

Dr. Trekker made eye contact with Mom. "Anna did very well during surgery and is resting in the ICU. We were able to remove 97 percent of the tumor, which we believe was a huge success. We hadn't anticipated being able to remove so much due to the fact it was near vital organs. The remaining 3 percent should be able to be treated with chemotherapy. Overall it was considered a success. I don't think we could have had a better outcome."

Mom, Grandma Jess, Dad, Kelly and Aunt Ella all had tears in their eyes. Mom composed herself. "Thank you so much, Dr. Trekker. God bless you. We're so lucky to have you as Anna's surgeon!"

He continued to wear a straight face. "I'm glad today went well. The nurse will come out to tell you when you can see Anna." Dr. Trekker walked out of the waiting room.

All of us formed one big hug right there in the cramped little room. There were tears and chants of "Thank you, God, Thank you, God" coming from Mom. We undid our group hug when we heard someone coming. A younger, Latina nurse with emerald-green eyes wearing blue scrubs walked up to our group. "Mrs. Galvin?"

"Yes, that's me, and this is my husband."

"Great. Anna's in the ICU and can have visitors, but only two at a time. She is still asleep, but you can see her."

Mom glanced over at Dad. "Okay, we'll go first." Dad agreed.

The nurse continued to explain that the ICU was down the hall and that she would escort us there. We left the waiting room and followed the nurse down the bright, white hall and stopped when she did. She reiterated that only two could go in at a time. She said to Mom, "If you don't want to leave Anna by herself, you can have one person come out and swap out for the next visitor." Mom told her she understood. Dad glanced back at us. "I'll be out in a little bit."

Sam sat down on the ground and leaned against the wall. Grandma Jess and Aunt Ella huddled and spoke quietly. Kelly paced down the hall back and forth while I paced side to side. This went on for quite a while before Dad came out. Grandma Jess asked if she could go in next. Dad obliged and gave her the directions to where Anna's bed was. Aunt Ella gave him a hug and asked how Anna was doing. He glanced over at Kelly and me and motioned for us to come near. "She's okay. She's sleeping, but she's okay."

Kelly made eye contact with Dad. "Can I go next to see her?"

Ella jumped in. "It's okay if Kelly, Casey and Sam want to go next. I can wait."

Dad thanked Ella and told Kelly that she could go next. We continued to pace in silence. Sam asked if I wanted to play tic-tac-toe on the floor with him; I agreed. It was nice to have something to do to help pass the time.

Grandma Jess walked back out through the double doors with tears in her eyes. She walked up to Dad and gave him a hug. Dad then motioned for Kelly to come over. "Kelly, it's your turn to go in now."

Kelly's mouth twisted. "Okay."

She glanced over her shoulder at Sam and me and then walked through the double doors. About five minutes later, Kelly came out and walked over to us. She peered down at Sam with tears in her eyes. "It's your turn to go in. Mom said we should each only stay a few minutes. Okay?" Sam leaned toward me.

"You can go next if you want. You did win the last game."

I agreed and got up off the floor and walked toward the double doors. I stepped through the doors, and the temperature seemed to drop by ten degrees. Along the corridor there were rows of beds and cribs, and soon I saw Mom, who was sitting next to Anna's crib. I walked up and gazed at Anna lying there quietly, sleeping with tubes going into her little nose as well as tubes coming out of her chest and arm. I glanced down at Mom in the chair. "How's Anna doing?

"Oh, she's doing well. She is resting, which is a good thing."

"How long will she be in here?"

"Just for a few days or so, assuming all goes well. Then she'll be transferred to a room on the fifth floor."

"That's good, right?"

"Yes."

I stood there for a few more minutes staring at Anna, not saying a word. She still appeared to be the strong little baby that nearly pulled my finger out of its socket the day before, now with just a little extra medical equipment. I gave Mom a hug. "Sam's next. I'll tell him how to find you." She waved as I left.

I walked out and went up to Sam. "Hey, it's your turn." He got up off the floor while trying to pick up all the tic-tac-toe papers and dropped the pencil. I bent to pick it up and hit my head on the wall. He chuckled. "Luckily you have a hard head, otherwise I might be worried."

I scrunched up my face. "Thanks, bro."

"No prob. So how do I find Anna?"

"It's easy, just go through the doors and walk straight ahead. You'll see Mom. She's sitting next to the crib."

"Thanks. See ya."

After everyone had a chance to see Anna, Dad took us all out to dinner. Over dinner we asked when Anna got to come home. He said he wasn't sure but that it would be a while because she needed to heal from surgery and then start chemotherapy. I didn't know what that meant. All I knew was that the surgery went well, according to Dr. Trekker, and that Mom and Dad seemed hopeful.

CHAPTER 5

SAM

I WAS SO FREAKIN' happy to get out of the hospital. I was bored to tears. I don't know what I would have done if Casey wasn't there to play tic-tac-toe with me. I mean, I can only draw pictures of Super Mario for so long. Not only was I happy to get out of the hospital, but Jasper—for the record, he's not my Dad—took us out to Sizzler for dinner, which is my favorite restaurant. I'm sure he was just trying to be nice, since Grandma Jess and Aunt Ella were there. He's always so nice in public and in front of other people. Little do they realize what a jerk he really is. I can't believe Mother has stayed with him all these years. Anyway, I'm glad we got to go out to dinner. Grandma Jess and Aunt Ella were pretty cool.

During dinner I stared down at my massive plate filled with one of everything from the salad bar and my mix of cola and root beer. It always made me laugh when Kelly and Casey got grossed out when I'd mix my drinks. Tonight they didn't even glance in my direction. Kelly was too focused on grilling Jasper for all the details on Anna. She was obsessed. She asked Jasper, "When does Anna get to come home?"

Jasper fidgeted in his seat. "I don't know. After she heals from surgery she will start chemotherapy. She won't come home until after her treatment. It could be quite a while. Anywhere between one and two months, they said."

Kelly covered her mouth as tears formed in her eyes. Aunt Ella put her arm around her and hugged. Grandma Jess stared straight ahead at Jasper. "Well, when can we visit? I can come by every day after work if necessary. She needs us right now!"

Jasper pursed his lips together. "I think in a few days to a week, once she's moved from the ICU, she can start having regular visitation. We'll just have to wait and see."

Everyone was so upset, it was like our table was the "doom-and-gloom table." I tried to cheer up Kelly and Casey by adding salt and pepper to my drink so they'd at least look at me and say, "Ew. Totally gross, Sam," like they normally do. Kelly just flipped her hair and went back to giving Jasper the third degree. Casey grimaced and said, "Eww, are you going to drink that?" and went back to chatting up Grandma Jess and Aunt Ella. It figures. I swear, she talks nonstop. Always goofing around and making everyone laugh or impressing them with her good grades and grown-up talk. Once she started getting those Gifted Children Monthly magazines, she went from dork to super dork, real fast.

I swear, if I wasn't making a mess or getting in trouble, I'm not sure they'd even notice I was here. I bet Casey wouldn't be so bubbly and great if she ever got beat like Kelly and me. I don't think she could handle it; she'd end up just as messed up as the rest of us.

It's weird to think someone as sweet and funny as Anna could have come from a guy like Jasper. I think our lives would have been better if he'd never gotten out of prison. What a home-coming that was! We had to move again, and oh guess what? Not only is our stepfather an ex-convict who beats us, but Mother let us in on a little secret. He's a drug addict too! Are you kidding me? She told us that he was getting clean for the baby and for us. Sure. For us. Right. Mother explained that we had to be strong as a family to support him while he went to rehab. I mean, good for him for trying to get clean, but then to regularly drag us kids down to a methadone clinic in downtown Oakland? Who does that?

I glanced back at the table of sad people. I mean, I get it. Anna had surgery and is in the hospital with cancer. I was sad too, I just didn't drone on like these guys. Honestly, I don't know what I'd do if she died. Although, I was feeling hopeful she'd be okay.

Dr. Trekker seemed positive about the situation, and he seemed like a pretty cool dude with his green scrubs and crazy hair. I always thought those surgery caps were supposed to cover the hair, but his was just all over the place—maybe he fussed with it after the surgery was over? Anyway, it was cool. My hair does the same thing in the morning. I wonder if I could ever be like Dr. Trekker; he's like a real-life hero. I never thought about doctors or what they did. I mean, I go to the doctor every year before baseball starts to get a physical. I certainly never thought of my regular doctor as a hero, but Dr. Trekker for sure is. Based on how Mother and Grandma Jess talked, he saved Anna's life. That is so badass. I think as long as Dr. Trekker is around, Anna will be okay even if there is "still a long road ahead," as everyone keeps saying over and over.

When I went to see Anna in the ICU, she seemed like she was doing pretty good. There were tubes everywhere, but overall she appeared normal; I mean, she wasn't deformed or anything. I didn't say much to Mother when I visited mostly because I didn't know what to say. I just stared at Anna and thought back to that day we laughed when she made that funny face. It wasn't funny at all; it was her cancer. We laughed at her cancer. It makes me sick to think about it. I don't know if I'll ever be able to forget.

After we said our good-byes to Grandma Jess and Aunt Ella, we drove home. Within seconds of walking through the front door, Kelly was back in her and Casey's room and Jasper had gone upstairs. I guess we weren't talking anymore for the night except for Casey. She's always talking. She asked me how I was "handling" everything and if I wanted to play Monopoly or rummy. I shook my head at her. "I'm fine. Not in the mood. Sorry, I'm gonna play Nintendo in my room."

She mumbled, "Okay then, good night," and walked into her room, defeated. This was one of those times that I was glad I had my own room. The girls always complained that they had to share a room and that it wasn't fair. Mother always said I got my own room because I was the only boy. Whatever the reason, I'm glad that I had my own room. I spent the rest of the night playing Super Mario Brothers until I got too tired and went to sleep.

Over the next week things started to change at home. For starters, Jasper had informed us of the change to our daily routine. "So, guys, you are going to start taking the bus to school 'cause I'm not going to be able to get off work, and we don't know how long Mom will be in the hospital with Anna."

Casey cocked her head to the side. "Did you get us bus passes?"

"Your mom called the school. Tomorrow you can take the bus and tell the driver your new pass is in the office. You and Sam will pick them up."

"Okay, cool." Casey grinned.

Kelly glanced at Jasper. "What about me? We don't have a school bus."

"You'll have to take the County Connection. I'll give you some bus and lunch money for the week."

Kelly perked up. "Okay."

I started to get excited. I asked Jasper, "What about us, do we get lunch money too?"

"Yep, I'll give you and Casey money too."

"Cool."

I hadn't expected anything good to come out of Anna's cancer, but now we got to buy our lunch and didn't have to drive to school with Mother. I mean, nobody enjoyed the morning drive to school with Mother. She'd either make us listen to her terrible music or lecture us about doing well in school so that we'd go to a good college. She would on occasion follow up with how she had always wanted to go to college and that it was her dream but she had gotten pregnant with Kelly instead. I think we heard the story about a million times. Not to mention, as soon as we'd step out of the car to go to school, she'd yell out the window, "Have a truly academic day!" with a silly grin. It was so embarrassing.

Without Mother and Anna around, Kelly was moody and spent most of the time in her room. Casey was usually doing her homework on the kitchen table, reading or watching TV. When she was bored, she tried to chat me up or get me to play games with her. Mostly I said I'd rather play Nintendo in my room. After school Mom wasn't there to make us dinner, so when Jasper got home, he'd either bring take out or order a pizza. After dinner, Jasper would disappear either upstairs or to run errands. That was fine by me.

Saturday morning, a full week after Anna's surgery, I woke to Kelly knocking on my door. She yelled through the door, "Sam, it's time to get up, we have to go the hospital to visit Anna."

I yelled back, "Fine, give me a minute. Jeez."

Of all the days Anna was getting transferred to her regular room it had to be today. Today was our first baseball game of the spring season, and I was going to miss it. I don't get why we can't just go later in the day. It's not like Anna will care if we are there bright and early or later in the day. I think Anna would have wanted me to go to my game. She always likes to hear my stories about baseball and any other story I tell her. One time I was telling her about the home run that I'd hit at my game earlier in the day, and she stared at me and then cracked up. I think that is proof she likes my stories and would want me to play.

I knew there was no point trying to fight Mother or Jasper about it. I'd just get in trouble. I got dressed and packed my backpack with a deck of cards, pen and paper for another long day at the hospital. Breakfast and the car ride to the hospital were pretty uneventful. It was our new thing, I guess. Get up early. Pack bag. Eat cereal. Drive to hospital. Get badge. Take Elevator. Sit down. Be quiet.

CHAPTER 6

IT HAD BEEN a month since Anna's surgery, and we were getting pretty used to the ins and outs of the hospital. On this particular visit we practically sailed past the information desk attendant, Lou, and up to Anna's room.

In Anna's room on the left side was a little girl about three years old with pale skin and dark circles under her eyes and a tube coming out of her arm connected to an IV pole, asleep in her crib. Past the crib and curtain, there was a bathroom on the right and Anna's crib on the left. Anna was also asleep with a tube coming out of her chest connected to an IV pole. Mom was on the window seat reading but glanced up when she saw us, instantly putting a finger to her mouth to let us know we needed to be quiet to not wake Anna. Her efforts were useless, as the noise from all of us walking in woke her almost instantly. Anna rolled over and sat up in the crib. When she saw all of us, a huge grin spread across her face, and her arms reached out to be picked up. Mom picked her up and held her in the chair next to her crib. I think we all chimed in at once. "Hi, Anna!" "Good morning, princess!" "Anna, we are here to play with you!" She made some cheerful, yet indistinguishable noises followed by a

"Dadadada." Dad took that as a cue that it was his turn to hold Anna and took her from Mom's arms.

In the midst of our greeting Anna, a petite nurse with dark hair, brown eyes and olive skin wearing lavender scrubs and a stethoscope walked in. "Well, hello, everyone. You must be Anna's dad, sisters and brother!" We bobbed our heads up and down. She continued. "I'm Karen, and I am one of Anna's nurses today."

Dad extended his hand. "Nice to meet you."

Nurse Karen asked Mom, "How has Anna been? When did she wake up?"

Mom chuckled. "Oh, she woke up about thirty seconds after the gang arrived! She's been okay. I fed her before her nap."

"Good. It seems like she's pretty happy to see everyone!"

"Yes, she is."

Much to our surprise, Nurse Karen then faced Kelly, Sam and me and asked us our names and what grade we were in.

I beamed. "I'm Casey and I'm in fifth!"

Nurse Karen angled her head toward Sam. "How about you?"

"I'm Sam and I'm in sixth."

Kelly leaned toward Nurse Karen. "I'm Kelly, I'm the oldest and I'm in seventh, junior high."

"Cool. Anna's lucky to have all of you." We nodded as she continued to tell us about herself. "Me, I'm from Oakland, not too far from the hospital, and I've been a nurse for seventeen years, and I absolutely love it!"

I asked, "What school did you go to?"

"UCSF School of Nursing. It is one of the oldest nursing schools in the Bay Area!"

I said, "That's pretty cool."

I liked talking to Nurse Karen, but Kelly and Sam were less than interested. Nurse Karen changed the subject back to Anna to ask if we had any questions about the room or the equipment or what she did to help her. Up until that point we hadn't been comfortable talking to the hospital staff and didn't want to bother Mom. I was thrilled to finally have the opportunity. "I have lots of questions. What is the tube in her chest? I first saw it in the ICU, but I still don't know what it is or why she has it."

Nurse Karen began to explain. "Anna has what is called a Broviac catheter. It's a tube that goes into one of her veins that goes to her heart. It's used for administering her chemotherapy and other medicines. We can use a syringe to inject the medicine right into the line or hook it up to the IV. No extra poking, so Anna won't feel any pain."

"How long will she have it?"

"I'm not sure. Most kids have it throughout their chemo-therapy regimen, so maybe a couple of years. Any other questions?"

We shook our heads from left to right. "Well, if you have any more questions, Anna's oncologist will be here later. Dr. Baker is very nice and I'm sure will be happy to answer any questions you might have."

Sam peered over at the wall. "Well, I have one more question. What are all those faucets and knobs on the wall—actually, what is all the stuff on the wall? It looks very high-tech and futuristic."

She was about to explain when a tall and freckled, redheaded nurse walked in and told her that the patient in 5260 was beep-ing. "I've got to take care of this, we can talk later, okay?"

Sam gave a smirk. "Yeah. Sure."

After she left, Sam stared at Kelly and me. "Wow, Anna has a tube going to her heart! That's crazy!"

We averted our attention back to Anna, who was now being held by Mom. We crowded around trying to talk to Anna and get her to laugh. After a while Anna started to fuss, requesting "num num." It was lunchtime, and the rest of us were hungry too. Dad took us down to the cafeteria, while Mom nursed Anna.

By the time we came back up to Anna's room, she was asleep. Mom glared at us and mouthed for us to be quiet. I decided to sit on the window seat and read a book, Kelly sat on the seat next to me and stared out of the window silently as Sam sat in the chair across the room doodling in a notebook. Mom sat in the chair next to Anna's crib, and Dad left the room saying he'd be back in a little bit.

The silence was interrupted when Anna's oncologist, Dr. Baker, walked in. She spoke quietly to Mom and then after a few minutes, they walked over to Kelly and me as well as motioned for Sam to join us.

"Dr. Baker, these are my other children: Kelly, Sam and Casey."

"Hi there! I'm Dr. Baker, Anna's oncologist." She was polite and appeared friendly as expected, since that is what Nurse Karen had told us. What I didn't expect was for her to be so pretty. She was tall with shoulder-length blond hair, fair skin, blue eyes and cool dark-rimmed glasses. I instantly thought that Dr. Baker was someone to know. Someone to be like. Dr. Baker interrupted my thoughts by asking if we had any questions for her. I, without letting anyone else speak, started in. "What is neuroblastoma? How did Anna get it? My dad said that it is a rare childhood cancer and Anna had a big tumor. Is it like leukemia? I've only heard of kids with leukemia. What is it, really?"

Dr. Baker tried to suppress a chuckle. "Like leukemia, neuroblastoma is a cancer. Cancer starts when cells in the body begin to grow out of control. Any of the cells in our body can become cancer and spread to other parts of our body. Neuroblastoma is a type of cancer that starts in the very early forms of nerve cells, or neuroblasts, in an embryo or fetus, before a baby is even born. Usually it only occurs in young children, like your sister. The neuroblastoma can form in any part of the nervous system; in the case of your sister, they were formed in the sympathetic nerve ganglia in the abdomen, hence the abdominal tumor. This is the case for about one out of four neuroblastoma patients. Are you following? Do you want me to go on?"

I think Mom, Kelly, Sam and I were all in a trance just

listening to Dr. Baker because it was so fascinating. A little, or maybe a lot, intimidated, I replied, "Yes, I follow. Um. Yeah. I think we follow. So how's this different than leukemia?"

Dr. Baker grinned. "Unlike neuroblastoma, leukemia isn't found in just children, but it is the most common type of childhood cancer. It can be found in adults too. Leukemia starts in the early blood-forming cells found in the bone marrow, the soft inner part of your bones. Most often it is a cancer of the white blood cells, but sometimes it is started in other blood cell types too. The leukemia cells build up in the bone marrow, crowding out normal cells and can go into the bloodstream quickly. From there they can go to other parts of the body like the lymph nodes, liver, brain and nervous system, where they will stop other cells from doing their jobs. So if you compare leukemia to neuroblastoma, among other things, leukemia is formed in young blood cells, whereas neuroblastoma is formed early on in the nervous system. As for how anyone gets either leukemia or neuroblastoma, it's unknown. Now, I realize that is a lot of information. Do any of you have any other questions?"

I was awestruck. Mom quickly jumped in. "Thank you, Dr. Baker. It is very kind of you to take the time to speak with me and my children."

"Of course. If you have any more questions, please don't hesitate to ask."

Kelly nearly in tears, blurted out, "So what about the chemotherapy? Will it make her better? When will she be better? Will she get better?"

"With the results of the surgery promising, we are optimistic that the chemotherapy will be effective at getting rid of the cancer."

Kelly calmed down. "So, she won't die?"

Dr. Baker's face straightened. "There are no guarantees, but we are optimistic that Anna will get better. We will know more in the coming weeks once she starts her first round of chemo."

Kelly wiped the tears that had formed around her eyes, seemingly satisfied with Dr. Baker's answers. Dr. Baker glanced at Mom. "Are you ready to go over the chemotherapy protocols and discuss what's going to happen next?"

Mom pressed her lips together. "Yes."

"Okay, great. For each round of chemotherapy, Anna will need to be admitted to the hospital for treatment. Additional oral treatments may be administered at home after the first round. After a few rounds of chemo, testing will be performed to determine the effectiveness of her treatment. Agatha, you and I can re-review each of the drugs a little later if you'd like." Mom had a straight face as she bobbed her head up and down.

"Are there any more questions?" We shook our heads.

"Based on how Anna is recovering from her surgery, we are on track to start her first round of chemo tomorrow."

Kelly's face twisted in horror, and tears began to form in the corner of her eyes. Sam didn't appear to be paying attention to anything but the zipper on his jacket, but I knew he was. Although his face was tilted down, I could see a single, lonely tear near the corner of his eye.

CHAPTER 7

ANNA STARTED CHEMO ON A SUNDAY. During breakfast, before Dad left for the hospital, Kelly pleaded to let us go and be with her but Dad insisted we had to stay home. Kelly wouldn't let it go. She glared at Dad. "So why is it that you can go and we can't?"

"Because I'm her father. She can't have a bunch of commotion around her today. Not today."

Kelly shook her head. "You don't think she needs our support too? We are her siblings!"

Dad got up from the table. "I'm not discussing this anymore. I've already told you, she can't have a bunch of commotion going on. I don't want to hear another word!"

Kelly responded by storming down the hall to our room and slamming the door. Sam and I sat there a little stunned and continued to eat our cereal. I glanced up at Dad and spoke softly. "So . . . when will you be back from the hospital?"

"I'm not sure. I might be late. I'll leave you guys some money to order pizza." Sam's eyes lit up.

Dad left shortly after breakfast, leaving us kids the house to ourselves. Kelly mostly stayed in our room (I didn't dare go in), Sam played Nintendo and I read the latest book in the Sweet

Valley High series. When it was time for dinner, Sam came out of his room to order the pizza, and Coke, we couldn't forget the Coke. Kelly didn't come out of our room until she heard the doorbell ring to see who was at the door; she hadn't realized we had ordered dinner. I'm not sure who else she thought would be there. The three of us sat around the table eating our pizza. Kelly was already in her pajamas and had pink puffy eyes like she had been crying, whereas Sam had red eyes from a day of staring at the TV playing video games.

Shortly after we began to eat, Kelly put down her fork. "It's so unfair that we can't be with Anna today. They just don't want us around. They wish it was just them and Anna."

I nervously chewed my inner cheek. "I don't know if that's true. I know it sucks, but maybe her doctors told them to not have us there. We are a bit of a crowd. Maybe it's best for Anna?"

Sam shook his head. "It's all bullshit. I agree with Kelly. They don't care about us. Just Anna."

I wrinkled my nose as I continued to pick the pepperoni off my pizza. Kelly and Sam continued on about how nobody cared about us, just Anna. They seemed to fuel each other's anger.

It made me sad to sit there and see how we'd begun to unravel as a family. I remember moving into the very house we were sitting in. Everyone was so excited. It was right before I started fifth grade, the very week, actually. I was stoked that although we were moving, we didn't have to change schools. Also, we'd always rented, which meant we moved around a lot; Mom and Dad had bought this house, which meant we wouldn't have to move houses or schools anymore. It wasn't our first house, but it was definitely our first home.

It was two stories, was yellow with white trim and had a lawn out front. When we first saw the inside, Kelly, Sam and I ran into all of the bedrooms trying to claim which would be ours. Of course, Mom decided that she and Dad would share the master upstairs, and Kelly and I would share one of the bedrooms downstairs next to Sam's. It had a big living room and kitchen. After the initial tour we did somersaults and cartwheels from the hall to the front door. I was so excited the day we moved in, despite still having to share a room with Kelly.

Dad came home around nine o'clock that night. A few moments after walking through the front door, everyone, as if choreographed, ran to ask about how Anna did during her first day of chemo. He seemed more agitated than normal and told us to calm down. "Let's just all go in the kitchen and we can talk about it, okay?"

We agreed, headed into the kitchen and sat down at the table. I stared at him. "Well, how is she?"

"Anna is okay. She's pretty tired from the chemo and isn't feeling good. She can't play or read and doesn't want to eat. She mostly sleeps and throws up. According to Dr. Baker and the nurses, all of this is normal. Chemo is some nasty stuff, but we need it to get rid of the cancer."

Confused, I asked, "So if it's so bad, how does it help Anna? She sounds like she's sicker than before she went to the hospital and had surgery. I don't get it."

Dad nodded. "I know it's confusing. The doctors say that the chemo drugs fight the bad cancer cells, which we need so that we get rid of the cancer, but at the same time it also kills some of the healthy, good cells too. It also causes all kinds of nasty side effects like vomiting, pain, hair loss, and mouth sores, just to name a few. Not to mention, the chemo weakens her immune system, so she'll have a harder time fighting infections like a cold or the flu."

"What happens if she gets a cold?"

"She could get really sick and possibly die. If any of you aren't feeling well at all, you need to tell me. You can't visit if you even have a sniffle. Understand?"

Kelly eyed Dad. "When can we visit her again?"

"The doctors think its best if we wait a few days before she has a lot of visitors."

Kelly impatiently shook her head. "When can we see her?"

"Most likely Wednesday after school and after I get off work, I'll pick you guys up and we'll go to the hospital."

Kelly's eyes opened wide. "But that's three days away!"

"Look, Kelly, this is hard on all of us. We have to think of what's best for Anna, and this is what's best. Stop fighting me on everything. I'm getting really tired of it!"

Sam and I exchanged glances. After that, Kelly burst into tears and ran back into our room, and Dad stormed upstairs. I smirked at Sam. "Well, that went well."

Sam shook his head. "Dad's such an asshole. I'm going to my room. G'night."

I lifted an eyebrow. "G'night."

The next morning we all got ready for school, Dad for work. Kelly left for her bus to the junior high, while Sam and I left to catch our bus to our school. On the way to the bus stop Sam decided he'd rather walk to school because "the bus is for dorks." I told him "whatever" and kept on to the bus stop.

The day was a typical day at school and a typical day after school with the exception that Mom and Anna weren't around. I made a snack and read. It took me a while to realize neither Kelly or Sam were home. It wasn't until almost dark that they both came home. We didn't talk much; Sam just asked what was for dinner. "I don't know. Dad's not home yet."

Kelly rolled her eyes. "Well, I'm hungry, so I'm going to make a sandwich. You guys want one?"

I glanced over at Sam. "Sure."

Sam smirked. "Yeah, okay."

I wondered if Kelly was trying to fill in for Mom; she had never made us dinner before. It was nice.

Dad came home much later when we were all in bed. He apologized the next day for not being home earlier but that it was hard to leave Anna. Kelly explained that she had made dinner, so it wasn't a big deal. We asked about Anna, and he said she was the same as the day before. He promised to leave money for tonight's dinner in case he was late again. After breakfast we all left to go to our bus stops.

We didn't get to visit Anna until Wednesday after school, as Dad had predicted. He picked us up at the house, went through the drive-thru McDonald's to pick up dinner and drove to the hospital. We got our badges and headed up to Anna's room. We walked into the room, passing the same little girl from our last visit, asleep in her crib, and headed toward Anna, who was lying down in her crib with Mom standing next to her.

Anna saw us and then sat up, grinned and reached out her arms. Dad picked her up and gave her a hug and kiss on the cheek. As usual, we all began talking to Anna at once. Mom gave Kelly a hug when she noticed the tears in her eyes. Sam was doing his monkey face for Anna, and she started cracking up. Mom, shocked at the laughter, told us it was the first time she had laughed since she'd started chemo.

Kelly glanced over at me and mouthed, "Told you." At that point it did seem like she wanted us to visit and that it didn't make sense they kept us away. Hello, she was cracking up after just having major surgery and chemotherapy. I piped up. "They do say laughter is the best medicine!" Anna seemed to think that was funny too. Her laughter was contagious. Soon we were all laughing—including Sam, with his laugh honk. I think at that point we were laughing so hard, we were crying.

In the middle of our laugh fest, Nurse Karen walked in. "What's all this commotion in here?" I told Sam, "Show her the face." Sam did the monkey face, and Anna started to giggle uncontrollably. Nurse Karen chuckled. "It's good to see all of you. I can tell Anna is very happy to see you too! I hate to interrupt, but I've got to check on Anna. Dad if you can put Anna in her crib, I'll only be a minute."

Dad put her down, and Nurse Karen took Anna's temperature and checked her IV and Broviac. As promised, she took only a few minutes and handed Anna back to Dad. On her way out she stopped in front of Sam and me. "I believe we got interrupted last time. I know you had a lot of questions. Do you still have questions?"

I said, "I did, but Dad filled me in on most of the stuff. I do have another question though. Who is the girl next door? Does she have cancer too?"

Nurse Karen glanced at the girl. "That is Katya, and she has leukemia."

"How old is she? Does she have a family that visits? I've never seen them?"

Nurse Karen gazed sadly over at Katya. "She's three, so a little older than Anna. Her family visits sometimes, but they have to work most of the time, and they have other kids at home to take care of. She is mostly by herself."

My eyes widened. "Do they not want to be here? We'd never leave Anna!"

"Of course they do. They just can't afford to take time off work, and her brother is just a baby and can't be left by himself. Katya's mom is usually very sad when she visits because she knows she has to leave Katya. Anna is very lucky to have a family that can be with her all the time. A lot of kids aren't that lucky. Most actually."

I stared at the ground. "Oh."

Nurse Karen cocked her head to the side. "I've got to check on some more patients, I'll see you later, okay?"

"Okay."

I waved to her as she walked out. Even with cancer, Anna was a lucky little girl.

We didn't get to visit Anna again until the weekend. Kelly, Sam and I had spent all day Saturday and Sunday at the hospital; we were certainly learning the lay of the land. Anna slept a lot, so we spent a lot of time roaming the halls and different floors. First floor: Admitting and Emergency. Second floor: cafeteria. Third floor: Surgery. Fourth floor: Burn Unit. Fifth floor: Oncology. During one of Anna's many naps, Sam and I figured out we could race elevators to pass the time. We'd pick a floor, and the first person to get there was the winner.

On Sunday, Anna seemed to regain some of her strength and kept putting her arms up, indicating she wanted to get up and walk around. Although nervous, Mom allowed it. Anna clumsily walked as Mom pushed the IV pole around the halls with us kids in tow. Anna thought it was fun to bang on the walls and to grip the pole and try to make it shake. Despite Mom's warning to stop because it was unsafe, us kids encouraged all of her little monkey business, mostly because of the smiles from Anna that came along with it.

The next few weeks were pretty much the same as the previous. Although Mom and Dad were there every day with Anna, we got to visit only once or twice during the week and all day on the weekends. Dad took us grocery shopping once a week, and we were getting pretty good at making sandwiches, heating up frozen TV dinners, ordering pizza and essentially running the house. We were like grown-ups. Although, Kelly did try to boss Sam and me around; I think she thought she was in charge, but in reality we were all pretty much flying solo.

One day after school, I was home alone and Sam walked in. "Hey. I didn't see you at school, did you go?" I asked.

"No, I decided to just ride my bike for a little bit and play video games."

"Aren't you scared you're going to get in trouble?"

"Nah. I've only gone to school a few times since Anna's been in the hospital. It's been almost two months and nobody even calls home. Once Mother and Anna are back, I'll go. Not a big deal."

I wasn't sure that it wasn't a big deal and wondered if I should tell someone. I decided I'd better not. We were kind of on our own, and I didn't want him to get mad at me. I wondered if Kelly was going to school. I didn't know where she was most of the time either. She wasn't usually home until dinner.

WE WERE happy when Anna was on her last week of chemo. We had asked Dad if we could pick up some balloons for Anna to celebrate the occasion. He agreed. When we got to the hospital, we picked out balloons from the gift shop and brought them up to Anna. We walked up to Anna with the balloons, and her blue eyes widened as she pointed. "Bablooms!"

Mom grinned. "Yes, Anna. Balloons, very good!"

Dad took Anna from Mom. "How's she doin'?"

"She's doing pretty good. A volunteer came by earlier and invited Anna to go to the playroom. She had an absolute blast! Oh my gosh. She colored, painted, played with stickers and met some other kids."

Dad's face brightened. "That's great!"

"Also she's getting more used to walking around with her IV pole." Mom pulled out a Polaroid.

"The nurses took a picture! How cute is she?"

She showed us the photo: it was Anna with a huge grin and her newly bald head, sporting a hospital gown and slippers, clutching her Ernie doll in one hand and the IV pole in the other. She was officially a "chemo kid." It seemed as though all of us, even Anna, were getting used to our new arrangements.

CHAPTER 8

SAM

ANNA FINISHED her first round of chemo nearly two months after her surgery and was finally ready to come home. Things were about to change. For starters, I was going to have to start going to school again. I can't believe I slipped up and let Casey catch me coming home late. Ugh. That goody-goody better not tell on me. Was it really that big of a deal if I wanted to take some time off to play video games, ride my bike around town and go to the arcade? It's not like school was hard or even that important. It's sixth grade, for Pete's sake. I don't get why Casey acted so concerned.

Next change was that Mom finally reached the next level in insanity when it came to cleaning the house. In preparation for Anna's homecoming, Mother went on a crazy cleaning spree. This wasn't our usual "clean team" Saturday cleaning where Mom lined us up and had us clean the house top to bottom while she wore a tool belt full of cleaning supplies. Not that that wasn't crazy too. I mean, who does that? Our mother, that's who. This was even crazier than that. This was a frenzied "clean every nook and cranny with a thick brown liquid called Betadine." She poured the dark brown goop all over the floors and counters. It looked like blood that changed to yellow when it was wiped down. It was pretty gross and kind of cool at the same time. Mother insisted it was sterilizing the house so that Anna wouldn't get sick. Not only did the house have to be dirt- and germ-free, we needed to be too. She felt it necessary to constantly remind the girls and me to wash our hands and that shoes were no longer allowed in the house.

I think she was a little paranoid, but what do I know? She was so obsessed with cleaning the house that I think she forgot my birthday was the next day. She said she didn't forget, but I over-heard Kelly asking Mother, "What are we doing for Sam's birthday tomorrow?"

Mother made a heavy sighing sound. "Dinner and a cake I guess."

Rad. My own mother didn't even remember my birthday. I could tell my twelftth year on the planet was going to be just great. After the house was scrubbed clean, Mother called Jasper at the hospital to give him the okay to bring Anna home.

When Jasper arrived at the house with Anna, he brought with him a carful of supplies from the hospital. There were huge boxes of gauze, syringes, changing pads, tape and a whole bunch of other things I didn't recognize. He had the girls and me bring in all the boxes while he got a sleeping Anna out of her car seat. He mouthed for us to be quiet as he carried her inside and upstairs to their room. We neatly, on Mother's orders, stacked all of the boxes at the bottom of the stairs to be brought up once Anna was awake.

It was kind of a letdown that she was finally home but was asleep. It had been tough not having her around, not that I would have admitted that to anyone. She was the one bright thing in our house before she got cancer; she made us a family. Without her there, we were all just people living in the same house going about our separate lives. It seemed as though the only one of us who didn't change after Anna's cancer was Casey. She was still the same chatty, book-reading nerd that she always was. Kelly now hid out in her room and moped around instead of being her normal bossy know-it-all teenage self. Jasper was hardly ever around. He said he was visiting Anna, but I'm not sure I bought it.

It was music to all of our ears when Anna started to cry, indicating she was awake from her nap. Finally, we got to see her in our house! We could play with her and her toys. We could ride around on her train. We could play at her pretend kitchen. We could have a reason to be happy.

While Mother went upstairs to get Anna, the rest of us waited at the bottom of the stairs in anticipation. While Mother walked her down the stairs, we waved and began in with our usual commotion. "Hi, Anna!" "Welcome home!" "We love you, Anna!" The expression on Anna's, now thinner, face was of pure excitement. She squealed and grinned from ear to ear; she was definitely happy to be home with all of us. When they got to the bottom of the stairs, Anna put out her arms and said, "Dow dow." Mother put her down, and she ran over to the girls and me and then to her basket of toys under the stairs. She was home and she was ready to play.

THE NEXT DAY was fairly normal like it was before Anna got sick. I decided to go to school, since Mother was home and she'd probably notice if I didn't go to school or if I didn't arrive home at the same time as Casey. I went and that was just great. My homeroom teacher, Mr. Bing, who was a tall dude with brown unkempt hair and dorky glasses, held me after school because he said he needed to talk to me.

"Sam, I'm concerned about the amount of school you've missed. To pass, you'll need to do a lot of makeup assignments."

He handed me a large, thick yellow envelope. "Sam, I'm

serious about this. I've put together the work for you to make up."

I took the envelope. "I'll work on it."

Mr. Bing forced a grin. "I hope you will. How's your sister? Is she home from the hospital yet?"

"Yeah. She got home yesterday."

"Glad to hear it." He paused. "Oh and Sam, I hope you have a happy birthday."

It was the first happy birthday of the day, and it was from my teacher. I half smiled, thanked him and walked out of the classroom.

When I got to the bus stop, Casey was already in line. She waved me over. "You can cut if you want."

"Okay, cool."

"Wanna sit together?"

"Sure."

On the bus ride home I drew in my notebook and told Casey that I didn't feel much like talking. She didn't seem bothered by that. On the walk home from the bus stop Casey started in about Anna. "Do you think Anna will be awake?"

"I don't know. Maybe."

When we walked in the house, Mother and Anna were both in the kitchen. Casey ran straight to Anna, giving her a hug and a hello. Mother came up to me and gave me a hug. "Happy birthday, Sam!"

Casey's eyes widened in surprise. "Happy birthday!"

She tried to get Anna to say it too. "Anna, can you say happy birthday to Sam? Happy birthday? Say it, Anna. Say happy birthday!"

Anna just stared at Casey like she was a loony tune. Later, when Kelly got home, we went through the same scene. Anna still couldn't say happy birthday. My guess was that she was quite a ways off from being able to say happy birthday, since she was only sixteen months old.

Later that evening, Jasper came home with a pizza, Cokes and a cake from the grocery store. The cake had white frosting and a "Happy 12th Birthday Sam" written in blue icing. It was chocolate, my favorite, with raspberry filling. Mother said that she would have liked to take us out to celebrate, but Anna's immune system was weak and she didn't want to take her out in public. I told her I didn't mind, and I didn't.

We had dinner followed by singing and cake. The best part wasn't necessarily the party or the cake. It was watching Anna eat the cake. Like all of the other cake-eating celebrations in the past, she got cake and frosting all over her face. She had white-and-blue frosting streaks on her chin, nose, and cheeks. It was too funny. In addition to cake and pizza, Mother gave me a birthday card, signed by everyone, with a fifty-dollar bill inside. She said that this weekend we could go shopping, and I could get whatever I wanted. I already knew what I was going to get. I was going to get the new Pro Wrestling game for my Nintendo. It was just released, and I was going to be the first person I knew who had it. I guess this birthday wasn't so bad after all.

THE NEXT WEEKEND Mother took me out to get the game with my birthday money. I couldn't wait to get home and play; Mother also seemed to be in a hurry. It was odd. I asked, "Why are you in such a hurry to get back?"

"It's not that I'm in a hurry. It's actually the opposite. I'm just a little nervous about having to change Anna's Broviac dressing today."

"What does that mean?"

"You remember what her Broviac is, right? The tube that goes to the vein in her chest so that she can get medicine without a poke each time?"

"Yeah."

"Well, I have to change the dressing while we are home. The dressing is the tape and bandage that goes over it so that it doesn't get dirty or infected. I was taught at the hospital how to do it. I'm just nervous that I might mess it up and there won't be a nurse there to help."

"So you kind of have to be a nurse to Anna too?"

"Pretty much. I have to flush the line with Heparin everyday too, to prevent blood clots, and I'm going to have to administer medication and draw blood."

I didn't know how to respond, but I don't think she intended for me to. I had no idea my mother had to do all this. I just assumed all of Anna's medical stuff would be done at the hospital. It was impressive. The rest of the ride was in silence. When we got back home, I went straight to my room to play my new game.

THE NEXT WEEK things settled down a bit. Everyone seemed to be in a better mood than when Anna and Mother weren't home. Kelly came out of her room more, mostly to play with Anna or talk to Mother about Anna. Casey was the same old Casey. Anna seemed happy to be home, as she was back to running around everywhere and getting into things, mostly trying to open and close all the doors and cupboards in the house and bang them shut. Her toys were all over the living room. It was as if she had claimed the house as her personal playroom that she invited everyone to join in on.

Mother's cleaning with the Betadine was a daily event. It didn't bother me any, as it meant that we didn't have to clean, other than picking up our rooms and putting our dishes in the dishwasher. According to Mother, our cleaning skills just weren't up to par. Fine by me.

Things were finally starting to get better, until they weren't.

Later that week, in the middle of the night, we all woke up to Anna's crying. It wasn't her normal, middle-of-the-night cry indicating she was hungry or needed a change. When it was that kind of cry, Mother would attend to her right away, and the crying would stop in a minute or so. This was a continued cry that went on for too long. I listened as both Mother and Jasper were up walking around.

I then heard the door open from Kelly and Casey's room and someone coming downstairs. I got out of bed and went into the hall to see what was going on. Nobody was there. I continued past the living room and into the kitchen. Kelly and Casey were in one corner of the dining room, and Jasper was on the phone talking to someone. I walked over to the girls. "What's going on?"

Kelly spoke quietly. "Anna has a fever, and Dad's calling the hospital to see if they needed to bring her in tonight."

Jasper turned around and put his finger to his lips, telling us to be quiet. We exchanged glances and stood quietly in the corner until he got off the phone. After he got off the phone, Casey asked, "What's going to happen?"

"We've got to take Anna back to the hospital right away. I'm going to drive Mom and Anna. You guys need to stay here."

Kelly started to protest.

"I don't want to hear it, Kelly. You guys get back to bed. I'll be home in a few hours." We didn't argue.

The three of us went back to our rooms. Shortly after I heard the front door close and the car drive off, I heard the door from the girls' room open. I went out to the living room to see what was going on. Casey and Kelly were in the living room talking. Kelly glanced up at me as I walked in. "Did they really expect us to just go back to sleep? Our sister is being rushed to the hospital in the middle of the night and it's no big deal—just go back to bed?"

I shook my head. "Oh, I know. So typical."

Kelly continued. "It's as if they don't think we worry about

Anna. All I think about is Anna! Just go back to sleep! They're so delusional!"

We stayed up for another hour or so talking about Anna and eating all the good snacks we could find. When Casey fell asleep on the couch, Kelly and I decided we should probably go back to our rooms to avoid getting into trouble for staying up. We woke up Casey to get her to go to bed. Kelly and I said good night and closed our doors.

CHAPTER 9

KELLY

I SAT up most of the night just thinking about Anna. Every so often I would glance over at Casey sleeping in her bed across the room. I wished I was able to sleep. I still can't believe Anna had to be rushed to the hospital; it must be serious. I felt so helpless not being able to do anything.

How was I supposed to sleep? How could my parents expect that I could sleep? I don't think I've slept through the night since Anna's diagnosis. I wondered when Dad would get home and let us know how Anna is doing. What if this fever kills her? I remember Mom saying that something as minor as a cold or flu could kill her. How did she even get sick? The house is sterilized, and none of the kids are sick. How could this have happened?

Dad didn't get home until four o'clock that morning. I waited a few hours before getting up so that he wouldn't know I never went to sleep. Once I heard him moving around upstairs, I got up and went into the kitchen for breakfast and waited. I heard footsteps toward the kitchen and hoped it was him, but it wasn't. It was Casey coming in for cereal and Sam shortly after. "How did you sleep?"

Casey yawned. "Fine."

"Sam?"

Sam glanced over at me as he pulled down a bowl. "Fine."

"Are you guys ready for school?"

Casey furrowed her brow. "What's with the twenty questions? Obviously we're ready, since we're dressed."

Just then Dad walked in dressed for work and with bags under his eyes. I asked, "How's Anna? Is she okay? What's going on?"

He motioned for me to settle down, like he always did. "She's in the hospital, in isolation. They are trying to find a way to get the fever down."

"How did she get a fever? We did everything Mom told us to do to make sure she didn't catch anything!"

"It may not be from anything we did. We don't know why she has a fever."

"How long will she be in the hospital? When can we visit?"

"We can't visit while she's in isolation."

"Is Mom with her?"

"Yeah."

"Well then, how come we can't visit?"

"They want to limit exposure. A fever is very serious for a child on chemo. It kills healthy germ fighters along with the cancer. So any fever or infection means we have to take every precaution to make sure we can beat it. Mom had to scrub down and gown up before entering isolation. It's just too risky right now for you guys to visit."

"So you get to visit too?"

"Yes, I'll visit."

It was unbelievable, we were getting shut out again. "So it's just us who can't visit?"

"For now. Yes. I'm sorry, but we need to make sure she gets better and the doctors have advised us against having any children visit."

"I'm not a child!"

"Kelly, I'm sorry. You just can't. This is very serious. Please don't fight me. I'm just too tired."

"Fine."

"You guys want a ride to school?"

I think he thought it was some kind of consolation prize. No, you can't visit your sick sister, but you don't have to take the bus. Whatever. We all agreed we'd take the ride.

Since we got a ride to school, I was pretty early. I went to my homeroom class to see if the door was unlocked. When I walked in, I saw that Ms. Green, my teacher who was a tall woman with long, wavy gray hair and blue eyes, was already there. I waved as I walked up to her. "Good morning Ms. Green."

"Good morning, Kelly. You're here early!"

"Yeah, Dad dropped me off. We had a long night last night. Anna got rushed to the hospital with a fever."

"I'm so sorry to hear that."

"Thanks. I've been meaning to ask you, do you know if there are any books in the school library that would have information on neuroblastoma?"

"There may be a few books, but you may have better luck at the public library. It's much bigger and will have a wider selection."

"Okay, thanks."

I went to the school library at lunch to see what books they had on Anna's cancer. As Ms. Green had warned me, there weren't very many. There was some information in the encyclopedia, but I wasn't able to check out the encyclopedia, so I read through it during lunch. It seemed a little complicated. Luckily, I did find one other book on cancer that was available for checkout. I figured if I studied it at home and had more time to go through it, I would be able to understand it.

When I got home, I went straight to my room. Casey was already in there reading. I said hi and then walked back to the kitchen. I sat the big cancer book down on the dining table and began to read. Sam walked in a few minutes later. "Wow. Hell must be freezing over! You're reading a book." He thought he was so funny.

"For your information, I was reading books before you could even walk." He just laughed and made a face at me. "When's Dad coming home? What's for dinner?"

"I don't know."

The phone rang, and Sam rushed to answer it. I asked who it was, and he wouldn't answer. Finally, he turned around. "It's Dad-Pete! He's going to pick us up this weekend!" I was as surprised as he was.

Shortly after, Casey walked into the kitchen and asked who was on the phone. I quietly explained, "It's Dad-Pete. He's going to pick us up this weekend."

She replied with a disinterested, "Oh."

After a few minutes I tapped Sam on the shoulder and told him I wanted to talk to Dad-Pete. After some resistance he gave the phone to me.

"Hi, Dad!"

"Please remind your brother and sister that I'm Dad, not Dad-Pete."

"Yeah, okay." I continued to tell him about Anna and everything going on. I was surprised to hear that Mom had called him and already told him. I guessed that is why he had called and was picking us up. He told me he'd pick us up at 6 p.m. on Friday after school, said good-bye and hung up. Casey stood in front of me with her hands on her hips. "Hey! You didn't let me say hi!"

I rolled my eyes. "We'll see him this Friday after school, chill out."

We hadn't seen Dad-Pete since Christmas, and I could tell Sam was pretty excited about the upcoming visit. Hopefully, he actually showed up this time. Dad-Pete usually told us he would pick us up and then we'd anxiously wait by the front door with our bags, looking like idiots, until Mom gets a call that he isn't going to pick us up. It's happened so many times I've lost count. It totally sucked. Mom usually tried to cheer us up by taking us out to dinner, which distracted us from being sad but didn't take away our disappointment that we didn't get to see Dad-Pete.

Later that night Dad came home and walked into the kitchen. I stood up from the table. "How's Anna?"

"She's hanging in there. The doctors are giving her some heavy-duty antibiotics to fight the fever."

"When can she come home?"

"I'm not sure. They say it could be another week or two. They just don't know yet. These things are tricky."

"Oh." I picked up the cancer book and went to my room to read the book and write in my journal.

THE NEXT DAY I stayed home from school with head and body aches. I spent the day watching TV, mostly soap operas and boring game shows. I surprised Sam when he got home around noon. "What are you doing here?"

"I was about to ask you the same thing."

"I have a bad headache, what's your excuse?"

"I just decided to come home early. I was tired."

"Ohhh-kay. Since when does tired get you out of school?"

"Since now. Get off my back. You're not my mom."

He stormed off to his room after that. I don't know what his problem was. When Casey got home from school, I told her that Sam had come home because he was "tired."

"Oh. That. Yeah he doesn't always go to school."

"What do you mean?"

"Well, I found out that he wasn't always going to school when Mom and Anna were in the hospital. He says it's not a big deal."

I was shocked. "What do you mean? How much school has he missed?"

"I'm not sure."

Casey was less than interested in continuing the conversation. I thought to myself, Well, isn't this just great. Anna's in the hospital. Sam's ditching school. What is it all coming to?

When Dad got home later that night, I was still on the couch watching TV. He walked up to the couch. "Hey, Kelly. How are you feeling?"

"I'm a little better, I think."

"Good. You should call your mom—she's worried."

"Maybe later. How's Anna?"

"Her fever is down a bit, so that's good news."

"Can she come home soon?"

"They don't know. We aren't quite in the clear yet."

"Oh."

"Have you had dinner yet?"

"No. Not hungry."

"You should eat. It'll help." He smiled like he cared.

To avoid further harassment, I got up and made a turkey sandwich. I ate a few bites and then went back to watching TV. I didn't feel like eating or doing anything at all. The next few days I gathered all the energy I had to get up and go to school.

ON FRIDAY NIGHT at six o'clock, Sam and Casey had already packed their bags and were waiting by the front door for Dad-Pete. Luckily, and to my surprise, Dad-Pete actually showed up. I wasn't convinced he was going to pick us up and hadn't packed a bag. I quickly threw a few outfits, some makeup, a hairbrush and hair spray into my backpack and headed out the door.

Casey and Sam were chatting up Dad-Pete all the way to dinner. I just sat in the backseat staring across the car at him. Dad-Pete had a big beak-like nose, inherited from our Italian family, olive skin, blue eyes, and a full head of straight brown hair. Our relatives thought that Sam was a spitting image of him.

We ended up going to dinner at Lyons in Antioch, which was close to Dad-Pete's apartment. It's kind of our usual dinner spot with him. I think he takes us there because both Sam and Casey love it. I don't know why they think it's so "cool" to be able to get hot chocolate and breakfast all day. It was basically just a diner with mediocre food. I don't know if I'll ever understand those kids.

During dinner Dad-Pete asked why I was so quiet, in contrast to Sam and Casey, who were talking nonstop about school, music, what we were going to do that weekend and any other little thing that came to their mind. I told him it was nothing, I just had a headache. He said he'd get me some Tylenol when we got back to the apartment.

When we got back to Dad-Pete's apartment, we set up our sleeping bags on the floor in front of the TV and put in a movie, The Karate Kid Part II, to watch. Dad-Pete had gotten us some popcorn and candy to eat during the movie too. Sam and Casey were thrilled. Those two are a couple of sugar fiends. The weekend was pretty cool, since I got to visit with my old friend, Tanya, who lived in the same apartment complex as Dad-Pete. I usually talked to her on the phone from time to time but hadn't seen her in a while.

The rest of the weekend was spent watching TV and movies. Saturday night we went out to an actual movie theater and saw Beverly Hills Cop II. It was totally hilarious. I think we all laughed during the movie, even Dad-Pete. Sam was crazy laughing, he even went into fits of honking. It felt good to not think about anything and laugh for a while.

Dad-Pete dropped us off at home on Sunday night. He promised he'd see us again soon, but I wasn't holding my breath.

When we walked in the door, Dad was already there in the

entryway waiting for us; all three of us said hi, walked in and put our bags down in the hall. "How's Anna?"

"She's doing a little better."

"Will she be home soon?"

"The doctors think it could still be a few weeks before she can come home."

My mouth dropped open. "Seriously?"

Dad grimaced. "Yeah. It sucks."

I shook my head at Sam and Casey. "It totally sucks."

Sam and Casey agreed. I picked up my bags and put them in our room. What a let down. I hoped that we'd get good news when we got home, but no, just more bad news. I wasn't sure how much more of this I could take.

CHAPTER 10

WHEN WE WALKED through the door after the weekend with Dad-Pete, it felt different. I think it was because Anna and Mom weren't there. Usually Mom would ask how it had went and what we did. This time all we got was the bad news that Anna and Mom weren't coming home for a few weeks.

It had been a while since we'd seen Dad-Pete, but we still had fun. I know that Sam was pretty happy to spend time with him. He is always going on about how Dad, Jasper, isn't our real Dad and that Dad-Pete was really our dad. I get it, I guess, but Dad-Pete just isn't there that often. I see him as more of the guy who takes us to see our other family, which are practically strangers, on Christmas Eve. If I had a problem, he isn't who I would call. He's like the fun-time Dad, not the take-care-of-you kind of Dad, like our Dad. I don't even remember Dad-Pete ever being with Mom and us. I was too young to remember when the five of us were a family.

The only family I knew was with Mom, Dad, Kelly, Sam and Anna. Mom and Dad would never take us to the movies and let us get popcorn and candy. Mom always said candy was bad for our teeth, and Dad said it was too expensive at the movies anyways. Mom certainly wouldn't allow us to stay up all night watching TV and movies while camped out in the living room, like Dad-Pete. Mom always insisted that TV rotted your brains and hardly ever let us watch it. It was just different over there with him.

I know that Kelly liked going over to Dad-Pete's too, mostly because of all the neighbor kids. She was such a social butterfly. Like this last weekend, she spent most of the day with a group of teenagers across the complex and then again after we went to a movie. I guess I liked to go because it was part of being Sam's and Kelly's sister. It was the unique thing that we shared; it was what made us special. We had a Dad-Pete and a Grandpop and a big Italian family we saw once a year. It was cool. I was always excited to visit but almost as excited to go back home to tell Mom, Dad and Anna all about it. This was the first time since Anna was born that Mom and Anna weren't there. It didn't feel right.

———

MOM AND ANNA came home a few weeks later and things quickly got back to normal. It wasn't the old normal, before Anna got cancer; it was the new normal. The normal where Mom and Anna were home with us. The normal where Mom scrubbed the house with Betadine. The normal where Sam started going to school again and I wouldn't get pestered by his friends asking where he's been. The normal where Kelly didn't spend every minute of every day on the phone or in our room. The normal where Dad went to work and then came home and we had dinner together. We continued to add to what our new "normal" was.

For example, one day Mom let me watch her change out and

flush Anna's Broviac. It was pretty scary and cool at the same time. She told me that I had to be still and sit back about three feet, wash my hands (with Betadine of course), and wear a face mask. While she began prepping all the materials, it was as if Mom's bedroom had just transformed into a hospital room and her bed was now a hospital bed.

First she put down a mat and put Anna on top of it as if she were going to change her diaper. She then pulled out a kit of materials. She put down what appeared to be a big paper towel, but was called a drape, and started taking out all of the items from the kit. She put on a mask and gloves, got out the tape, gauze, syringe, wipes, swabs and a bottle of Heparin. I was surprised that Anna lay so still while she did all of this. Mom continued to remove the old tape and dressing very slowly. I stared at the Broviac tube that went into Anna's chest; it was weird. It was like a tiny arm, or some other appendage, that was supposed to be there. Mom cleaned the area carefully in a circular motion and then let it air-dry. She glanced up at me. "It's okay to talk, you know."

"Oh, it's just so weird. How did you learn how to do all this?"

"The nurses at the hospital showed me how. They wouldn't let us leave until they thought I could do it on my own. I was quite nervous the first time I had to change it at home by myself."

"I can imagine. Aren't you afraid you are going to pull it out or something?"

"Kind of. Sometimes. I'm pretty careful, and by now it's in there pretty good."

"That's good. How often do you have to change the dressing?"

"A few times a week or as needed." I nodded as if I understood.

Mom finished another round of cleaning and then carefully put on Anna's new dressing. She continued to talk to Anna during the procedure, telling her what a great job she was doing.

Next she filled a syringe with Heparin, being careful to remove any air bubbles by tapping it and pushing up the plunger. Next she unclamped the tube on the Broviac and injected the Heparin. She was like a real nurse or doctor. "Why do you have to inject that into her?"

"I have to flush the Broviac with Heparin so Anna's blood won't clot. If she gets a blood clot, she could die."

"Is something wrong with Anna that her blood clots wrong—is that part of the cancer?"

Mom laughed. "No. Actually, it's very normal. When our bodies heal themselves, like when you cut your finger, the blood clots so that you don't bleed to death. Anna's Broviac goes to her vein that wants to clot because that is what a healthy body does; the Heparin stops that from happening. If she gets a blood clot in her vein, it could kill her."

"So it's really, really important. How often do you have to do it?"

"Every day."

I was amazed that something that seemed so simple was actually quite serious. When Mom was done, she put the rest of Anna's clothes on, gave her a hug and a kiss and said to her, "All done! Great job, Anna!" I mentally added this to our list of new "normal" activities.

The three of us headed downstairs. Mom put Anna down on the ground, and she walked over to her toys under the stairs. She grabbed a book, walked back over to me and we sat down and read Bert and the Broken Teapot.

Shortly after we finished reading, Kelly came out of our room and sat by Anna and me. Next thing I knew, Sam was there too. They both started to get other books and toys of Anna's to get her to play with them too. It worked. She liked the books and toys, but I think she liked being with us more.

Sam and I decided we should put on a skit for Anna. Kelly

instantly tried to take over. "I think we shouldn't just do a skit but a whole show. I'll be the director."

Sam and I exchanged glances. "Okay. What are you going to do?"

Kelly grinned and fluttered her eyelashes. "I thought you'd never ask. I think you two can do your skit, and then we can do a dance routine. For the finale, I'll sing." She studied our faces.

"A solo."

It was clear she didn't want us stealing her spotlight, so we agreed. Sam and I worked on our skit. We were a monkey and street performer who was trying to train the monkey. It was mostly Sam doing his monkey impression and me pretending to be frustrated that the monkey wouldn't do what I told it to do. Next, Kelly, Sam and I did a dance routine, that wasn't so much as a routine as it was dancing crazy and lip-synching to "Walk This Way" by Run-DMC. Anna danced along, clapping her hands. When it was time for Kelly's solo, "Greatest Love of All" by Whitney Houston, she insisted we sit down on the floor with Anna before she would begin. She stood in front of us, waved to imaginary fans and began her performance. "This is dedicated to my most beautiful little sister, Miss Anna Banana."

I protested. "Hey, what about me!"

She pretend cleared her throat. "If I may start over. Thank you. Thank you. This goes out to my youngest sister. The strikingly beautiful and intelligent toddler, Miss Anna Banana."

She paused and began a dramatic solo performance. Sam's and my eyes met. She sounded terrible, like a cat dying. Still, Anna was thoroughly entertained as were we, especially when Sam stood up and went behind Kelly and mimicked her every exaggerated move. By the end I thought I was going to die of laughter.

A few minutes later Mom came in to check on Anna. Kelly explained everyone was doing just fine. "What about your cleanliness levels? When was the last time you washed your hands?"

Kelly rolled her eyes. "All good here. We washed before our performance."

Mom seemed to believe her and went back into the kitchen.

When Dad got home, we gathered around the dining table in the kitchen for dinner. Shortly after we were seated, Mom glanced around the table. "Have you all washed your hands? If not, get up and wash your hands." We all got up, even Dad, and washed our hands in the kitchen sink. Before sitting down, Mom asked, "Who will set the table? Who will clear? Who will load the dishwasher?" This used to be a normal routine before Anna's cancer, but since she'd been in the hospital and we mostly ate takeout, we hadn't done it in a while. I said I'd set the table, since it was better than the other jobs. Once I set the table with our blue goose dishes and glasses, which matched the curtains, walls and decorations in the kitchen, we were ready to sit and eat.

Mom had made her famous lasagna with carrots. No, not a lasagna with a side of carrots; the carrots were in the lasagna. Despite our complaining about having carrots in our lasagna, Mom kept putting them in, declaring that it was healthy and that we had to eat it. We did. Dad asked us how school was, and we all said the standard "good" or "fine." We were all happy that there was only a month left until summer vacation. The rest of the conversation was around Anna and how she was doing and when she had to get testing for the next round of chemo. Mom said that she was going to take in Anna's blood for testing at the end of next week. I was shocked. "You have to draw her blood too?"

Mom smirked. "Yep. I have to draw it out of her Broviac."

"Can I watch?"

Sam was suddenly interested. "Yeah, me too, can I watch?"

"Sure."

"Cool." Sam sat back in his chair, satisfied.

After dinner, Mom put Anna to bed and told us kids to do our homework and get ready for bed. Sam and Kelly said they didn't have any homework, which Mom didn't believe for a minute.

Sam said he guessed he could work ahead on some stuff, and Kelly said she "guessed" she could too. I shook my head at them.

After I finished my homework, I went into our room and found Kelly in bed with her eyes closed. "Are you asleep?"

"No, I'm just resting. I'm not feeling very good."

It seemed as if she was always "not feeling good" or just all-around mopey, except for when she was playing with Anna.

THE NEXT WEEK seemed to fly by. Sam and I got to watch Mom draw Anna's blood. Like the dressing change and flush, it was quite the production. She had to sterilize the cap and then flush the line with two syringes of saline, draw the blood and then flush the line again. When Mom was doing the flush at the end, I explained to Sam, "She has to flush the line with Heparin so that Anna doesn't get a clot in her Broviac. If she gets a clot, she could die."

Mom beamed. "That's right, Casey."

After the blood draw and cleanup, Sam and I went with Mom and Anna to drop off the blood samples to the lab. On the way to the lab, Sam and I were both tasked with inverting the test tubes of blood so that the blood didn't clot before the lab could test Anna's blood. It was clear that Sam took the job seriously. He carefully moved the vial from left to right over and over; his eyes didn't leave the test tube until we arrived at the lab.

Sam and I stayed in the car with Anna while Mom went to drop off the tubes of blood. On the ride home, Sam asked when Anna had to go back to the hospital again for chemo. "If the test results are okay, she will have to go back to the hospital next week for her next round."

"Oh. How many rounds does she have to do?"

"They aren't sure yet. It will depend on how well the treatment is working. Unfortunately, there aren't any established protocols for what Anna has."

"Oh."

He put his head down and then turned to Anna in her car seat. "Anna, we are going to have to play a lot before you go back, okay?" Anna cheerfully clapped her hands.

CHAPTER 11

A FEW DAYS LATER, Anna was cleared to start her second round of chemo. Mom packed a bag of her things as well as Anna's favorite toys, books and clothes. It was as if Anna and Mom were going on vacation, but we all knew they weren't. It was such a different feel from the last two trips to the hospital. Nobody was yelling or freaking out. It wasn't rushed. It was as if it was just something that had to be done, like going to school. Like it was normal.

After Mom and Anna left for the hospital, the house went back to being quiet. It was as if the moment they drove off the rest of us scattered. Kelly and Sam went back to their rooms, and Dad left to run errands. I figured I would learn to get used to this too.

Later that week, Dad picked up Kelly, Sam and me after school to visit Anna in the hospital. Four months had passed since our first visit to the hospital, and we were becoming regulars, so much so that we now practically breezed through the front desk and badge-creation process. This day was no different. We walked into the hospital and went directly to the information desk, with confidence. "Hi, Lou!"

His face lit up. "Hey there, kids! Here to see your sister again?"

"Yep, second round of chemo, here we go!"

He chatted with us as we gave him our names and he filled out our badges. He no longer told us how to get to the elevator or other tips that he knew me must have memorized by now.

We walked into Anna's new room. On the left there was a boy sleeping in a hospital bed who looked to be about five years old with dark messy hair and pale skin as well as a breathing tube coming out of his mouth. Similar to Katya, Anna's last roommate, he seemed to be all alone. When we got to Anna's half of the room, we were happy to hear that Anna was awake and had already spotted us. Anna gave us lots of laughter and squeals. We proceeded toward her with our usual chaos of greetings, hugs and kisses.

Dad gave Anna and then Mom a kiss on the cheek. "How's she doing?"

"She's doing pretty good. It was a bit rough the first couple of days."

Mom glanced at Kelly, Sam and I. "She needs lots of rest. So be careful not to tire her out."

Just then a young woman with stick-straight dark hair and green eyes, wearing a bright blue coat, like a doctor's coat, walked into the room. Mom saw her and waved her over. She bounced up to Anna. "Hi, Anna! How are you?"

Mom replied for Anna. "She's good. Happy to have the rest of her family here. These are her sisters and brother, Kelly, Casey and Sam, and dad, Jasper."

"Nice to meet you all. I'm Patricia. I'm a volunteer here at the hospital. I can tell Anna is quite happy to see you. I just came in to let you know that the playroom is open for another hour if you'd all like to come and check it out!"

Sam perked up his chin. "What kind of stuff is in the playroom?"

"We have paints and markers, games, books, toys . . . all kinds of things! It's really fun."

Mom stepped in. "Thank you for letting us know. Maybe we'll head down in a little bit if the kids want to."

"Okay, hope to see you there. Bye, guys. See ya later, Anna!"

After Patricia left, Kelly exclaimed, "Wow. She has a lot of energy."

Mom handed Anna to Dad and then joined our conversation. "Anna met Patricia at the playroom earlier today. I told her you guys were coming in case you'd like to go with Anna. She said she'd stop by, which I think is very nice, don't you?"

Sam glanced at Mom. "Did Anna like the playroom?"

"Yes, the sandbox and the stickers are her favorite."

Sam responded, "Sounds cool. Can we go? I mean, it's got to be better than this hospital room."

Mom asked, "Girls, do you want to go?" Kelly and I both agreed.

"Okay, then. I'll get Anna situated, and then we can go."

Mom put Anna down on the ground, straightened out her tubing and glanced up at us. "Okay, we're ready. Let's go."

We followed behind Anna and her IV pole. Our group proceeded down the hall and around the corner. It probably took us about ten minutes, since we were moving quite slow. It didn't help that we all tried to play with Anna as we walked. When we arrived at the playroom, we saw that there were a few other kids and more volunteers.

On the right side of the room there was a counter, sink and cabinets above and below. There were three tables and chairs. The walls were adorned with previous playroom visitors' art projects. The back wall was made of glass and overlooked the city. Next to the back wall were toys and bookshelves. Anna quickly navigated us to a table full of cornmeal and beach toys. Apparently, the "sandbox" was actually full of cornmeal.

I glanced around the room to see all the other kids, who were obviously patients. One girl, about six, with an IV pole and peach-fuzz hairstyle, similar to Anna's, was sitting at one of the tables with paper, markers and a bucket full of stickers. At the same table was a boy, about five years old, in a wheelchair, with a bald head and giant scar going all around his head. He was sitting with a volunteer that was helping him pick a sticker. When he picked one he liked, he put it on his hospital gown. He had about six stickers so far. I wondered how many he'd have by the time the playroom closed.

Across the room were some younger kids reading books on the play mat on the floor in front of the window. Patricia was on the floor with them helping them turn pages and saying the words. All of the kids seemed to be having a good time.

After Anna tired of the cornmeal box, she moved us over to one of the empty tables. Mom brought over paper, markers and a tub of stickers and stamps from the cabinets along the wall. Sam, Kelly and I decided we would each make a piece of art for Anna to hang in her hospital room. We worked on our projects until the playroom closed.

Dad carried Anna back to the room as Kelly pushed the IV pole. When we got back to the room, Mom said Anna was tired and needed to eat and go down for a nap. Dad and us kids went down to the cafeteria for dinner. As usual, we got to pick out whatever we wanted. Sam did his normal mound of ice cream and sundae toppings. Dad was giving Kelly a hard time about her lack of eating, so she gave in and had some fried chicken and french fries. I don't think she took more than two bites of the chicken. but she did eat all the fries. I had my normal mac 'n' cheese but added some fried chicken this time, since they were out of mashed potatoes.

At dinner, Kelly asked, "When can we come back to visit?"

"Well. It's hard to pick you guys up at the house after work and then go back out to the hospital. So, while you guys are in school, only once or twice a week, but you can come out on the weekends. School is almost out, and once it's out, you can come almost every day if you want."

Kelly wouldn't give up and asked, "What if we meet you at the shop? We could ride our bikes. That way you don't have to come all the way home to pick us up."

Dad hesitated. "I don't think that's a good idea. Plus, Grandma Jess is going to start coming out to stay with Anna for a few hours, a few days a week so that Mom can get a little bit of a break."

I jumped into the conversation. "Anna will love to see Grandma Jess. Also, I think Mom needs a break. Do you see the stuff she does? The dressing changes and flushes and blood draws?"

Dad grinned. "I agree. She needs a break. You kids need to be on your best behavior when she comes home. No back talk . . . Kelly . . . Sam . . . I'm serious."

Kelly and Sam ignored him.

After dinner we went back up to Anna's room, but she was still asleep, so Mom suggested that maybe we should just go home because it was likely she'd be sleeping for a few hours. Dad lifted his eyebrows and peered at Kelly and then glanced over at Mom. "Okay, we'll go. Do you need anything?"

"No, I'm fine. Thanks."

"All right. C'mon, kids. Get your stuff. Let's go—and be quiet."

We gathered our things, waved good-bye to Mom as we left the room and then headed down to the car. We didn't speak much on the car ride home.

At home everyone went into their rooms, except for me. I stayed in the living room so that I could give Kelly some space. After I finished my homework and read for a little bit, I went to bed.

THE REST of the week was similar to other times Anna was in the hospital. We got up in the morning, got ready for school, came home from school and had pizza, Chinese or frozen meals for dinner. We didn't get to visit Anna again that week, and Mom didn't make it home until the weekend.

When Mom walked into the front door, she placed her bag in the entry and let out a deep breath. I walked up to her. "Hey! Welcome back."

"Hey, Casey. I can't wait to go upstairs and take a long shower and put on some clean clothes!"

"I bet. How long are you home for?"

"Just for a few hours."

"Isn't Grandma Jess with her?"

"Yes, but I don't want to be gone long in case she needs me. I'll start coming back a few hours a week though. Grandma Jess can stay with Anna in the evening and weekends, which will give me a chance to come home and check on things, change my clothes and take a real shower instead of the quick hose down I do in Anna's hospital-room shower."

"Will you be home for the last day of school?"

"We'll see. I don't want to leave Anna. So if I can get someone to stay with her, I might be able to."

"I understand."

I tried to not show how disappointed I was. Mom had always picked us up on the last day of school and taken us out for ice cream: it was a tradition for us. I didn't fight her or try to guilt her into being there. I knew Anna needed her.

Later that afternoon, we all went to the hospital with Mom, and Dad told Mom he'd be out later to visit and take us kids home. When we got to the hospital, we were all excited to see Anna and Grandma Jess. When we walked into Anna's room, the little boy was still in the bed next to her, and straight ahead was Grandma Jess holding Anna, reading her a book. Grandma Jess peeked up, saw us and flashed a wide grin. Once done greeting Anna, we showered Grandma Jess with hugs and hellos too. Mom went to Grandma Jess to get the update on how Anna had been doing. After that, Grandma Jess sat with us for a while, asking how we were all doing. I said to her, "You aren't wearing any lavender? It's your signature color."

Grandma Jess laughed. "Wouldn't you know it, I completely forgot to do laundry, and all I've got is aqua." She glanced down at her watch.

"Oh heavens. That reminds me. I've got to go soon."

We all gave her hugs, and she picked up Anna and gave her a hug and kiss. On her way out, she told Mom she'd be back on Monday around five o'clock. Mom thanked her, and she waved good-bye to all of us as she exited the room.

Moments after Grandma Jess left, Nurse Karen walked in and told us she needed to do a quick check on Anna. After she finished checking Anna's vitals, she spoke with Mom for a few minutes. While she was walking out she waved to us. I stopped her. "Hey, wait. Can I ask you about the little boy in the bed?"

"Of course."

"Who is he? Does he have leukemia?"

"That's Tony, and yes, he has leukemia."

"Doesn't he have family to stay with him?"

"Most of his family lives far away. His mom visits sometimes, but she's sick too."

"Does she have leukemia?"

"No. No. Something else. It makes it hard for her to visit."

"Oh. Okay. Do you know what happened to Katya, Anna's old roommate?"

Nurse Karen took a few moments to answer. "She isn't with us anymore. She passed during her last visit."

"Oh. Sorry."

"She's in a better place now. Anyhow, I've got to run. It was good to see you."

I waved as she walked briskly out of the room. I couldn't believe that little girl who was only three years old had died. It was so sad. I always thought death was for old people, like our great uncle who'd passed. We had gone to his funeral. Never did I think about young people passing away. It didn't seem right.

Mom must have overheard my and Nurse Karen's conversation, because after Nurse Karen left, she walked over and sat next to me. She lowered her voice and said, "Tony's mom is a drug addict and not in great shape. Tony is by himself most of the time. It's so sad. He's such a sweet little boy."

"Do you ever talk to him?"

Mom chuckled. "Yes. He's so sweet. Anna tries to say his name. It's so funny. She calls him 'toe,' and he thinks it's hilarious. He always laughs."

All of a sudden we heard Anna say, "Toe!"

We all laughed, as did Anna. I asked Mom if Tony would always be Anna's roommate when she had chemo or was in the hospital. Mom explained that they never knew what room she'd be in or who Anna's roommate would be. It wasn't like a dormitory; it was more like a parking spot at the mall. Whatever was available is what you got.

We spent the rest of the day taking turns reading books to Anna and playing in the playroom. After the playroom, us kids went to the cafeteria for dinner, and Anna went down for her nap. Later that night Dad came to pick us up and take us home. We hugged Mom good-bye and left.

The next week was the last week of the school year. I was ecstatic when during one of our hospital visits Mom said she would pick up Sam and me on the last day of school; Aunt Ella had offered to stay at the hospital with Anna. It was nice that some things didn't change. At the same time, I was quite excited that I was officially going to be a sixth grader in the fall. For the first time ever, I was going to be the only Galvin at my school. People at school would no longer refer to me as Casey, Kelly's little sister, or Casey, Sam's little sister. I was going to be Casey, just Casey.

CHAPTER 12

THE LAST DAY of school was finally here, and we got up in the morning like any other morning and headed off to school. Sam decided to take the bus with me, and on the way to the bus stop he started talking to me. "You know, Casey, this is the last time we'll ever walk to the bus stop together."

"Well, we'll be in the same junior high in another year, so maybe not. It will definitely be our last time walking to a school bus stop together, since the bus to the junior high is a public bus."

"Oh yeah. I didn't think about that." I was surprised when he continued talking.

"Isn't it weird that Anna has cancer? I mean. Who would've ever thought?"

"I certainly never would've thought that in a million years. I've never even known someone with cancer until Anna. Now I feel like we're surrounded by cancer."

"Do you think she is going to be okay? Like, not die?"

"I don't think she'll die. Do you?"

"I don't know."

Just then the bus pulled up, and we got on for our last school bus ride together. Sam sat with one of his friends, and I sat with mine.

It ended up being like every other last day of school. We got our yearbooks and had everyone sign them at lunch and recess. I never liked to write KIT (keep in touch) because I didn't usually keep in touch. I preferred to write a more heartfelt Have a great summer! to those I wouldn't be seeing or talking to over the summer.

At the end of the day, I walked down the ramp from my classroom to go to the front of the school. I noticed Mom was already next door at Sam's classroom. She was on the ramp talking with Sam and Mr. Bing. I rushed over to meet them. When I walked up, I heard Mr. Bing say, "You'll have to talk to the principal or superintendent, but that is what normally happens. It's unfortunate that it has come to this, but it is what I recommend. I think it's best for Sam."

Mom's mouth dropped open. "I had no idea. Why didn't the school send anything home or call or anything? This is outrageous that I'm just hearing about this now!"

"I'm sorry, Mrs. Galvin. Like I said, if you'd like to discuss this further, you can speak with the principal or the superintendent."

"I'll do that."

She shook her head at Sam. "Come on, let's go."

She hadn't noticed I was standing there before, but when she turned around, all she said was, "Oh, hi, Casey. Let's go. We're going now."

Sam waved to Mr. Bing, and he waved back. "Bye. Good luck next year."

We continued across the campus to the front of the school, where Mom had parked. When we got to the car, Sam said I could sit in the front. On the way home I asked Mom if we were going to get ice cream, but she didn't respond. I wasn't sure what was going on, but Mom seemed upset and Sam was quiet.

All of a sudden, Mom started yelling at Sam. "Sam, is this true? Have you been missing school? Have you gone to school at all since Anna's been sick? Tell me, now!"

"I didn't feel like going."

"That is no excuse. You have to go to school. I can't believe this. I can't believe you did this. Why? Why would you do this?"

"I didn't feel like it. What do you care, anyway? You're never around."

"I am gone because I'm taking care of your little sister with cancer who is in the hospital fighting for her life. What is wrong with you? Did you realize you failed every class? They want you to repeat sixth grade! Do you get that? I can't believe this shit. I can't believe you did this."

Sam sat quietly with his head down. I now understood why he let me sit in the front seat. I started to think about the last few months. I knew Sam wasn't going to school, but he had told me it was no big deal. I just assumed because he always got pretty good grades, he was keeping up. I had no idea he'd fail. I wondered if I'd get in trouble for not telling anyone. Who would I tell? I wasn't going to tell Mom when she was in the hospital and caring for Anna. Dad wasn't around much either, and when he was, I didn't want to make him mad or get Sam in trouble. I guess it's too late for that now.

When we got home, Mom told Sam to go to his room and that he was grounded until further notice. I decided it was better to hide out and read in my room. I knew there would be more fighting once Dad got home.

Kelly got home a few hours later and, as was her usual routine, went straight into our room. "Why aren't you reading in the living room like you normally are?"

"Oh. Mom is mad and Sam is grounded. He failed all his classes. They want him to repeat sixth."

"What? How did he fail? He's never failed anything!"

"I don't know, but Mom is really, really mad. Cussing and everything."

"I can't believe it."

"I know."

"Dad's going to be so mad."

"I know."

I guessed the conversation was over because she pulled out a notebook and started writing. I went back to reading my book.

A few hours later, I heard the front door open and close. Dad was home. I could hear talking in the kitchen and then it turned to yelling. Kelly went to open our door, so we could listen in on Mom and Dad's fight. We heard Mom say, "You didn't notice he wasn't going to school? How could you not notice? You are supposed to be taking care of them, not doing God knows what else!"

Dad retorted, "I have been working to put food in our mouths and a roof over our heads. I'm at work all day. How could I know he wasn't going to school?"

"You didn't ask if they were doing their homework? Did you notice he never did any homework?"

"No. Between work and going to the hospital, I wasn't checking their homework! There's been no time. When would I do that? While I'm grocery shopping? While I'm working? While I'm at the hospital?"

"Well. I'll tell you this. Things are going to change around here. I just can't believe all of this is happening and you just let it!"

"Oh yeah, this is all my fault. It's always my fault. This is just bullshit. I'm gone."

I heard the front door open and then it slammed closed. Kelly and I decided to stay in our room until we were called for dinner.

About twenty minutes later, Mom knocked on our door, opened it and told us dinner was ready. Kelly stared out the window. "I'm not hungry."

Mom stood in the hallway with her hands on her hips. "I made you dinner, and you will eat it."

Next she went across the hall to Sam's room and told him dinner was ready and to come and eat. We all sat at the kitchen table and ate our spaghetti and broccoli. Mom told us she had to leave soon to go back to the hospital and then reminded Sam he was grounded. She glanced up at Kelly and me. "Kelly, Casey, how did you do this semester? Am I going to get any surprises from you guys too?" Mom glared at Kelly.

Kelly answered, "I did fine."

"So you passed all your classes?"

Kelly rolled her eyes. "Yes. I. Did. Fine."

"Casey?"

"I did good. All As and two Bs, I think."

"Good job, Casey. You guys need to realize how important school is. It isn't something you just 'don't feel like going to.' It is your future. Without education, you'll be nothing."

Mom seemed satisfied with her closing statement and that Kelly and I hadn't failed our classes.

After dinner, Mom told me to clear the dishes and for Kelly to wash. Sam was instructed to go straight back to his room. We didn't argue, although it seemed odd Sam was grounded but didn't have to do any chores. After we finished our chores, Mom left to go back to the hospital to be with Anna. Dad must have gotten home pretty late, since we didn't see him until the next day.

WE ALL SLEPT in the next morning. I think we were all a little relieved to not have to go to school or deal with Mom. The three of us got our cereal and ate in front of the TV watching our favorite Saturday-morning TV shows. Nobody seemed to mind they were all reruns. Sometime midday Sam decided he wanted to play Nintendo, even though he knew he wasn't supposed to. I tried to reason with him. "But you're grounded. You'll get in trouble."

"So what. Mom's not even here."

"But Dad's here."

"Like he's paying attention? What are they going to do, ground me some more?"

"I don't know."

"I'm gonna play Super Mario. See ya."

He went into his room, and Kelly and I continued to watch TV until Dad came downstairs. He walked right past us toward Sam's room. Kelly and I exchanged glances.

We first heard Dad yelling at Sam about school and then about playing Nintendo. I told Kelly I was going to go in our room, got up and started to close the door. Almost immediately after the door shut, I heard it. The yelling seemed to be getting louder, but this time Sam was yelling back.

Sam yelled at Dad, "What do you care? You aren't my Dad. Fuck you!"

"What did you just say to me?"

"You heard me. I don't have to listen to you. Why don't you just go and do whatever you go off and do and leave me alone!"

"I pay for the food you eat. The roof over your head. The Nintendo you are playing. I own everything."

"You don't own me. Get out of my room!"

"You don't tell me what to do, you little piece of shit. You will start listening to me and your mother."

"Fuck you!"

That is when I heard the first scream. It was followed by more screams and more yelling from Dad. "You like that! You want to talk back to me again?" Another scream.

"You start listening or you'll get the belt next time."

"I don't care. I hate you," my brother sobbed.

More screams. More crying. More hateful yelling. I curled up on my bed and put my headphones on and waited for it to stop. I stayed in my room the rest of the day because I didn't want to see anyone, especially Sam. It was too difficult to look at him after he had gotten in trouble. I felt like there was something I should have done to help Sam, but I didn't know what or how. It made me feel so sad and helpless. Kelly came in later in the day to tell me that she had checked on Sam when Dad left, and he seemed okay.

The rest of the weekend nobody really talked to each other. We didn't go visit Anna or have meals together. I assumed, like me, everyone just had eaten whatever was in the cupboards. I ate mostly cereal and peanut butter and jelly sandwiches. I wondered if this is how it would always be when Anna was in the hospital. Usually after Sam and Kelly got in trouble, things went back to normal pretty quickly. Without Mom and Anna around, the silence and solitude seemed to last a lot longer.

MOM CAME HOME a few days later to take a shower and change her clothes. She told us Anna was coming home the next week so we, as in us kids, needed to prepare. She showed us how to clean with Betadine and told us we had to make sure it was done properly. She had us take notes. Before she left to go back to the hospital, she told us we could go with her and that Dad would bring us back later that night; Kelly and Sam said they didn't want to go. I went because I wanted to see Anna, but mostly I just wanted to get out of the house.

We anxiously awaited Anna's homecoming. Us kids did as instructed and scrubbed the house with Betadine, cleaned our bedrooms, living room and kitchen. Anna walked through the front door, holding Mom's hand, glanced up and saw the three of us kids. She grinned as she ran toward us, and we greeted her with our normal commotion.

The household seemed to go back to normal for a while. We got to spend most of our days playing with Anna, reading and doing chores. The only time the house seemed to be tense was when Dad was home, which wasn't often. He began working a lot and wasn't usually home for dinner. When he was home, he spent most of his time playing with Anna.

At home, Anna seemed to be her normal happy, little toddler self. She began taking some of her chemotherapy drugs at home, which brought more new things into our house, like wheatgrass. Mom started buying flats of grass, juicing it and giving it to Anna. She let us kids try it, and we unanimously thought it was totally gross. One day while she was prepping her next batch, I asked her, "Why do you have to make wheatgrass?"

"It's pretty healthy. I think it tastes great! Don't you?"

"Um. No. It's gross. It tastes like grass."

She laughed. "You get used to it."

"Does Anna like it?"

"I don't think so, but it cuts the bitterness of her medication. It's basically that or orange juice, and the wheatgrass is a lot healthier. Orange juice is full of sugar. Sometimes I'll mix them together for her so that she'll take it better."

"Oh. Yeah, I think orange juice would definitely improve the taste. I think almost anything would make it taste better, since it couldn't be much worse."

Mom laughed again and continued to cut another patch of grass and put it through the juicer. Once it was done juicing, she crushed Anna's pill and put it in the wheatgrass, added a little orange juice and stirred it with a spoon. She then helped Anna drink it from the tiny cup. As usual, Anna was a trouper and drank the whole thing in about a minute.

Things were going okay until report cards came. It was official: Sam had failed every class. Along with his report card was a letter from the school district recommending that he repeat the sixth grade. Kelly's grades weren't great either. She passed, but barely. My grades were as I had reported before. Kelly was instantly grounded for the rest of the summer, along with Sam.

After many phone calls with what I assumed was the school, it was decided that Sam would need to go to a new school. I was happy to hear that he and I wouldn't be in the same grade at the same school. It would have been too weird and awkward. However, things only got worse from there. Since Sam had to go to a new school, St. Ann's in Lafayette, a private school closer to the hospital, Mom had made the decision that Kelly had to go too.

Kelly pleaded with Mom. "This is ridiculous! I don't want to leave my friends. I'll get my grades up, I promise. Just don't make me go!"

Mom shook her head. "Oh, you're going. I talked to your school and come to find out you have missed a bunch of classes too! I was also informed that you are hanging with a bad crowd that spends most of its time getting in trouble. You're going."

"That's so untrue. I don't hang with a bad crowd. That's ridiculous. Who did you even talk to?"

"It doesn't matter. It is settled: you are going."

Mom insisted that having Kelly and Sam at the same school gave her the ability to keep better track of them. Also, the private school had small classes to help them get more of the attention they needed to get their grades up.

After the decision was made, Kelly barely spoke to Mom and continued to spend most of her time in our room, even when Anna was home. Sam was angry and insisted he didn't need to repeat sixth grade. It was a constant argument. Things didn't seem to get better. Even at Kelly's fourteenth birthday celebration dinner, that she insisted she didn't want, the only time anyone spoke was to talk to Anna or to sing "Happy Birthday." I think the only time Kelly laughed was when Anna got cake all over her face. After Kelly got her birthday card and accompanying birthday money she asked to be excused and went back to our room and listened to her Walkman all night.

CHAPTER 13

THE NEXT MONTH Anna was cleared for her third round of chemotherapy. Mom and Anna packed for the trip to the hospital, said their good-byes and were gone. A few days later Dad asked who wanted to go out to the hospital to visit Anna with him. Sam and Kelly both decided they would rather stay home, so I went with Dad by myself.

On the drive to the hospital I thought about the last six months, since Anna's diagnosis. Mom and Anna now spent half the time in the hospital and half the time at home. In the beginning, things at home were bad when they were in the hospital, but now it was bad all the time. I couldn't wait for Anna to be done with chemo and cancer so that we could all go back to the way things were before.

When we entered Anna's room, I saw that she had a new roommate in the first bed, a girl, who appeared to be about twelve, with a peach-fuzz hairstyle; she was alone, like all of Anna's other roommates. Anna was in the second half of the room, like usual. I started to wonder if Anna always got the second bed in the room because she always had company with her. The first bed usually only had one chair for visitors compared to Anna's half, which had at least two chairs and a large window seat that Mom slept on.

When we reached Anna's bed, she was awake but was lying on her back in the crib with one of her nurses standing next to her. It was a new nurse who I hadn't seen before. She wore light blue scrubs and was average height and weight with mousy brown hair tied back in a messy bun and thick glasses that magnified her bright blue eyes. Anna tried to get up to see Dad and me, but Mom told her she had to wait.

When the nurse was done taking Anna's temperature she told Mom, "Okay. I'm all done. I'll be back later. Let me know if there is anything you need." Mom thanked her, and she left. The nurse must have been busy, as she didn't even acknowledge that Dad and I were there. Maybe she knew we were no longer new to all of this and felt she didn't need to be friendly like Nurse Janet or Nurse Karen; that, or she just wasn't very friendly. Either way, we were happy that Anna was ready to visit with us.

Anna was happy to see us and, I was surprised when she started calling me "Cay-hee." She had never said my name before. Anna started to point her arms down, saying, "Dow wa." I glanced at Mom. "What's she saying?"

"She's saying she wants to get down and walk the halls with her IV pole."

"Really?"

"Oh yeah. It's her new favorite thing. She's becoming quite famous here on the fifth floor!"

I soon found out what she meant. After Mom got Anna out of the crib, straightened out her tubes and put her on the ground, she began to follow behind Anna pushing the IV pole. We walked up to Anna's roommate, and Anna stopped. "Hi! Hi! Hi!"

The girl, who had been watching TV, replied, "Hi, Anna!"

We continued out the door. There were two nurses talking outside the door. Anna stopped. "Hi! Hi! Hi!"

The nurses laughed. "Hi, Anna!"

We continued down the hall and ran into one of Anna's previous roommates, Tony. He was strapped into a small wheelchair. His dark hair needed to be combed, and his glasses were dirty, practically hiding his light brown eyes. Anna stopped. "Hi, Toe! Hi, Toe! Hi, Toe!"

Tony's face lit up. "Hi, Ann-na! Hi, Ag-ag-atha!"

I had never heard him speak before. I wasn't sure if he could. The last time I saw him he had appeared so weak in his hospital bed, and Mom had explained that he was seven years old but he was developmentally delayed, which meant he acted more like he was three or four.

Mom walked up to Tony and placed her hand on his. "Hi, Tony. How are you today?"

"Goood."

"I want to introduce you to Anna's sister, Casey."

He arched his neck upward at me. "Hi, Casey."

"Hi, Tony. It's nice to meet you."

Mom pointed at Dad. "Also, this is Anna's dad, Jasper."

"Hi, Tony, nice to meet you."

"Hi, Jassssper."

Mom leaned closer to Tony. "What are you doing out here?"

"I like to watch ev-ery-thing going on."

Mom told him that Anna liked to watch everything too. He grinned and said Anna's name again. Mom told him we'd see him when we came around again.

We continued down the hall and stopped at every person we saw. If it was someone Anna didn't know, she'd still say, "Hi, hi, hi," followed by Mom introducing Anna and then her, Dad and me, but it seemed that almost everyone knew her. We did the entire loop around the fifth floor, three times before Anna started to get tired. Back at the room Dad read Anna a book, and she fell asleep. Once Anna was asleep, Dad left to run errands. I stayed behind, but instead of sitting in the room watching Anna sleep with Mom, I decided to explore the hospital.

I left Anna's room and walked around the fifth floor, first stopping in front of one of the posters describing leukemia and the signs of leukemia. I must have read the poster five times. I started to wonder if I had leukemia. Pale skin. Yes. Bruise easily. Yes. I had never had any problems with my nose or gums bleeding, no rashes or fever, no weight loss and no headache. The only similarity between myself and leukemia was my pale skin and that I bruised easily. I decided that I did not have leukemia. I continued to wander the halls. I walked passed the colorful pictures of balloons and rainbows that I remembered seeing during Anna's first time in the hospital. It seemed like it was years ago. I headed back to Anna's room to see if she was awake yet. She wasn't, so I sat in one of the chairs and read while Mom slept on the window seat.

Dad came back from running errands with a McDonald's dinner. He put the adjustable-height, narrow bed table near the window seat, lowered it and pulled up the two chairs. The four of us dined on chicken nuggets and fries. Anna sat in Dad's lap as she tried to feed herself; she dropped half of her fries on the floor, but Dad was able to help her get some food into her mouth. During dinner Anna surprised us when she said, "Fry, fry." Dad tried to get her to say nugget too. It came out as "Nuggie." We laughed, and that made Anna laugh. While we cleaned up the dinner mess, the no-nonsense nurse came back and said she needed to examine Anna. Dad said it was getting late and that we should head back to the house. We said our good-byes to Anna and Mom and went home.

The next day Dad went to work and us kids were at home. We didn't talk or hang out together. Sam stayed in his room or went outside on his bike. Kelly was either on the phone, writing in her notebook, sleeping or out of the house. I wondered if this is how it would be the rest of the summer; it sure did seem like it. Sometimes both Kelly and Sam wouldn't be home, and I wasn't sure where they went. Neither of them seemed to want to go to the hospital and visit Anna anymore. The only time they went was when Mom or Dad said they had to. I didn't understand why. I know, the hospital isn't the most fun place. It's a hospital. Everyone is sick or working. The food isn't that great. Actually, it's mostly boring, but Anna was there. Mom was there. I went as often as they'd let me.

My eleventh birthday was coming up, and Mom asked if I wanted to postpone my birthday dinner to when Anna was out of the hospital. "Can we just have it here? Like, we could bring pizza or something?"

"Are you sure?"

"Yeah, why not?"

On my birthday we all, even Kelly and Sam, went to the hospital, bringing with us pizza and cake. When we got to Anna's room, Nurse Karen was there. "Hi there, Anna's family! Looks like a party!"

I explained, "It's my birthday. I'm eleven now."

"Happy birthday!" She glanced over at Mom and Dad.

"You are welcome to celebrate here, but unfortunately you can't light any candles in here. You might want to get a table down at the cafeteria."

Mom thanked Nurse Karen for the suggestion and then returned her attention to us. "C'mon, folks, let's go!"

Dad picked up Anna, Kelly pushed the IV pole, Sam carried the pizza, I carried the cake, Mom carried a bag of Anna's things and we headed to the elevators. When we got to the cafeteria, we found an open table, and Mom set up the party. Dad got Anna a high chair; I got to sit next to her. We all ate cheese pizza from Domino's and drank soda from the cafeteria. When it was time for cake, Mom put the candles in the white-frosted cake that had "Happy Birthday Casey" written in pink cursive letters, but before she could get a chance to light the candles

Anna stuck her hand in the frosting and squealed. We all laughed.

It instantly reminded me of Anna's first birthday, eight months prior. She had a pink sparkly cake that she practically dove into. Frosting and cake was all over her hands, face, hair and clothes. Kelly, Sam and I had egged her on to make the biggest mess possible. She didn't disappoint.

Mom chuckled. "Anna, you can't put your hand in Casey's cake. It's Casey's."

Anna giggled. "Cay-hee."

Mom proceeded to light the candles, they sang and I got my birthday card. "Thanks, Mom and Dad! Now I can get some more books; with all the hospital visits and no homework I only have one Sweet Valley High book left." Dad promised he'd take me to the bookstore the next day, after work.

I suddenly remembered something. "Mom, school starts next week, and we haven't gone back-to-school shopping yet. When can we go?"

"Oh, I don't know. Anna will still be in the hospital when school starts."

Kelly chimed in, "What about our school uniforms?"

"I ordered them when I signed up you and Sam for school. They should get here any day."

I glanced at Kelly. "What do you buy at back-to-school shopping if you have a uniform?"

Mom answered for Kelly. "They have some free dress days where they don't wear a uniform, so they do need some clothes."

Kelly interjected, "We still get shoes, sweaters, jackets, tights . . . all kinds of things, right? They just have to be a certain color."

Mom bobbed her head up and down. "That's true."

I didn't like where this was going. "Oh. Well, can Dad take us?"

Dad turned his gaze to me. "I'm not sure we have time. Mom will take you when Anna's out of the hospital."

Kelly and I didn't fight it, and Sam didn't seem to care either way. After the party we headed back up to Anna's room, said our good-byes and went back home.

That night I woke to a window opening in our room. I glanced over and saw Kelly was getting ready to climb out the window. "What are you doing?"

She spoke quietly, "I'm going out."

"When are you going to be back?"

"Later."

"How much later? What if you get caught?"

"Don't worry, I'm just going down the street. I'll be back before anyone's up."

"Well, I'm up now!"

"Just read until you go back to sleep."

"Fine." I pulled out my book light and book and read until I fell back to sleep. It wasn't too surprising that I was awakened a few hours later as Kelly climbed back through the window. I didn't ask her about what she did or where she went; I just rolled over and went back to sleep. I soon figured out that Kelly liked sneaking out at night, since she continued to sneak out every night until school started.

The first day of school arrived and we all struggled to get up. We started the day by fighting over who got to use the bathroom first. Kelly insisted that she should get to go first because not only was she the oldest but they had to leave earlier than me to get to their new school. I sarcastically told her she ought to put less hair spray in her hair, it would likely save her at least ten minutes. She responded by telling me her hairstyle was fashionable unlike my boring straight hair. I thought she looked like a poodle with her poofy curls and bangs that were plastered straight up, like a wall. I ate my cereal as she hogged the bathroom.

Before they left with Dad for their forty-five-minute car ride to school, I told them, "Have a truly academic day!" in my best

Mom impression. While I was getting ready for school, I started getting butterflies in my stomach about the first day of sixth grade. I was excited to see my friends and that I got Mr. Bing for homeroom. Both Kelly and Sam had Mr. Bing and said he was totally cool; all the kids liked him. When I finished getting ready, I walked to the bus stop and started my last year of elementary school.

CHAPTER 14

SAM

WHEN WE DROVE up to St. Ann's, I felt sick to my stomach. On the right was an old white church and on the left was a row of classrooms. There were a bunch of kids all wearing blue pants and white shirts. They looked like a bunch of sissies. I guess I wasn't much better, since I was wearing the same thing. A bunch of privileged white robots. They didn't know what life was really like. I got out of the car, slamming the door behind me. Kelly grimaced. "Watch out!" she yelled at me after she narrowly avoided being hit by the door. While we walked toward the school, I noticed that she instantly fit in with her plaid skirt and white polo. Kelly had always tried to fit in, wanting to be like everybody else, and now she was.

When I walked into my new classroom, I found a seat and sat down. There were a few kids there that seemed to already know each other. Mother warned me that I was probably going to be the only kid that didn't go to the school from kindergarten on but also assured me no one would know I was repeating the sixth grade. It was such bullshit. I didn't need to repeat sixth grade. I only failed because I didn't take the tests or turn in my homework. It wasn't like I didn't know how to read or do math at my level. It was totally unnecessary.

I know that if I lived with my real dad, Dad-Pete, he would never have made me repeat sixth. Then again, where was he? Usually not with us. He's a jerk too. Not as big of a jerk as Jasper but a jerk nonetheless. And Mother? She lets her junkie of an asshole husband beat on her kid. Who does that? She's even worse than Jasper for letting it happen. She's only with him because he has money. Why else would she be with him? This is all her fault. She only made me repeat sixth because she thinks she knows everything. She didn't have to allow it. She could have let me go to seventh grade with my friends. Not to mention that because we now have to go to school forty-five minutes away I can't play football or baseball anymore. Nope, she just wanted to put Kelly and me in a fancy private school so she can feel rich. Whatever, at least school would be easy, since I already did everything last year.

Kelly and I were both surprised that Mother picked us up from school. After she stopped the car, we got in. Mother was more cheerful than normal and beamed at us. "How was your first day?"

Kelly grinned. "It was great. I've already made three friends, and they invited me to go to the mall this weekend. Can I go?"

Mother ignored her question. "What about school? How was school?"

"Oh, fine. The teacher, Ms. Kline, seems really cool. . . ."

Kelly droned on about her class and the kids in her class for what seemed like an eternity. When she finally stopped yapping, Mother asked what I thought of my new school.

"Fine, I guess. The kids seem young and snobby. Dorks, mostly. Not to mention we're stuck in the same class all day. That sucks."

Mother's mouth turned downward. "Ohhh."

I'm not sure what Mother expected to hear. I didn't want to

be there. Mostly ignoring my lack of enthusiasm, she continued talking about how great the school was supposed to be and how lucky Kelly and I were, the entire drive home.

We pulled into the driveway, and then Mother told us that Anna was coming home this weekend, so we had to start cleaning. Great. When we walked in the house, Casey was already home and in the living room reading one of her lame Sweet Valley High books. She jumped as we walked in. I guess she didn't expect us. She got up to say hi and asked us how our first day was. Kelly started in again about all her new friends, and then Casey told us all about her first day. Apparently, everything is great in the world of Casey. Never in trouble. Good grades. Sooo smart. Why can't we be more like Casey, they always say. Maybe because we don't want to be a fucking dork.

The week didn't get any better. All the kids at school were lame and the teachers were annoying. After school wasn't much better. Especially when Jasper got home. I could at least play Nintendo until he got home, but once he was there I had to pretend to be doing my homework or start cleaning per Mother's instructions. Mother was totally whacked about all the cleaning. Anna seemed fine.

When Anna got home, things got marginally better. There was less focus on me and what I was doing and more on Anna. Anna was at least cute and innocent. She always seemed to lighten the mood. Mother and Jasper hardly ever fought with us or each other when Anna was home.

It was kind of cool learning about all of Anna's medical stuff. The Broviac and blood draws were pretty cool. However, I could definitely do without the wheatgrass and Mother's obsession with so-called health food. I was glad when Anna started to regain her strength and Mother stopped fussing about her so much. She finally let her go outside to the park across the street. Casey had been bugging her about it for weeks. Casey would say, "It's right across the street. It's practically our backyard!"

Mother would shake her head. "It's too risky. God only knows what kind of germs could be there. Teenagers go there at night, doing God knows what!"

However, the doctors recently told Mother some fresh air would be good for Anna. So that weekend, Mother, Casey, Kelly and I walked across the street to the park. It wasn't much of a park. There was grass, some sand, a few benches and a big log to sit on. I always wondered how they got that big log there. It was long and wide enough to sit on. I wondered if there used to be a tree where the park was and they chopped it down for the park and left it there or if they brought it from somewhere else. Either way, it was peaceful. Sometimes I would go there by myself and sit on the log and gaze out at nearby Mount Diablo.

Anna seemed to like it too. She liked walking and playing in the sand. Kelly picked her up and put her on the log. She thought that was hilarious. She laughed. "Gen! Gen!"

Kelly was puzzled. I said, "I think she is saying 'again.' Try picking her up, put her on the ground and then back on the log."

Sure enough, Anna liked being lifted and put on the log and wanted to do it again, or "Gen," as she said it.

THE NEXT WEEK SUCKED BIG-TIME. This kid at school was mouthing off about something stupid, so I punched him. Much to my surprise, the kid hit me back. He was short with sandy-brown hair and pretty dweeby looking. I assumed he was going to cry and then go tell a teacher, but he didn't. I respected the kid for that. Unfortunately, some little kid nearby went and ran to tell a teacher. After the teacher broke up our fight, we both had to go to the principal's office. While waiting in the chairs outside her office, I faced Mark. "You have a nice right hook."

"Thanks."

"You're pretty good too."

"I'm sorry for starting the fight. Friends?"

"Sure."

Mark and I were friends after that. We were cool, but Mother and Jasper were not. St. Ann's called home about every little thing. No surprise that when Mother picked me up, she lectured me the whole car ride home. I was grounded again. Big deal, it wasn't like I ever go anywhere other than school and the hospital. When we got home, I was told to go straight to my room until Mother and Jasper could come up with the rest of my punishment. I knew I wouldn't get beat because Anna was home. I wasn't sure what they'd do.

When Jasper got home, Mother came in my room to tell me they were taking my Nintendo away. I shook my head. "I don't care." She started to pull at the Nintendo, and I tried to stop her. "You are going to break it that way! You have to unplug it first!" She didn't listen. She pulled the box and then the whole TV crashed to the ground and split the power cord on the Nintendo. Fucking great. She destroyed my Nintendo. She jumped back with wide eyes but quickly composed herself. "Well, that is what you get!" After that she walked out of my room. Seriously? I didn't even hurt the kid. We were friends now, for Christ's sake. She was such a spaz. I couldn't wait to get out of this house.

I swear I couldn't do anything right. A few days later, Anna came down with a fever and what appeared to be chicken pox. Somehow this was our fault? Yes. Mother started yelling at the three of us that we hadn't washed our hands and brought chicken pox germs home. Casey said, "We've all had chicken pox. A long time ago. How could we have brought it home?"

"On your hands. Germs. Someone at your schools must have chicken pox. I told you guys you have to wash your hands all the time. You never listen. Ever. I don't know what is wrong with you kids!"

Kelly clenched her hands into fists. "I think you're wrong. She could've gotten the germs from the hospital."

"Don't talk back to me, Kelly. Go to your room. Now." Casey peered over at me like, You know she is crazy, right? And rolled her eyes. I glanced back like, Oh yeah. I know. Mother must have noticed, because she yelled at Casey and me to go to our rooms too. From my room I heard her packing up and leaving the house with Anna. We didn't even get to say good-bye.

Later that night, Jasper told us we could come out of our rooms for dinner. Over dinner, pepperoni pizza again, he told us that Anna was admitted to the hospital and was now back in isolation. He went on to explain that chicken pox could kill Anna because of her weakened immune system. It sucked, but it wasn't our fault. Mother had no right to yell at us like that. She was such a lunatic.

We had no idea Anna would be in isolation for six weeks just because of chicken pox. We weren't allowed to visit her. I was okay with it, but Casey was upset and Kelly was near hysterical. Kelly kept saying that she could die and we wouldn't be able to see her or say good-bye. I kept telling them I thought Anna would be okay. She was tough, despite being so little. I tried to remind them of her walking the halls with her IV pole and how she powered through her wheatgrass shots. I told them, "I mean, I could barely stomach the wheatgrass. Anna was a champ. She chugged it!"

Casey laughed and then said, "That's true. I agree. I think she'll be okay. I just wish we weren't stuck here."

Kelly arched her eyebrows. "Yeah, maybe."

I said to them, "Hey, maybe in the spirit of Anna we all take a wheatgrass shot! I dare you!"

Casey perked up. "I'll do it! Do you know how to work the machine?"

Kelly glanced over at the juicer. "I do."

I stood up. "Come on. Let's do it!"

The three of us ran to the juicer. Kelly cut the grass and started the machine. She handed the first cup to me and started up another batch for Casey and then one for herself. Once we all had a shot, I looked at them. "Okay, on the count of three we chug. 1, 2, 3." I chugged it and watched Kelly and Casey; both of them nearly gagged. When we finished, we slammed the tiny cups down and I yelled, "For Anna!" We all cheered. Since no parents were home, we decided to watch TV after that. It was better when no parents were around.

CHAPTER 15

I HAD no idea that chicken pox would put Anna in the hospital for six weeks. Kelly, Sam and I always washed our hands, and I wasn't convinced that even if we hadn't washed our hands it was our fault Anna got the chicken pox. I don't know why Mom got so mad at Kelly for suggesting that it wasn't our fault; she must have been pretty stressed-out. I guess it made sense. She has a baby who is in and out of the hospital all the time. She says every visit is like a new fight for her life. I guess if you fight all the time, you'd get pretty tired and stressed-out. I only wished Anna's cancer brought us together instead of pulled us apart.

I was surprised when Sam suggested we do wheatgrass shots in support of Anna. It was totally cool. I liked it when the three of us stuck together. It was too bad it was now a surprise when it happened instead of it being the norm. It's even worse now that they go to school so far away. Sam hates it, even though he has already made new friends and apparently is doing well in school, according to Mom. Kelly too. Maybe the idea for them to go to private school wasn't so terrible after all.

Anna's homecoming after chicken pox was more stressful than previous times. Instead of making us clean the house, Mom hired professional cleaners and inspected before she gave the okay to let Anna step foot into the house. I'm not sure what the cleaners thought of Mom as she had Dad sit in the car with Anna while she inspected every nook and cranny. I guessed that if that was all it would take to keep Anna out of the hospital, then it was worth it.

Once the house was clean and Mom watched us wash our hands, Dad let Anna walk into the house. Anna held Dad's hand and made her way up the step as fast as she could. Once on level ground she ran to the three of us waiting for her. We gave her hugs and kisses while she led us over to her toys under the stairs. We read books and played with her little pink piano. In that one moment, we were all happy.

While sitting and playing with Anna, I asked Mom when we would go shopping for our Halloween costumes, since Halloween was at the end of the week. She grimaced. "I have no idea, Casey. We just got home."

I decided to drop the shopping idea, since Mom was clearly annoyed and asked, "Are you going to let Anna trick-or-treat with us?"

"You assume that all of you get to go trick-or-treating!"

I cocked my head to the side. "Why wouldn't we be able to go?"

"Well, if you do all your chores and there are no problems at school, you can go, I guess."

Kelly chimed in. "Well, we will do our chores and we're all doing good in school. So we can go, right?"

Mom rolled her eyes. "That is what I just said."

Kelly dismissed Mom's irritation. "If we are going to go, we'll need costumes. The stores are going to run out if we don't go soon."

"We'll go when I say we'll go. It can wait a few days."

Sensing that things were going to get bad soon, I tried to get Anna to laugh in order to break the tension. I started making funny faces and had Sam join in. Soon she was laughing, and it appeared the subject was closed for now.

A few days later it came back up, since none of us had a costume and Halloween was only three days away. Mom finally agreed to take us to Kmart to check out their selection. I decided on punk rocker. I got pink hair spray and black net gloves and used some of my regular clothes to finish off the costume. Kelly decided on being a witch and got the full costume in a bag. She had a big, black floppy hat, green face makeup and a black gown. Sam decided he was going to be a vampire ninja again and told Mom he didn't need a new costume, just some new vampire teeth and fake blood. We spent most of the time trying to decide what Anna should go as. Kelly thought she would be a cute bumblebee and I thought she'd like being a Care Bear more. In the end, Mom decided she would be a fuzzy pink-and-white bunny. It was cute and doubled as pajamas.

WHEN HALLOWEEN ARRIVED, we were all excited. It was my favorite holiday and I was psyched that Anna got to go with us. Mom said Anna could go only for a little bit; it was better than nothing. When we headed out for the night, we shuffled out to the front of the house. We moved at a snail's pace, similar to walking the halls of the hospital. We headed next door first, having Anna lead the way. She was finally big enough to walk up to the door by herself and put out her plastic pumpkin to get treats. We said "Trick or Treat" for Anna, as she hadn't quite figured out that part yet, which was understandable, considering she was only twenty-two months old. However, I was confident by the end of the night she'd catch on, at least a little bit.

We proceeded to go around the court and then down the street to the other little clusters of houses, make a U-turn and head back up the street and end at our house. Mom said it was time for Anna to get ready for bed, but she let Kelly, Sam and me keep trick-or-treating. After we hugged Anna good-bye, we ran up the street to the nearest house and continued for the next hour or so.

When we got back, the three of us went into the living room and dumped our pillowcases full of candy onto the floor and counted our loot. We conducted our candy trades until Mom said it was time for bed. It was a good night.

The next day at dinner, Mom told us she had to take Anna to the hospital the next week for testing. I asked, "Why can't you just bring her blood sample like last time? Why does she have to go to the hospital?"

Mom explained, "This isn't just her regular testing to see if she can do another round of chemotherapy. This is to see if the chemotherapy is working."

It sounded serious. I asked, "Is it more than just blood testing?"

"Yes, she has to get a CT scan and visit with her surgeon, Dr. Trekker, and her oncologist, Dr. Baker. It's going to be exhausting for Anna."

"Does she have to go overnight?"

"No, just the day. It's a lot to do in one day. That is why she'll be tired, but at least we don't have to stay in the hospital. Anything is better than having to stay in the hospital."

"How do they think she is doing?"

"So far Dr. Baker says that she seems to be doing well, but we won't know for sure until we do the testing."

"When will they have all the results?"

Kelly's eyes arched. "Yeah, when will they know if she's going to be okay?"

"It will take a week or so before they have all the results ready to review. We'll go back and talk to Dr. Baker when they're ready to share the information with us."

Sam faced Anna. "You'll be all right, Anna. You're a fighter, aren't you?!" He followed up with a monkey face. She laughed and said, "Sa! Sa!" and then laughed some more. It always amazed me how Anna could transform any serious or tense conversation into giggles and laughter.

We were thrilled the next week when we found out the chemotherapy was working. Dad brought home Anna's favorite "nuggies and fri fries" for dinner along with cake, ice cream and balloons. I'm not sure Anna knew why we were celebrating, but the rest of us did and we were all in a good mood. Sam asked Mom, "So does this mean she is done with chemo, now?"

"No. She's not ready for that yet. She can't go off the chemo until there are absolutely no traces of the cancer left."

Kelly's mouth dropped open. "She still has cancer?"

"Yes, there is still a small amount, according to Dr. Baker. They are hopeful that chemo will get all the rest based on how she is doing so far. This is great news! God has truly blessed us!"

We all were in agreement. For the rest of the night, everything was as it was before. Mom and Dad asked about school. We played with Anna. Sam, Kelly and I joked and made fun of each other. We laughed until we had tears in our eyes.

RIGHT BEFORE THANKSGIVING ANNA had to go back to the hospital for her next round of chemo. Because Anna was going to be in the hospital for Thanksgiving, we had to miss our annual family Thanksgiving at Aunt Marney's. There was always tons of food as well as all of our aunts, uncles and cousins on Mom's side. Us kids would play and hang out, and the aunts and uncles would ask us about school and any sports or other activities we were into. We all liked to go.

This year Grandma Jess and Aunt Ella were going to join us for a portable Thanksgiving in Anna's hospital room. Our Thanksgiving table consisted of a bed table and borrowed chairs from other rooms. Dinner consisted of preprepared ham, mashed potatoes, green beans and rolls from the grocery store as well as sugar cookies and a pumpkin pie that Grandma Jess brought. We huddled around the makeshift table and took turns saying what we were thankful for. The consensus was that we were thankful for Anna and that she was doing well. After we ate dinner we walked Anna around the halls. We stopped at each person we saw and told them, "Happy Thanksgiving" in addition to Anna's, "Hi Hi Hi." It wasn't nearly as fun as going to Aunt Marney's.

By mid-December, Anna was still in the hospital. We had hoped she'd be out for the holidays but weren't sure so a few days before Christmas, Dad and all of us kids went to the hospital to visit Anna and celebrate. When we walked into her room with food and gifts, I noticed that Tony was Anna's roommate again. He was sleeping, so we walked quietly past him.

When we reached Anna, she was sitting up in her crib "reading" a book with Mom standing by her side. Us kids did our normal greetings with Anna, and then I heard Mom quietly ask Dad, "Did you bring the gift for Tony?" He nodded and pointed to one of the bags.

A little bit later we ate cookies and had Anna open gifts. She had a hard time tearing the paper, so Kelly and Sam helped her. Of all her gifts, I think her favorite was the My Little Pony, a purple plastic pony, about the size of a deck of cards, with big, beige eyes and a single rainbow painted on the cheek as well as little rainbows painted on the body and a long yellow mane and tail. After gifts we walked Anna around the halls with the My Little Pony clutched in her hand.

When we got back to her room, Tony was awake. Anna stopped at his bed. "Hi, Toe! Hi, Toe! Hi, Toe!"

Tony saw us and his face brightened. "Hi, Annna!" "Hi, Agaaatha!"

Mom cut in and reminded him the rest of our names. She went on to tell him, "Merry Christmas, Tony! We got you something." Mom handed him a large wrapped gift. His eyes widened as he accepted the package. With Mom's help, he quickly tore off all of the paper. "Bowwling! Thank you! Thank you!"

Dad started to help take off the plastic wrap. "Do you want to play?"

Tony's eyes lit up. "Yes! Cannn we?"

Dad gave a friendly smirk. "Of course. Agatha will get a nurse to help you in your chair."

Mom went and got one of Tony's nurses. The nurse, one I didn't know, had gray hair, wrinkly tan skin and big brown eyes. She checked Tony over and then helped him into his wheelchair.

We followed Tony and Mom out into the hall. Dad set up the plastic bowling pins and then walked to Tony and said, "So you just have to lower your arm and throw it. Got it?"

"Yeees!"

Dad handed the black plastic ball to Tony, and he proceeded to lower his arm alongside his wheelchair, as instructed, and roll it. We all cheered when the ball knocked down a few of the colorful pins. Sam, Kelly and I took turns resetting the pins after each roll.

It seemed as though Tony would never tire of playing, but eventually his nurse came by and told him he needed to go back to the room and get some rest. We packed up the set and put them on Tony's side table, told him to get some rest and that we'd see him soon. The nurse thanked us, and we went back over to Anna.

When we walked up, Mom wore a giant grin and was hugging Anna. "Dr. Baker was just here. Anna is going to be discharged tomorrow!" We quietly cheered. Anna would be home for Christmas.

CHAPTER 16

CHRISTMAS EVE HAD ARRIVED and the house was buzzing. We had decided to wait until Mom and Anna were home before getting our Christmas tree and decorating the house. There was a lot to do! That morning we got bundled up and went to the Christmas tree lot to buy our tree. We found out, much to our surprise, that if you go to buy a tree on Christmas Eve, they were all free! Sure, there wasn't much of a selection, but this allowed us to get more than one tree. We ended up with two: a big one for the living room and a small one for the kitchen.

Once we got back from tree shopping, Mom pulled out the decorations, and we got to work on the trees. Anna insisted that she was going to help with everything, including hanging the ornaments. However, it was more like: Anna hangs ornament on the tree. Ornament falls on the ground. One of us picks it up and hangs it on the tree. We all say, "Good job, Anna!" She claps her small hands and moves on to the next ornament. After we declared the Christmas trees finished, we hung small Christmas lights on the fireplace mantel and along the stairs. Anna loved the lights and so did we.

The decorations were finished, so we moved into the kitchen

to make cookies. Mom sat Anna in her high chair and I showed her how to mix the ingredients for the cookie dough and how to roll it out. Kelly, Sam and I took turns cutting out the shapes and placing them on the cookie sheet to bake. Anna put both arms up in the air. "Num num!"

Mom laughed. "Anna, you have to wait until they're baked! You can't eat raw cookie dough, silly girl!"

Anna protested. "Num num!"

"Sorry, Anna, you have to wait!"

Mom gave her a half grin and started doing the dishes. While her back was turned, Sam snuck her some dough. Anna's face lit up in delight. He snuck her a little more and told her not to tell. We had to pretend like nothing happened when Mom had finished the dishes; she didn't like it when we would taste the dough, she certainly wouldn't like it if we gave it to Anna. After baking, Anna had to go down for a nap, so we put the icing and sprinkles on while she slept.

Later that day, Dad-Pete picked up Kelly, Sam and me for our other family's annual Christmas Eve celebration. The three of us were happy to see Dad-Pete and couldn't wait for some crab cioppino. When the doorbell rang, we said good-bye to Mom and Anna. Kelly opened the door with Sam and me behind her. In unison, we said, "Hi, Dad!"

"Hi! You guys ready to go!"

We all said yes, waved to Mom and headed out to his car.

On the way to Grannie and Grandpop's, Dad-Pete asked us about school. Kelly said, "Our new school is kind of lame, but I've made friends and they're cool."

"That's good. How about you, Sam? What do you think of the new school?"

Sam shook his head. "It's lame, but whatever."

"Casey, how 'bout you?"

"Things are good. I'm a sixth grader now, and sixth graders rule the school!"

Dad-Pete laughed. "Sounds good. So what did you guys ask Santa to get you for Christmas this year?"

Kelly grinned. "Well, I asked Santa for the new Ice-T, NWA and 2 Live Crew albums and of course clothes and money."

I chimed in. "I asked for George Michael, Debbie Gibson and Rick Astley albums and some new books and clothes!"

"I see you guys are all into music! Sam, what did you ask for?"

Sam replied, "I was hoping for Michael Jackson's Bad or the Def Leppard Hysteria album and a new Nintendo, since mine got broken." Sam's face contorted.

Dad flashed us a sneaky grin. "I called Santa earlier and he hinted that you might be getting some cash so that you could pick out whatever you wanted."

I wasn't surprised that Dad-Pete was going to give us cash, since that is usually what he got us with some candy or other small gift.

When we got to Grannie and Grandpop's we hugged them and wished them Merry Christmas. Grannie was a tall, stately German woman with cropped, curly gray hair and Dad-Pete's blue eyes. She wasn't a woman you'd want to mess with, whereas Grandpop was a small, Italian man who seemed to always be in a good mood. He had dark tan skin and big brown eyes usually hidden behind his dark-framed glasses and a nose twice the size it probably should've been. As we approached our aunts, Dad-Pete's sisters, we did the same. I leaned in to Kelly and quietly asked, "Which one is Gina and which one is Maria?"

"The one with the dark, straight hair is Gina and the one with curly hair is Maria."

I shook my head. "I always get them confused."

"Me too. I just try to remember, curly hair is Maria so the other has to be Gina."

"Ah. Thanks."

We were late, so there wasn't a lot of sitting around and eating appetizers. We got straight to the main event, the crab cioppino.

More specifically, buttered bread dipped in the cioppino broth. It was the best part. During dinner we got to talk to our cousins, a trio of rowdy older boys and the eldest cousin, Kathryn, who was mostly tending to her newborn baby girl. I remember thinking it was funny because it was the opposite of Mom's family. In Mom's family we were the oldest kids, but at Dad-Pete's we were the youngest.

The big deal that year was that our cousin Kathryn, who was seventeen and unmarried, had just had a baby. While sitting with the cousins, they all talked about how cute the baby was. When I moved over to the other room for dessert and to talk to the adults, I quickly found out that they were far from happy about Kathryn having the baby, and they weren't shy about it. Grannie made it clear that she felt Kathryn made a mistake by having "it," and all the adults seemed to agree. She glared at Kelly. "Now, don't you be goin' and doin' the same thing. Be smart!" I was glad I wasn't Kathryn. At times it got a little uncomfortable, and I hoped Kathryn couldn't hear the adults from the other room.

After dinner we all sat around the tree and opened presents while nibbling on cookies and Andes mints. Most of the gifts we got from our relatives were pretty lame. One of my aunts gave me a pair of socks, and the other gave me a shirt that was about three sizes too small. We thanked them anyway. Like Dad-Pete had hinted, he gave us kids each fifty dollars in our cards along with some See's candy. Shortly after presents it was time for us to go home. We said our good-byes and Merry Christmases to all.

We got home to Mom, Dad and Anna sitting around the Christmas tree. They were eating cookies and waiting for us to get home so that we could open our one gift, as it was our tradition, and then get to bed. Each of us carefully selected the gifts, as if trying to guess which one was the best. Mom and Dad didn't know that earlier in the week Sam and Kelly had figured out how to unwrap and rewrap the gifts and taught me how too. We knew what each and every one of our gifts were but acted surprised when we opened our one gift. After gifts and our excellent performances, we went to bed.

The next morning the presents under the tree seemed to have grown exponentially. What was a small pile on Christmas Eve was now a massive mound of gifts on Christmas morning. Mom and Dad said it must have been Santa Claus. Right. Kelly, Sam and I tore through our gifts in about five minutes, but there was still a giant pile for Anna. Sam called out to Mom, "We each got like five presents—Anna got like thirty!"

"You all got the same amount. It just looks like Anna has more."

"No, I counted. She really has six times more than us."

"I spent the same on all of you."

Sam smirked. "Yeah right."

Dad started to get angry. "Stop being so ungrateful. What a bunch of spoiled brats. Some kids don't have any presents. How about I take yours and give them away to those kids. Huh?"

Sam ignored him and went into his room. Kelly and I kept our heads down and played with Anna and her new My Little Pony figures. After we finished helping Anna open her gifts, we got ready to head out to Aunt Marney's in San Jose to celebrate with Mom's family. From Aunt Marney's we would go over to Grandma Jess's in San Leandro.

Everyone at Aunt Marney's told us that they had missed us at Thanksgiving but were glad we made it to Christmas. All inquired about Anna's health and toasted to the fact the chemo was working. Aunt Marney had always been my favorite aunt on Mom's side, so no matter the event, I was happy to go to her house, even if most people were concerned with Anna and not the rest of us kids. Aunt Marney always seemed to be in a good mood and on any occasion was ready to get a dance party started. She was a petite brunette with shoulder-length hair, freckles and brown eyes. She and Mom looked nothing alike. During the party, I overheard Mom talking to Aunt Marney. "Yes, it's been rough. I just wish it would end already!"

Marney shook her head. "I bet. How long's it been?"

"Nine terribly long months since Anna's diagnosis. I had no idea we'd spend half the time in the hospital. Our lives have been flipped upside down!"

"How are things with Jasper—is he helping out too?"

"He comes by the hospital, but he has to work. Unfortunately, the kids are kind of on their own. I just don't know what I can do about it."

She sounded so sad. My eavesdropping was interrupted when a cousin shot me with his laser gun and I had to run and pretend to be injured.

We ate our usual dinner of turkey, green bean casserole, salad, rolls and assorted appetizers. We didn't usually exchange gifts, since there were so many of us. Instead we played the white elephant game, where everyone brings a wrapped gift and draws a number. The highest number gets to pick the first present and unwrap it; the next highest number gets to pick a gift or steal the now-unwrapped gift. It repeats until everyone has gotten a chance to open or steal a gift. The family enjoyed the game, but I didn't. I thought it was weird to steal each other's gifts. After dinner we left for Grandma Jess's house.

When we got to Grandma Jess's house, Aunt Ella and Aunt Katie had already arrived. We said hi and Merry Christmas to everyone. They seemed happy to see us, but like most places we went, Anna was the main attraction. They fought over who got to hold her next and joked that Grandma Jess was hogging the baby. I tried to explain that she prefers to walk around, but they didn't listen. We sat down to eat another huge meal but had to apologize for not eating more, since we just ate at Aunt Marney's; Grandma Jess didn't seem to mind.

After eating we went into the living room for gifts. Aunt Ella decided that she would hand out all the gifts that year, so she organized piles based on who the gifts were for. There were a bunch of piles that had three to four gifts each, and one pile that had about twenty. I saw Sam go up to the biggest pile and check the name. He walked over to me and said, "Guess whose pile that is?" I told him not to think too much of it. Baby toys were cheaper and that it wasn't favoritism. I don't think I convinced him; I wasn't sure I had convinced myself.

The rest of Christmas break was pretty good. Us kids got a lot of Christmas money and Mom let us go to the mall to spend it. Sam said that he didn't want to shop with girls and left Kelly and I to shop at all the clothing and music stores by ourselves. We went to all the trendy teenager clothing shops in the mall. I pretty much just followed Kelly around, trying to be cool like her. While she tried on all the latest styles, I told her she rocked it, and she did. I was jealous of her tall, thin frame and beautiful curly hair ever since I could remember. I was short, chubby and had stick-straight hair. I'd never had any boyfriends, yet she always had boys interested in her, even when she was my age.

We both bought some new clothes with our Christmas money and some new cassette tapes. When we were done shopping, we met back at the entrance as instructed and waited for Mom to pick us up. Back at the house we showed Mom and Anna what we bought. Kelly and I took turns giving fashion shows wearing our new clothes. I played Debbie Gibson's tape for them, and Anna started dancing when "Shake Your Love" played. We laughed and danced with her. We had no idea she'd want to listen to it over and over again. She kept saying "Gen! Gen! Gen!" She was so cute, we couldn't refuse. Although by the end we couldn't wait to shake that song.

During break Kelly started sneaking out in the middle of the night again. One night, after being woken up I asked, "What are you doing?"

"I'm going out."

"I know that, but why? You're gonna get caught one of

these days."

"I'm just catching up with my friends from my old school. It's not a big deal. Sam goes sometimes too. Not to mention, Mom sleeps like the dead. She'll never hear."

"Sam goes?"

"Yeah, there are guys from baseball and football, so he hangs with them. You can come too if you want."

"No thanks. I prefer sleep."

"Suit yourself. Bye."

She climbed out the window. I shook my head and went back to sleep.

A few days later there was a loud knock on the front door, at three in the morning. I glanced over at Kelly's bed and saw that she wasn't there. I heard Mom come downstairs and open the door and talk to someone. Next thing I knew Kelly stormed into our room and closed the door. She said she didn't want to talk and went to sleep. The next day she confessed that her and some guys were picked up by the police. She said they weren't doing anything wrong, but the police insisted on taking her home and talking to Mom. Kelly was grounded for an entire year.

We celebrated New Year's Eve at home. Mom, Anna, Sam and me drank sparkling apple cider and watched the ball drop on TV. Kelly was too mad that she was grounded to celebrate and stayed in our room all night. Dad went upstairs around ten o'clock with Anna, who had fallen asleep. At midnight we yelled and hollered as quietly as we could.

At last, it was 1988. Mom, Sam and I agreed 1988 had to be better than 1987. In 1987 Anna got cancer. We decided that we needed to make sure 1988 would be a good year. Mom's eyes widened as the corners of her mouth curled upward. "How about the three of us, at the same exact time, cross our fingers and say, 'In 1988 Anna will go into remission and all of our friends and family will be healthy.'" Sam and I agreed. The three of us crossed our fingers and said the words.

CHAPTER 17

HOLIDAY BREAK ENDED and we quickly got back to our regular routine. The excitement of the holidays had faded, but we still had one celebration to look forward to. Anna was turning two and Kelly and I were going to help Mom plan the party. Sam wasn't interested.

During one of our planning sessions, Kelly said, "We should definitely have the theme be My Little Pony."

I agreed with her. "Yes! Everything has to be pink and purple. Balloons too."

Suddenly Mom's eyes widened. "You know what? We should have an actual pony! There are ponies that you can rent for the day. They come with a handler that will help the kids ride the pony. What do ya say?"

Kelly's face lit up. "Wow! That would be totally rad. Anna would love a real pony."

It was decided. Anna would have a real live pony at her second birthday party. I beamed at Mom. "Can I be the party DJ?"

"Do we need a DJ?"

I opened my eyes wide. "Of course!"

"What kind of music will you play?"

"All of Anna's favorites."

Kelly laughed. "Oh no! Not more 'Shake Your Love'!"

I formed an evil grin. "Lots of Debbie Gibson and of course 'Shake Your Love.'"

I was happy that Kelly was planning with us. Since she got grounded she'd hardly spoken to Mom and Dad.

When the day of Anna's party arrived, everything was ready. Dad had gone out that morning to pick up the cake and the pink and purple balloons filled with helium. Kelly set up the tables with My Little Pony plates, napkins and tablecloth. Sam and Kelly arranged the balloons and hung pink streamers. The caterers dropped off the Mexican food. I set up my DJ booth in the living room, in front of the fireplace. My booth consisted of a stereo with two cassette players and speakers on the ground.

Before guests arrived Anna had insisted on listening to "Shake Your Love." I tried to show her how to rewind the cassette so she could play it over and over; she didn't quite get it but knew she needed to push the button. When guests started to arrive and knock on the front door, Anna would run to see who it was. She continued this for quite a while, since we had what seemed like an endless stream of grandparents, aunts, uncles, cousins and neighbors. She greeted each one with a grin and a "Hi! Hi! Hi!"

Everyone seemed to be having a good time catching up and playing with Anna. When the pony arrived, Anna was surprised, as were most of the guests. When Anna saw the pony, she pointed at it. "Pony!" The handler gave her a big carrot to try to feed to the pony. Anna held out the carrot, but every time the pony got close, she ran and hid behind Mom. However, when it was time to put the helmet on and ride the pony, there was no hesitation. She grinned from ear to ear and kept saying, "Pony!" When her turn was over and the handler set her back on the ground, she insisted, "Gen! Gen!"

Mom knelt down. "Anna, you have to let other kids ride too."

Anna didn't budge. She crossed her arms and shouted, "Gen!"

Mom stood up. "Okay, Anna, one more time, but then you have to share. Okay?"

Mom put her back on the pony. At the end of her second ride, Mom helped her off the pony as she protested, "Gen!" but Mom held her ground and then promised she could go again after everyone else had their turn.

At the end of the party, Anna had a pile of gifts even bigger than at Christmas. Mom decided it was best if she waited until after the party to open them. After the guests and pony went home, Anna went down for a much-needed nap while Mom and us kids cleaned up the party. Sam's idea of cleaning up was sucking the helium out of the balloons and talking funny. Kelly and I joined, as did Mom. Eventually the party got cleaned up.

A FEW WEEKS LATER, Anna was cleared for her fifth round of chemo. A few days after treatment, Dad picked us up after school and brought us to the hospital. On the way we stopped to acquire Anna's favorite dinner at McDonald's. As we walked into Anna's room, bags of food in hand, there was a baby sleeping in the first crib. For the first time, one of Anna's roommates wasn't alone. There was a woman, about Mom's age, with dark hair pulled into a bun, olive skin and sad brown eyes, sitting in a chair next to the crib reading. We politely waved as we walked past.

When we reached Anna's crib, she was up playing ponies with Mom. We broke into our normal greeting, trying to be quiet, since the baby was sleeping in the next crib. Dad set up the table for dinner, Kelly picked up Anna and Sam made faces as Anna laughed. When we sat down for dinner, Mom told us about Anna's roommates. "The baby's name is Caleb, and his mother is Deirdre. Caleb has neuroblastoma too."

Dad snorted. "Really?"

Mom lowered her voice. "Yes. Deirdre is a wreck. Caleb was

diagnosed a few months ago. I have been talking to her, and I think it helps her to hear how well Anna is doing after just under a year."

Kelly shook her head. "It's only been a year? It seems like so much longer."

"I know what you mean. It hasn't been quite a full year, eleven months. But who's counting?" Mom threw her head back and chuckled. Regaining her composure, she continued, "In that time, though, Caleb is the only other child we've met with neuroblastoma."

After dinner all of us walked the halls with Anna. Anna held her pony in one hand and the IV pole in the other, leading the way. Mom and Dad stood closely behind to help if the IV pole got away from her; us kids followed slightly behind Mom and Dad. It was as if Anna was the superstar singer and we were the back up dancers. We were Anna's backup dancers! The thought made me happy.

WE DIDN'T GET to visit Anna again until the weekend. When we walked into Anna's room, Mom was standing next to Anna's crib with tears in her eyes and rubbing Anna's back. Dad said hi to Anna, picked her up and then asked if something was wrong with her. Mom wiped the tears from her eyes. "No. Anna is fine. She's good."

She glanced up at Sam, Kelly and me. "Little Tony passed away."

Kelly burst into tears and Sam's face reddened, and then he said, "But we were just bowling with him. He seemed okay?"

Mom spoke softly. "Tony was very sick. He's at peace now."

Nobody spoke for a few minutes as we tried to process what had happened. Mom reached out to Kelly to give her a hug. I knew he was sick, since he was in the hospital so much, I just didn't expect for him to die. I then asked Mom, "What happened?"

"It wasn't any one thing. He was very sick. His body just stopped fighting. He's in a better place now."

She then reached out to hug me and Sam. Dad hugged Anna. I told Mom I was going to go on a walk. She waved as I left.

I wandered the halls and began to think about all the kids that had become so familiar to us that weren't there anymore. I wondered if they were at home or if they had passed away too. It was sad to think about. I approached the leukemia poster and read it again. I checked myself for suspicious bruises, confirmed I still didn't have leukemia and kept walking.

When I got back to Anna's room, Mom said Dad had left to run errands and that Anna wanted to go to the playroom. Kelly was going to stay in the room, but Sam agreed to go, so I went too. We made pictures and played in the cornmeal with Anna. After the playroom closed, we headed back to the room where Dad was waiting with dinner. We ate and then Dad drove us home.

THE NEXT WEEK, Dad, Sam, Kelly and I went back to visit Anna after school. When we got to her room she was asleep, so Sam, Kelly and I decided to go for a walk around the floor. We revived our game of elevator tag for a while and then went back to see if Anna was awake yet. When we got back to the room, she was still asleep so Sam and I decided to go to the playroom; Kelly stayed behind in the room.

It was the first time we had gone to the playroom without Anna. It felt a little weird, but we were greeted warmly by the volunteers. We sat at a table to make some art. There were a couple of skinny African American kids at our table. I decided to be friendly. "Hi. I'm Casey and this is my brother, Sam."

The older girl replied, "Hi, I'm Destiny. This is Opal. You look like you're visitors. Who are you here to see? We're patients. We've got sickle-cell. We're here a lot."

I smirked. "Yeah, we're here a lot too but just to visit our sister Anna. She has cancer."

"Leukemia?"

"No, neuroblastoma. It's rare."

"Hmm. Never heard of it."

She then continued to tell us that they were both from Oakland, describe where they lived and tell us all about their brothers and sisters. They also seemed to know everyone who walked into the playroom. During our conversation they stopped to greet everyone who walked in, by name. I had no idea what sickle-cell was, but I figured I could ask a nurse later.

When we got back to Anna's room, she was awake and playing with Kelly. Nurse Karen walked in to check on Anna. She began to walk out when I asked her what sickle-cell was. She stopped and chuckled. "You are quite inquisitive!"

Mom laughed. "Yes, very."

Nurse Karen explained, "Sickle-cell anemia is a blood disease. It's when there is a problem with a person's red blood cells, or RBCs. RBCs carry oxygen throughout the body, which is pretty important. Organs like the brain, heart and kidneys need constant blood flow to work properly. People with sickle-cell have funny-shaped RBCs that can keep the blood from flowing when it should. It can cause a lot of pain and exhaustion and a bunch of other problems."

"That sounds terrible."

"Yes, it is."

"Thanks for explaining it to me. Sam and I met some kids in the playroom and they told me they had sickle-cell and that they were in the hospital a lot."

"Yes, that's pretty common. Unfortunately."

"I'm guessing it's not contagious."

"No, it's inherited. It's mostly prevalent in the African American community."

"Oh."

After Nurse Karen left, I walked over to Anna and Kelly. I noticed Dad had picked up some dinner. The six of us crammed around the table and ate. Shortly after dinner we had to leave to go home, since there was school the next day.

WITHOUT MOM and Anna at home, we were back to living our separate lives. When we were separate, it was lonely, but at least it was quiet. I could read or have my friends, Sally or Heather, over after school. When the family was together, it usually resorted in Kelly and Sam fighting with Dad over what seemed like every little thing. Little things were fine, I guess. It was the big stuff that tore our family apart. The latest big fight was over Kelly being grounded. She had argued with Dad over being able to go out with her friends to the mall. Dad said, "You're grounded. You can't go."

"You can't tell me what to do! You're not my father."

"I may not be your biological father, but I provide for you a hell of a lot better than your so-called real father."

"You don't know what you're talking about. He does. He pays child support!"

Dad laughed bitterly. "Oh, is that what he told you? He didn't pay child support for years until your mom took him to court. He's a deadbeat!"

"He is not!"

"Oh, is that so? He doesn't pay child support all on his own. The courts have to have his employer take it out of his check. If it was up to him, he'd never support you or see you. When was the last time you saw him? Does he call to check on you guys? No. He's a deadbeat, and he doesn't care about anyone but himself."

"It isn't true! I'm so sick of you and Mom always trying to turn us against him. I'm going to go live with him instead!"

"Go ahead. Good luck with that!"

Kelly stormed out of the house. Sam and I exchanged glances and went back to our rooms before we got caught in any cross fire.

Later that night Kelly came home after everyone was asleep. When she walked into our room, I woke up and asked her, "Where have you been?"

"I was at my friend's house. I called Dad-Pete, and he's going to let me live with him."

"Seriously?"

"Yep."

"Well, when are you going?"

"He's going to pick me up tomorrow after school. I've got to pack, like now."

"Oh. Well, try to be quiet." I rolled over and went back to sleep.

The next day after school, I was shocked to see Dad-Pete pull up to the front of our house and then drive away with Kelly.

CHAPTER 18

KELLY

When I drove off with Dad-Pete, I knew everything was going to be okay. I was filled with excitement and hope for the future. Not to mention, I was finally going to be treated with a little respect. Come on, my real Dad wouldn't be so ridiculous as to ground me for an entire year.

When I got back to the house last night, I had hoped to sneak in undetected. However, when I walked in our room, it woke Casey and she practically gave me the third degree before falling back to sleep. Once Casey was asleep, I packed my things and went to sleep for the last time in that house.

When Dad-Pete picked me up the next day, I said good-bye to Casey and Sam, picked up my suitcase and headed out. They wanted to say hi to Dad-Pete, but I told them we were in a hurry and they had to stay in the house. They seemed dejected, but I just wanted to get out of there. I saw Sam and Casey peering out the kitchen window as we drove off. I figured once things cooled down I would call Mom and check on Anna and the kids.

When we arrived at Dad-Pete's apartment, he told me that since he only had a one-bedroom I would have to sleep on the couch. I didn't care. It was fine. He told me he was so happy I was there. I was a little surprised and asked him, "If you miss us so much, how come you haven't tried to get us to live with you or visit with us more?"

"It's your mother. I always want to see you, but she says I can't unless I pay her."

"She said that you didn't get us because you were a flake. I never believed her."

"Yeah, your Mom and Jasper have tried to turn you guys against me for years. She has been trying to kill me with child support. It's why I'm always broke. If I didn't have to pay child support, I would be able to buy a house. I'll never get ahead as long as I have child support to pay. Your mother is so greedy. She just wants all the money to spend it on herself. Tomorrow we can go to the court and file that you are not living with her anymore so they'll at least stop taking out your support from my paycheck."

"Oh, okay. How am I going to get to school?"

"You'll have to take the bus and BART, I guess. Eventually you'll have to change schools because it's too far and I can't afford private school."

"Once you don't have to pay child support for me, can we move to a bigger apartment so I can have my own room?"

"I don't know. Two bedrooms cost a lot more than one bedroom. We'll just have to wait and see."

"I can't live on the couch forever."

"I'm not rich like Jasper. This is it. Sorry, this is the best I can do."

I hadn't realized that living with him meant I wouldn't have a room or that I'd have to change schools. I was starting to make friends at school and getting good grades. I started to realize maybe living with him wasn't a great idea, but I hated Jasper, and Mom had been such a witch. I felt so trapped and helpless. I decided to call Mom at the hospital and see how Anna was doing. When she answered, I said, "Hi, Mom."

"Hi, Kelly."

"How's Anna doing?"

"She's fine. We're coming home on Sunday. It would be nice if you were there too."

"Uh. I don't know."

"Kelly. This is your mother. I love you. You're part of this family. We want you with us."

I started to cry, but I wasn't sure why. I told her I needed some time to think about it.

The next day I had to take the bus and BART to school. It took two hours to get there and two hours to get home. After school, I told Dad-Pete that I wasn't sure I should live with him and didn't want to go down to the court yet. I needed the weekend to think about it. He didn't seem happy about it but agreed and said that he couldn't make me do anything I didn't want to do.

I stayed the weekend and spent most of the time with my friend, Tanya, who lived in the apartment complex or on the phone with my best friends, Terry and Sasha. Dad spent most of his time with some woman he was dating. I called Mom on Sunday and told her I was coming home. She said she was glad and then reminded me I was still grounded.

When I got home that night, I was thrilled to see Anna running around, turning the house into a disaster; toys and books were everywhere. When I went to drop off my suitcase and backpack in the bedroom, Casey walked in and said, "Dang it. I almost had my own room! Just kidding. I'm glad you're back."

I flashed my best fake grin. "Thanks."

She waved and then walked back out to the living room to play with Anna.

Things at the house stayed calm for a while. Even Sam stayed out of trouble and was getting good grades again. Mom said that I could apply to go to Cornerwood, the Catholic high school where all my friends were going, next year. Maybe showing them that I could be gone in an instant made them finally appreciate me more.

Mom and Anna were getting ready to head out to the hospital for another round of chemo when Mom got a call from Anna's doctor saying that they thought she might have an infection. She would need to submit another blood sample and have it tested before they could start another round. They instructed Mom to bring Anna to the hospital for the testing.

After she got off the phone, she took Anna's temperature. Sure enough, she had a low-grade fever. I wondered if Anna would ever get better. I worried about her all time. She was all I could think about, most of the time. When she got sick, I felt her stomach ache. I felt her nausea. I felt her fatigue. I felt her headaches. It was like we were connected physically; nobody seemed to realize it but me. Before Mom and Anna left for the hospital, I gave Anna a big hug and told her I would always be with her.

With Mom and Anna out of the house, I stayed mostly in my and Casey's room. I didn't want to have to deal with Dad. In our room, I had privacy to talk to my friends on the phone, except when Casey was there. I could also come and go as I pleased, albeit out the window. It's not like Dad ever checked on us. At least Terry and Sasha were close by so that I could go and decompress with them over a few drinks or some weed. It was my medicine, and it made me feel good. I didn't think about Anna or Sam or Casey or Dad-Pete or Mom or Dad when I was out. I just chilled and had a good time.

With Anna in the hospital, it was up to me to plan Sam's birthday celebration, since nobody else remembered. I called Mom at the hospital and asked her what she wanted to do about it. She told me that Anna was still going to be in the hospital, so maybe we could do a celebration in the cafeteria like we did for Casey. I told her I'd talk to Sam and see what he thought about the idea. Sam said he didn't care. It was set. We'd celebrate Sam's thirteenth birthday in the hospital cafeteria.

Sam's birthday arrived, and we all got in the car to go to the hospital. When we got up to Anna's room, she was asleep. Mom told us that Anna couldn't go down to the cafeteria, so we had to go down, get the food and bring it back up. Great. The three of us went down and brought the trays of gross cafeteria food back up to Anna's room. I swear, if they didn't have the name of the food displayed, I'm not sure I'd even know what it was; everything looked like mush. By the time we got back, she was awake. She was a little sleepy but happy to see us. We took our food off the trays and arranged them on the table.

Over dinner Mom told us that another one of Anna's hospital friends didn't make it. She said that in the year Anna had been coming to the hospital, more kids died than those who didn't. I don't know why she was telling us this now. Was she trying to prepare us for Anna dying too? Sam jumped in with his wacky announcer voice, "And, Sam, what other cheerful topics do we have for your birthday dinner?"

Casey responded in a deranged, reporter voice. "Well, Sam. This just in. A plague has been reported just outside the very hospital we are in right now. This will be your last birthday. Dun. Dun. Dun."

Casey and Sam laughed, which made Anna laugh. They were so weird.

Mom gave a sheepish grin. "I'm sorry, Sam. It's hard not to constantly think about it when we are surrounding by so much death and suffering." She tried to change the subject and asked, "How's school?"

Sam replied in a monotone voice, "Fine."

"What do you want for your birthday?"

His eyes lit up. "I'd really like a new Nintendo, since mine accidentally got broken."

I'm sure he said "accidentally" instead of the truth that Mom went on a crazy tirade and broke it, in the fear that she'd get mad and not buy it for him.

At the end of dinner Dad brought out a cake for Sam. He didn't seem to care that we couldn't light the candles; he made his wish and then pretended to blow them out. Mom said she didn't have time to shop now but that when Anna got out of the hospital, she'd take him to Toys "R" Us and let him pick out a new game system. He was thrilled. Like, dancing around thrilled.

ANNA CAME HOME the next week. As promised, Mom took Sam to go get a new Nintendo. After they got back from the store he went straight to his room to hook it up. He didn't reemerge until it was time to go out to dinner. Apparently, Mom had felt bad that his birthday dinner was hospital food, so she let him pick out any place he wanted to go. It was no surprise he picked Sizzler.

We all loaded up in the car and made our way to the restaurant. Although Anna was allowed to go out, Mom insisted she wear a face mask. She was only allowed to take it off when eating dinner. I didn't blame her. God only knows what kinds of germs were at the restaurant. Sam ordered a big steak, baked potato and the salad bar option. He was a thirteen-year-old boy and ate like it too. You'd never guess by looking at him though. He was skinny and small for his age.

Anna was tested a few weeks later to see if she was ready for another round of chemo. We were happy that all her tests came back normal and that she could start. The sooner she could get through the whole chemo regimen, the quicker we could be done with it. I just wanted Anna to be better and for this whole nightmare to end.

CHAPTER 19

UPSTAIRS IN MOM, Dad and Anna's bedroom, Mom had pulled out Anna's small blue Cinderella suitcase and a navy blue duffel bag and then started packing for the hospital. Anna pointed to her chest. "I do it."

Mom laughed. "Oh, you're big now? You want to do it?"

She pointed at herself again. "Me big!"

"That's right. You're a big girl."

I tapped Anna on the shoulder. "Do you want my help?"

Anna cocked her head to the side. "Okay. I do it."

I wasn't sure if it was a yes or no. I started putting pajamas in her backpack, and she put her hand on my arm. "Cay-hee! I do it!"

I chuckled. "Okay, Anna. You do it."

Her whole face lit up. "I do it!"

Later that day, Mom and Anna were off to the hospital for Anna's sixth round of chemotherapy. While they were gone, our 'Mom's gone' routine started up again: go to school, come home from school and then you're on your own. It was pretty routine now, especially since Kelly and Sam had to be driven to their new school; no more cutting class for those two.

We visited Anna in the hospital a few days later. It was amazing how big she was getting, almost two and a half years old, telling us "I do it" and developing a little attitude. It was hilarious. I starting thinking back to how she acted and looked before her cancer, fourteen months before. She was adorable with chubby cheeks and wavy strawberry blonde hair. She couldn't say many words and liked to be held a lot. Now she was taller with thin cheeks and her head was covered with peach-fuzz. She was much more independent, insisting on doing lots of things by herself. Her favorite activities included playing with her colorful ponies, hanging out in the playroom and walking the halls talking to everyone, as well as trying to boss people around.

When the nurses came in to check on her, she would try to check their temperature and listen to their heart, insisting, "I do it!"—which was apparently her new favorite phrase. Not to mention, she ruled the halls of the fifth floor. Everyone knew her and was always happy to see her when she was making her rounds.

I started to realize how comfortable she was at the hospital. It had become her second home. It made sense. In the last year and two months she had spent more time in the hospital than at our house. I also realized that it kind of felt like a second home for us too. The nurses even let us kids go into the nurses' lounge by ourselves and get Popsicles and juice whenever we wanted. We were regulars in the playroom with or without Anna. The cafeteria staff knew us by name and always asked how Anna was doing. It had all become so normal.

From across the room, I watched Mom and Anna on the window seat as Anna "combed" Mom's long curly hair. I moved my chair over and asked, "How many more rounds of chemo does Anna have left?"

"It depends on her tests. As of right now, they think she'll only need a few more rounds."

"They don't know for sure?"

"Anna's protocol is brand-new and somewhat experimental. There just aren't a lot of kids with neuroblastoma, so there are no previously established protocols that have been effective. If the protocol works, she'll be done in a few more rounds; if not, we have to try a new regimen."

"So if all goes well, she could be done this year?"

"Cross your fingers, but yes."

"Wow. I think I forgot what it was like to not come to the hospital all the time."

"Me too! It seems like so long ago. I'm looking forward to a life without chemo. Fingers crossed." Mom crossed her fingers.

Anna finished another round and was back home the next weekend. Things got back to the normal "Anna's home" routine. Mom and Anna took Sam and Kelly to school. Dad worked what seemed like all the time; he was barely home even on weekends.

SCHOOL WAS ALMOST OUT for the summer with just a few weeks to go. One day after school, I was playing with Anna and telling her I was going to go into junior high next year. She wasn't nearly as interested in our conversation as she was watching Cinderella for the fiftieth time. She had seen it so many times, she had started acting out her favorite scenes. Her most favorite was when Cinderella is holding a tray of tea and her stepsisters are talking about the prince. Cinderella says, "The prince," and drops the tray. The tea spills everywhere, and Cinderella is called a "clumsy little fool" by her stepmother.

Anna insisted that we fill up her pink, plastic teapot and cups with water, put them on the tray and let her act out the scene. She would stand in front of the TV holding the tray with the liquid-filled teapot and cups and say, "The prince!" and drop the tray. She would do this over and over and would throw a fit if we suggested that we didn't put water in the tea set. It was funny to watch but a pain to clean up. She seemed to be doing so well, we couldn't believe it when she got chicken pox for the second time in nine months.

As they were packing up for the hospital, I asked Mom, "How can she get chicken pox, twice? I thought you could only get it once?"

"The doctors said that healthy people typically only get chicken pox once because after they have it, the body develops antibodies against reinfection. I didn't know this, but after a person has chicken pox the virus lives silently in the nervous system of the body for the rest of the person's life. Because Anna's immune system is compromised, being on chemo, she couldn't fight it a second time."

"Does that mean she could even get it a third time?"

"Yes, but let's hope this is the last time."

I agreed to.

While Anna was in the hospital fighting chicken pox for a second time, school got out for the summer. Kelly was super excited because she got accepted to Cornerwood, the Catholic high school that all of her private-school friends would be attending. Sam was excited to be done with school and that Mom and Dad agreed to let him play football over the summer. I was excited because I was going to be going into seventh grade and would start junior high school. I asked Kelly, "So, what is Mount Diablo Junior High like?"

"It's totally cool. You get your own locker and change class-rooms for every class. Not just math and English like in elementary school."

"That sounds so cool. What languages can you take?"

"French or Spanish. I was taking French until Mom made me change schools."

"Oh, I'd love to learn French! Ooh la la!"

Kelly laughed.

"What other stuff is there that they don't have in elementary school?"

"School dances! School dances are so fun."

"Oh yeah. That sounds fun. I can't wait to go!"

"Now that I think about it, I'm going to be in high school, Sam will be in seventh at St. Ann's and you'll be at Mount Diablo JH. We'll be in three different cities and schools. I wonder how Mom is gonna swing that."

"I was talking to Mom, and she said Anna may be done with chemo by the end of the year. So maybe it won't be that big of deal."

"She said that?!"

"Yeah, she said if everything goes well, she could be done by the end of the . . . Oh wait. That was before the second round of chicken pox. I'm not sure if that is still true."

"I'm so tired of worrying about Anna all the time. I feel like it's killing me. I just can't take it. I wish she would get better, like now."

"Me too."

Anna was in the hospital for another month due to the chicken pox.

Mom was so happy when they finally got to come home, and Kelly was happy because everyone would be home for her fifteenth birthday. She said to me, "I'm so glad I'm not going to have to spend my birthday at the hospital, like you and Sam. It was just so sad."

"It wasn't that bad. It was fine."

"Well, that isn't going to be me. I'm going to ask Mom if I can go out to dinner with the family and then have an after-party with my friends. We could go downtown and see a movie. It's going to be off the hook!"

"Do I get to go to the movie too?"

"No. Just teenagers. No kids allowed."

"Does Sam get to go? He's thirteen."

"No. No younger siblings. Just me and my friends chillin' out and seeing a movie. Sorry, kiddo."

I hated that she always referred to me as a kid. I was almost twelve, and she wasn't even three years older than me. Much to her surprise, her plans didn't work out as she hoped. There was no predicting that the next day Anna would come down with another fever. I thought back over the conversation and wondered if Kelly had jinxed herself and us.

Mom just about flipped out when Anna got sick again. I think she, and us, assumed the chicken pox was back. She took her straight to the hospital to get Anna checked out. Mom called the house to talk to Dad, but I answered. I asked, "How's Anna? Is the chicken pox back?"

"No. It's an infection in her Broviac. It's bad. I feel so guilty."

"Why do you feel guilty? I'm sure it isn't your fault."

"I'm the one who flushes it and changes the dressing. I must have infected her somehow. I just don't know."

"But you've been doing it for over a year. How could it all of a sudden be wrong? Did the doctor say it was because of what you did?"

"No. They insist it was normal and that it probably wasn't anything I did. I just have to wonder."

"I'm sure it wasn't your fault. Are they going to give her antibiotics for the infection?"

"Yes, but they also have to take out the Broviac and give her a new one."

"But they gave it to her when she was in surgery. Does she have to have surgery?"

"Yes. I'm terrified. They say it's simple, but no surgery is simple. Just the fact that she's going under general anesthesia means she could die."

"Seriously?"

"Yes. I'm sorry. I don't have a lot of time. Can you put Dad on the phone?"

"Yeah. Okay. Give Anna a kiss for me."

I ran upstairs to tell Dad that Mom was on the phone from the hospital. On our walk to the kitchen I told him that Anna's infection was in her Broviac. He grabbed the phone from the counter and began to talk. I watched as his face went pale.

CHAPTER 20

KELLY

WHEN I HEARD the news that Anna had an infection in her Broviac, I wanted to kill myself right then and there. How much more am I supposed to take? Not only does she have an infection and have to be admitted to the hospital, she has to have surgery too. All of this right before my fifteenth birthday. I swear it's like I can't catch a break! I guess it's my fault for starting to think I could have a normal life or at least a normal birthday party. I don't know why everything bad happens to me.

On the day of Anna's surgery all of us went with Dad to the hospital. When we got to the reception Lou told us that she was on the third floor; it was the same floor as Anna's surgery nearly a year and a half before. I remember it like it was yesterday. Now here we were going up the same elevator, to the same waiting room and once again hoping Anna would survive surgery and this terrible cancer.

When we walked into the waiting room, Mom was sitting in a chair talking to Grandma Jess. I went right up to Mom and extended my arms to give her a hug. Next I gave Grandma Jess a hug and a kiss on the cheek. I returned my attention to Mom.

"How did Anna do before surgery? Was she brave like the last time?"

Mom cocked her head to the side. "Well . . . Anna was so little at her last surgery, she couldn't say much. As you know, Anna is much more vocal these days. She made it clear to her oncologist, Dr. Baker, and her surgeon, Dr. Trekker, she did not want to go to surgery. It was a bit of a struggle to get her to cooperate."

I became nervous. "What happened? What did she say?"

Mom chuckled. "She kept saying, 'No. Go Way. Go Way. Go. Way.'" Everyone seemed to think this was funny. I just kept thinking, my poor Anna.

Casey, said, trying to contain her laughter, "How did you finally get her to cooperate? She can be quite stubborn!"

"Yes. That she is. We had to promise her a new My Little Pony when it was over."

"That's so Anna!" Casey continued to laugh. Not me, I was too concerned and I asked, "Well, so you got her prepped and she did okay, right?"

Mom explained, "Yes, the prep went fine. She is in surgery now. It shouldn't be nearly as long of a surgery as her first. They assured me it's a simple procedure. However, I'll feel a lot better once she's in recovery."

I said, "Me too." Everyone else agreed as well.

The conversation quickly changed when Casey started talking about Anna acting out scenes from Cinderella and how she had become so independent. The whole group was laughing and telling funny stories about Anna. All we needed was Sam and Casey to break into one of their bits, and it would officially be comedy hour.

I had to admit, Anna had become quite the little character. Even so, I couldn't believe they were joking around at a time like this. I was worried sick! Thinking back to her first surgery, maybe everyone talking and joking was better. Last time we hardly spoke as we waited for hours in this ugly old waiting room. It was absolute torture.

As promised, the surgery wasn't nearly as long as the first. Before we knew it, Dr. Trekker walked in the room calling Mom and Dad over. We all followed. Dr. Trekker spoke to Mom. "Anna is out of surgery. She did great." We all cheered. I hugged Grandma Jess as she declared, "Thank heavens!"

Mom gushed over Dr. Trekker, as usual. "Oh, Dr. Trekker. Thank you so much. I just wanted to tell you how grateful we are that you are Anna's surgeon. You saved our Anna's life, twice now. Thank you and God bless you."

Dr. Trekker maintained a serious face and tone. "Thank you. I am glad things went well, and I have to tell you, Anna's a fighter. I was happy to see how well she's doing."

"Yes. We owe it all to you. Thank you. Thank you." Mom beamed at him.

Dr. Trekker responded, "Anna is in the ICU. The nurse will come out shortly to start bringing in visitors. Bye, now."

We waved to him as he left. I was so relieved Anna was okay. It felt like a giant burden had been lifted, even if for just a little bit.

Anna had to stay in the hospital for only another week, but unfortunately it meant that we missed the annual Fourth of July celebration at Aunt Katie's in Santa Cruz. Not to mention, it was my fifteenth birthday. I ended up doing exactly what I had feared I would end up doing. My birthday party was at the hospital. I ate gross cafeteria food—I think it was fries and roasted chicken—and blew out non-lit candles on my grocery store cake that had white frosting and pink lettering, just like Casey's. At least Mom and Dad gave me one hundred dollars in my card, instead of the normal fifty they give the kids. I couldn't wait to go shopping and get some cool clothes and maybe some new music. Public Enemy had just come out with a fresh album; I could be the first of my friends to get it.

SOON ENOUGH ANNA was home from the hospital and things went back to normal. One night over dinner we started talking about how I was going into high school. I grinned at Mom and Dad. "You know, I'm grateful that you are letting me go to Cornerwood with my friends. I know it's expensive and everything, but I think it is going to be good for me."

Mom's eyes lit up. "Kelly, we are so proud of you for keeping your grades up and getting accepted. You should feel proud too."

"I am. You know they only accept so many students. I was lucky they chose me."

I glanced over and saw Casey rolling her eyes and making a face at Sam. I didn't care. I felt like I was on top of the world. I continued, "How are we all going to get to school? I'll be in Walnut Creek. Sam in Lafayette and Casey in Clayton. Talk about driving all over the Bay Area!"

Mom's expression changed from smiling to more apprehensive. "You're right, Kelly. It would be quite difficult to be able to drive all of you guys to all of your different schools. Especially with Anna in and out of the hospital. Dad and I have been talking." She paused and glanced over at Casey.

"We're thinking it might be better if Casey changed schools and went to St. Ann's with Sam."

I thought Casey's head was going to explode. "What?! Are you kidding me? I can't go to junior high with all my friends? Why? I didn't do anything wrong? I always get good grades. I never get in trouble. This is so unfair!"

Mom tried to defuse her. "Nothing is final yet. We haven't even talked to St. Ann's."

"But it's sooo unfair. I could just take the bus. Kelly used to take the bus!"

Dad grimaced. "Yeah, and we see how well that turned out."

Casey wouldn't let up. "I'm not Kelly. I've never gotten into trouble. I got almost straight As last year! This is ridiculous!"

Casey stormed out of the kitchen and went back to our room and slammed the door. I'm not sure I had ever seen her so mad.

Sam smirked. "That went well."

Dad started to get up and told Mom that he would talk to Casey. She told him to just give her some space and that she would calm down eventually. Dad sat back down.

Mom opened her eyes wide. "Actually, we do have some good news. I was going to tell everyone and then tell Casey about school, but that didn't work out. Clearly. Anyways, we're going on vacation! Anna's doctor cleared her to go to Disneyland and a cruise to Mexico! Surprise!" Mom displayed jazz hands next to her giant, goofy grin.

Surprised? Heck yeah. I couldn't remember the last time the family went on vacation together. Mom explained that we were going a few weeks before school started; it would be three days in Disneyland and five days on a cruise to Mexico. I couldn't wait to tell Casey. She was going to be thrilled. She was going to be in a different country for her birthday. It was going to be so much better than another sad hospital birthday party.

The rest of the night was spent asking Mom about details of the trip. It sounded like it was going to be totally cool. We were going to go drive down to Disneyland for three days and then take a cruise from Los Angeles to Mexico. I wonder what made Mom and Dad decide to go on vacation? It was so unlike them. I guess I didn't care why we were going. I just couldn't wait to go! I was going to take all kinds of vacation photos at Disneyland and on the beaches of Mexico. My friends were going to be so jealous.

CHAPTER 21

I COULDN'T BELIEVE they were making me change schools, again. It was the fourth time in six years! I don't know why they were doing this to me. I always did whatever anybody wanted me to. I never missed school or got in trouble. I always got good grades. I always did my chores and helped with Anna. Now, I could take being left behind when Anna was in the hospital. It wasn't even that I minded. I loved Anna and I knew she needed Mom and Dad more than me. I could take care of myself. What I couldn't take was doing everything right and still getting punished. Maybe Kelly and Sam were right about Mom and Dad. They only cared about Anna and themselves. I didn't even get to tell my friends I wasn't going to be at Mount Diablo Junior High in the fall. They could have at least told me before school got out. It was so unfair!

Kelly walked into our room and asked if I was okay. I gave her my rant about how unfair it was. She said, "Yeah. I know. It's typical Mom and Dad."

I shook my head. "Yeah, I guess."

Kelly's face lit up. "Guess what isn't typical?"

"What?"

"After you stormed off. Well done, by the way! Ha! I knew you had it in you to not be the goody-goody all the time!"

"Well, this was clearly a special occasion."

Kelly laughed. "That it was. But guess what? You'll never guess!"

"Okay, then tell me." I was growing impatient.

"We're going on vacation! Disneyland and a cruise to Mexico!"

"Get out. No way." I was in complete disbelief.

"Seriously. We leave in a couple of weeks. We'll be there for your birthday. You are going to spend your twelfth birthday on a cruise to Mexico!"

"I'm sure it was a coincidence."

"Oh, I'm sure. It's still totally cool though, right?"

"You're serious? We're really going on vacation?"

"Yep."

Okay. I was still totally pissed about changing schools, but a vacation? Disneyland? A cruise? I couldn't believe it. It was only a matter of time before something good was going to happen around here.

THE NEXT WEEK Mom told me that we were going to go register Sam and me for school and that it would be a good idea for me to come and check out the school. Reluctantly, and without a choice, I went. When we arrived at the school it all of a sudden seemed daunting, despite the fact I had seen it many times before when we had picked up Sam and Kelly on the way to the hospital. Mom parked the car, and then Sam, Anna and I followed her to the office.

The three of us sat in the hall as she spoke to the teacher or principal or nun or whoever it was. I didn't really care, since I didn't want to be there. Sam chuckled and then said to me, "This is where I sit when I get in trouble."

"Wow. Some real memories here for ya?"

"The best."

"I feel honored to sit here. It's like a historical site."

"Oh stop. I might tear up."

Sam pretended to sniffle and we both laughed. I quickly got up to follow Anna as she started to wander down the hall by herself. I brought her back over to the chairs and tried to get her to read a book. She appeared to be more interested in running off so I would have to keep chasing her.

When Mom came out of the office, Anna and I were down the hall playing our game of chase. She called to us and we ran back. "So? Am I registered here?"

"No. Actually they didn't think it would be a good idea for Sam to have his little sister in his class."

I grinned. "So does that mean I get to go to Mount Diablo Junior High?!"

"No. I explained to Sister Margaret our situation and that I just can't be driving all over the Bay Area with a sick child. She recommended the public middle school just down the road. It has great academics. We're headed there next."

I deflated. "Great. News."

I gave Mom my most obviously fake smile as we walked back to the car. I helped Anna into her car seat and got in my seat. Mom started the car and we drove down the road to Carter Middle School, home of the Wildcats.

The campus at Carter was a lot bigger than St. Ann's. It had a huge sports field, tennis courts and lots of classrooms. We headed to the office. Sam, Anna and I sat in the front of the office while Mom went back to talk to the vice principal. Sam smirked. "Hey, maybe this is where you'll sit when you get in trouble."

"Gosh. I hope so. It's really lovely."

"It suits you."

"Thanks. I take that as a great compliment coming from you."

"That's what brothers are for."

"Oh stop. Now you're going to make me tear up."

I pretend sniffled and we laughed again. Mom walked out with the vice principal. He extended his hand to me. "You must be Casey. I'm Mr. Skippy. Welcome to Carter Middle School."

I shook his hand with a straight face and said, "Thanks."

We walked out of the office and drove home. It was official: I was leaving behind all my friends and going to school forty-five minutes from our house. It sucked. I was fairly melodramatic in the following days and kept it up until it was time to pack for our big vacation.

WHILE WE WERE LOADING up the car with all of our suitcases, backpacks and other essentials, Sam and Kelly decided to commemorate the trip with a rap. Sam did beatbox as Kelly rapped a silly knockoff of Rob Base's "It Takes Two." Kelly started out by putting herself in the song. "I'm Kelly G and I came to get down. I'm not internationally known—yet—but I'll be known."

Sam beatbox.

Kelly continued, waving her hands around. "Stay away from man if you're contagious. 'Cause my lil' sis has cancer. Immuno-suppressed. Word."

Sam beatbox.

Kelly went on with her theatrics. "Mickey loves me, Goofy adores me. Even the ones on the cruise who never saw me like the way that I rhyme at a show. The reason why, man, I don't know. So let's go, bro."

They laughed and high-fived each other. Needless to say, they sounded totally stupid. However, they were happy and in a good mood; it was rare.

Once the car was loaded and everyone was buckled up, we

were on our way. The first thing Kelly, Sam and I did was put our headphones on, tuning out the rest of the car. About six hours later we had made it to the Disneyland Hotel.

While Dad checked us in, Sam, Kelly and I ran around the lobby checking out all the gift shops and restaurants. It was Disney everything. I couldn't wait for Anna to wake up and see it all. When we got up to the room, we were psyched to find out that we didn't just have one room for all of us. Mom and Dad booked adjoining rooms, one for us older kids and then one for Mom, Dad and Anna.

Upon entering our room, Sam quickly ran over to his bed, climbed up and started bouncing. Kelly and I joined shortly after, on our bed. We jumped on the bed until Dad started banging on our door telling us to "knock it off." We then knocked on their door, and Dad opened it. I asked, "Can we go to the park tonight?"

"No, we have to wait until tomorrow morning because Anna is still sleeping and it's getting kind of late. You guys need to keep it down."

"Okay. We will."

He gave a crooked grin. "If you get hungry, you can order room service and rent a movie if you're bored."

The three of us exchanged glances, told them good night and went back to our room. We dined on hamburgers and fries from room service and watched The Lost Boys on pay-per-view.

We woke up early the next morning and got ready. While Sam and Kelly were fighting over the bathroom, I heard a knock on the door; it was Mom and Anna. Anna was wearing a blue Cinderella dress and a backpack as she walked into our room. Anna walked up to me and gave me a hug and a "Hi Hi Hi" and then went over to Sam and Kelly to do the same. Mom asked if we were ready for breakfast with the characters. We said we'd be ready in two minutes. I knelt down to be eye level with Anna. "Are you excited to see Mickey Mouse?"

She put her arms up. "Mickey! Ya!"

After getting ready we headed downstairs to have breakfast with all the Disney characters. Anna loved Minnie Mouse and Goofy and smiled at every photo opportunity. When breakfast was over we headed to the park, got tickets and entered through the gates.

We walked into the park, stopped in front of the Disneyland flowers and took a family photo. From there we made a plan for us older kids to go off and then meet back up for lunch with Mom, Dad and Anna. At lunch, Anna talked nonstop about all the characters she met and the rides. It wasn't all coherent, but we got the idea. After lunch we split up again and met up at dinnertime. After dinner we watched the fireworks and went on a few kiddie rides together. We repeated this for three fun and exhausting days.

When it was time to pack up for the cruise, Anna said, "No Go! No Go!" We all took turns trying to calm her down and explain that the vacation wasn't over. I told her that we had more adventures to go on. I promised we'd go on a big ship on the water and that it was like a big ride. That seemed to do the trick. At last, she stopped whining. We finished packing, got in the car and drove to the port for our next adventure.

I was super excited about the cruise to Mexico. I had never been out of the country before or on a cruise, for that matter. It seemed to take forever to actually get on the ship; there was a line for everything. When we finally got to our cabins, us kids were happy to see that, like at the hotel, we had one cabin and Mom, Dad and Anna shared another. It was a good thing we didn't try to share, as the cabins were tiny.

Despite the exhaustion of getting on the ship, Kelly, Sam and I were jazzed and wanted to go off to explore. Mom agreed but also explained that there were set times for dinner, so it was okay for us to go, but we had to be back before dinner. We agreed to Mom's conditions and set off to check out the ship. We were amazed at how much there was to do. It had a movie theater, a casino, bars, lounges, dance clubs, restaurants, swimming pools and a gym. It was like paradise. All three of us agreed the most fun place to be was the casino.

While hanging out by the slot machines we met a couple of other kids near our age. Kelly introduced us to the guys, both tall, blond and tan. The older one replied, "My name's Kip and this is my brother Peter."

Kelly flirted. "Where are you from?"

"We're from down under. Australia."

"Oh, that is why you have an accent."

"Oh, no. I don't have an accent. You guys are the ones with an accent!"

I had never thought about that before. People outside of the United States thought people from the United States had an accent. It was difficult for me to comprehend. I guess it made sense. We hung out with Kip and Peter for most of the afternoon.

When it got close to dinnertime, I told Kelly and Sam we needed to head back to the cabin so we wouldn't be late. Kelly rolled her eyes. "Oh, come on. We don't have to leave yet. We have fifteen minutes."

"But it takes us ten minutes to get to the cabin. We don't want to be late."

"Fine."

She faced Kip and Peter. "So, we have to go but we're in Cabin 1423. Do you want to go to the dance party later?"

"Sure."

"Okay, call us when you're ready to go. Cabin 1423, remember, okay?"

They agreed and we waved as we headed back to the cabin.

To our surprise our assigned dinner table was also the captain's table. Mom and Dad thought it was pretty cool that we got to have dinner with the captain every night. I thought it was weird that we didn't have our own table and had to dine with strangers. However, I soon learned that was just how it was on a cruise ship.

Our first port was Catalina Island. We got off the ship and explored the island with a tour guide and later on foot. We walked along the shops, ate at a local restaurant, and went to the local history museum. The shops and restaurants were cool, but the museum was boring. It didn't help that Mom insisted we stop at each exhibit and have a family discussion about it. After Catalina Island, we went to Ensenada, where we took a bus tour of some of the city's villages. They had beautiful, brightly colored art and lots of woven blankets. At one of the souvenir shops Mom and Dad told us we could each pick out one thing. I decided on a lime-green poncho that I had planned to wear for my birthday dinner, later that evening.

At dinner, I was presented with a small, round white cake that simply read, "Happy Birthday" in red icing, and the whole ship sang "Happy Birthday" to me. It was quite different from my last birthday party, in the hospital cafeteria. Now here I was in a foreign country, on a cruise ship with over one thousand people singing to me. It's crazy how different things can be in just one year.

The next day was an "At Sea" day, which meant that we had to entertain ourselves on board. I guess Dad had drank a little too much alcohol and started arguing with Mom. It was weird to see Dad drinking, since they never drank at home or when we were out to dinner. I didn't realize how bad the argument was until later that night. Sam, Kelly and I were in our cabin and all of a sudden we heard yelling. Sam opened our door, propping it open with his body. To our surprise, it was Dad who was yelling at Mom. Dad was trying to force his way into the cabin as he yelled, "You're a stupid whore. You think you're so fucking great!"

She yelled back, "Get out of here, you asshole! You're a fucking low-life, cheating drug addict. Get out!"

Sam, Kelly and I stood there with our eyes wide and mouths

dropped open. Dad saw us standing there and starting yelling at us too. "Oh yeah, kids. Didn't you know? Your Mom's a whore. A dirty whore. You wanna know what she did . . ."

He continued to yell obscenities about our mother, and she yelled them back. He continued to try to get in the room with Mom and Anna. Scared that Dad might hurt them, Sam went back into our cabin to call for help. Soon there were other guests in the hallway staring at the scene too. We were terrified. Dad had never gone after Mom before, that we knew of, but we certainly knew what he was capable of.

Luckily, the onboard security arrived a few minutes later and took Dad away. One of the ship's crew asked Mom if she was okay and then asked us. We were scared and humiliated but said we were fine. The officer told us it was best if we stayed in the cabin until they could ensure our safety. We went into Mom and Anna's cabin and stayed there the rest of the night. At around two in the morning, the ship's officer called to let us know that Dad had been helicoptered off the ship and flown back home.

CHAPTER 22

WE SPENT the remainder of our trip like nothing bad had happened. The long, six-hour drive home was quiet and uneventful. Kelly, Sam and I had put our headphones on shortly after we buckled up and then proceeded to listened to our favorite music until we arrived home. When we got home, it was still light out, so we could see that Dad's car was parked in the driveway.

While we were unpacking the car, Dad walked outside and approached the driveway. "Hi, kids! Hi, Anna!" He proceeded to walk up to Anna, take her out of her car seat, give her a hug and kiss and then carry her into the house. Kelly and I exchanged glances and went back to unloading the car with Mom and Sam.

Once all the gear was unloaded, Kelly and I went back to our room to unpack. At first we didn't speak, and then Kelly said, "Can you believe this? Mom is acting like nothing happened."

"She always acts like nothing happened. Think about it."

"Yeah, but this was in public. He was forcibly removed from a cruise ship! In the middle of the ocean! Who does that? Wait until I tell Dad-Pete about this."

"Are you going to call him?"

"Heck yeah!"

"What do you think he'll do? He's never done anything to help before."

"But this was in public! It's not just he-said-she-said. We have the cruise line to back up the story if he doesn't believe it. "

I was not convinced Dad-Pete would do anything or that this was any different from any other time Dad had been abusive. I told her, "I'm not going to hold my breath."

"I'm still surprised Mom is letting him be around Anna. Sure, who cares if he hits Sam and me, but Anna? Mom would never let anything happen to her."

"He didn't hit Anna."

"Doesn't mean he wouldn't have just to get back at Mom."

"But she's his child. You really think he would have?"

Kelly's eyes got wide. "I don't know. He's freakin' crazy with a capital 'C.'"

I smirked at her and went back to unpacking. I never thought Dad would ever do anything to hurt Anna.

With the first day of school approaching, I realized that I still hadn't told any of my friends that I wasn't going to be at Mount Diablo Junior High. It's not like I could have called Sally; her family was on a summerlong vacation and wasn't due back home until the day before school started. She had been sending me letters from her cross-country trip, so I decided that I would break the news by writing her a letter and hoped she would get it before school started.

A few days later I was surprised to find a letter in the mailbox from Sally. In it she told me how much she thought it sucked that I had to change schools and that she would continue to write to me to let me know everything that happened at Mount Diablo Junior High. I wrote her back and promised I'd do the same, but with my new school.

The first day of school arrived quickly. The morning was a scramble. We all had to get up extra early to make sure we got to our three different schools on time. It was a real struggle to get some bathroom time. Mom intervened, dictating that we would go in order of age. By the time I got in the bathroom, we were down to only twenty minutes before we had to leave. I didn't even have time to dry my hair. I would surely make a great impression on all my new schoolmates looking like a wet dog.

When it was time to go, we rushed out of the house, piling into the car, including Anna. Once we were all buckled up, Mom popped in her favorite, and our least favorite, Al Jarreau cassette. We complained instantly. Sam started in first. "Ah, come on! Not Al Jarreau!"

Mom's response was to sing along loudly and then say, "C'mon guys, sing along. You know you want to!"

We declined, although we probably knew all the words.

First we dropped off Kelly at her new high school; it was an impressive two-story building with a brick facade. After dropping off Kelly, we drove an additional twenty minutes to my new school. I hadn't seen it since the day we went to register. It looked the same but now with hundreds of students all over the blacktop and in the halls. I waved good-bye to Mom, Sam and Anna, closed the door and headed to my first day of junior high.

With my printed schedule in hand, I set out to find my homeroom. I found it pretty quickly, as it was down the first hallway I walked down. I entered the room, which had about thirty other kids in it, and took a seat next to a girl with long brown hair, an oval face and blue eyes. Her eyes lit up as she extended her hand. "Hi, my name is Patty Garner. What elementary school did you go to? I went to Briarwood."

"My name is Casey Galvin. I went to school in Clayton, so you probably haven't heard of it."

"That's cool. Did your family move here?"

"No. It was just easier for my mom, since my brother goes to St. Ann's."

"Oh."

Just then our homeroom teacher told us class had started and that we had to pay attention.

Forty minutes later the teacher dismissed the class and Patty asked what class I had next. I glanced down at my schedule. "US History."

Patty grinned. "Me too! Wanna walk together?"

"Sure."

She asked me, "So what kind of music are you into?"

"I like mostly Tiffany, Debbie Gibson, Belinda Carlisle and some hip-hop."

"Me too! Have you heard that new song "Please Don't Go Girl" by New Kids on the Block? It is my current fave. I love it!"

I got excited. "Oh. My. Gosh. I love it too! I have the single and play it over and over! My sister gets so annoyed. She's always like, can you play something else? Anything else?"

Patty laughed. "That's awesome. I heard the whole album is coming out in a few weeks. I saved up and am going to the mall to get it!"

"So cool!"

Suddenly Patty got serious. "Okay. Hold on. I've got to ask. Haim or Feldman?"

I chuckled. "Totally Haim!"

"Me too! Cool."

We walked into our history class together, chatting and giggling until the teacher told us class was starting. I thought to myself maybe this new school wasn't going to be so bad after all. Before heading our separate ways to the next class, Patty stopped me. "Hey do you want to have lunch together?"

"Yeah, sure."

"Okay, meet me on the wall next to the office, okay?"

"Okay."

We said our good-byes, and then later that day, Patty and I had lunch together. During lunch time we walked around the halls, the basketball courts and the soccer field. She introduced me to practically everyone she knew. We didn't have any more classes together for the rest of the day but did exchange home phone numbers so we could talk on the phone.

By the time Anna had been cleared for her next round of chemo, a few weeks later, Patty and I were best friends. We shared a love of music and teen magazines as well as gossiped about the boys in school. We'd have lunch together and hang out by the Carter Middle School sign after school. Mom was often late, so we had a good fifteen to twenty minutes to hang out. Patty lived near the school and walked home, so it worked out well. Despite spending lunchtime and after school together, we also talked on the phone almost every day.

One day after school, Patty glanced down at her watch and said she had to get home. I told her not to worry; Mom would be there any minute to pick me up. I didn't realize the minutes would turn into hours. I sat on the ledge of the sign and read the book required for my English class while fending off teachers who kept asking if I had a ride. I told them not to worry and that my mom would be there soon. She finally picked me up around 6 p.m. When she got there, she apologized and explained that she had been at the hospital with Anna. From school we went straight back to the hospital, had dinner in the cafeteria and waited for Dad to come by and drive us home.

Little did I know that the late pickups would become another new normal. Since it was so difficult to pick up Sam and me, Mom and Dad decided to let Kelly start taking the bus to and from school. She was ecstatic. Sam's school and mine were so far away from home, we would have had to take a bus to BART and then another bus to get home. Mom and Dad thought it wasn't safe, not to mention it would have taken an hour and a half. Sam and I tried to convince them it would be okay just for when Anna was in the hospital so we wouldn't have to be left alone at school, but they refused. It's not that I would have minded hanging out or even waiting, if it wasn't so embarrassing. I constantly had to assure other kids, teachers and parents that I hadn't been abandoned.

One day I decided that I would walk over to St. Ann's and meet up with Sam. That way I wouldn't have to deal with questions from people, and I could find out if Sam had gotten any news of when we'd be picked up. I walked up the winding hills through the suburban neighborhood for about a mile before I got to St. Ann's. When I walked up, I saw Sam in his blue pants and white polo sitting by himself on a bench in front of the school. He seemed surprised to see me. "Hey. They forgot you too?"

"Yep. Again."

"Did they forget you and Kelly last year too?"

"No, but Dad used to pick us up sometimes. Now it's only Mom."

"Oh. I guess that makes sense."

"Do you want to walk back down to Carter with me? Mom usually picks me up first, so we'd have to wait less."

"Okay." He packed up his binder and book into his backpack. On the walk back to Carter, we commiserated over how we were always picked up late. Sam noted that nobody at St. Ann's was picked up more than ten minutes late. I told him at Carter it was about the same except that there was a second wave of pickups around 5 p.m. for the kids who did after-school sports, so I got two groups questioning if I was going to be picked up. We both agreed it was humiliating.

ANNA FINISHED the latest round of chemo on a Thursday, in early October. She had been discharged before the end of the school day, so Mom was at Carter already waiting for me when I got out of class. I was surprised not only because I saw her car at the front of the pickup line, for the first time ever, but also because Anna was with her.

I ran up to the car. "Hi, Anna! You're out!"

Anna waved. "Hi, Cay-hee!"

"Did she get out early? I thought she was getting out tomorrow?"

"Dr. Baker let her out a day early because she was doing so well."

"That's so cool! Is she done with chemo? Finally?"

"No, but Dr. Baker said that if all the testing comes back positive, she'll only have one round left."

I beamed at Anna in her car seat. "That's some good news, Anna Banana!"

She kicked her legs up and put her arms over her head. "Good news for Anna!"

I gave her a hug and kiss on the cheek.

From there we went to go pick up Sam at St. Ann's. He was just as surprised as I had been. I told him what Mom had said about the chemo. We both agreed it wasn't good news, it was great news.

CHAPTER 23

To celebrate Anna's homecoming, we went to dinner at our favorite Chinese restaurant. The restaurant was in the same shopping center as Dad's jewelry store, and we knew the owners personally. Whenever we'd walk in, especially with Anna, they'd practically roll out the red carpet. This time was no exception. The owners, Gary and Tina, a happy middle-aged Chinese couple with matching round faces, asked how Anna was doing within the first minute of our arrival. Mom told them that she had just gotten out of the hospital that day and that, fingers crossed, we only had one more round of chemo. Gary and Tina insisted that our dinner was a celebration. We didn't argue. Kelly, Sam and I got our usual Shirley Temples and Mom ordered a hot tea. Dad joined us a little bit later after he closed up the shop. Gary and Tina insisted we didn't need menus because they were going to make us something special.

Over dinner we discussed the possibility of Anna having just one more round of chemo. Kelly asked, "So if she only has one more round, she could be done this year?"

"That's right. Knock on wood."

Mom knocked on the table, and then in unison, Kelly, Sam

and I knocked on the table and then fell into a fit of laughter when Anna joined in too. We ate our dinner and went home.

Over the next few weeks everyone seemed to be in a better mood. I was adjusting to school and making more new friends. Once the New Kids on the Block (NKOTB) album came out, Patty and I went to the mall to buy it. When we got back to Patty's house, we listened to it over and over.

Patty and I soon found other girls, Sarah and Jasmine, at school who were equally enamored by the new album and singing group. Sarah was bookish with long straight brown hair, freckles and big glasses, and Jasmine was short and stocky with a bunch of dark curly hair and big brown eyes. Being the minority, with respect to being NKOTB fans, the four of us became known as the school NKOTB fans. We'd walk down the halls, and boys would sing to us. "Please don't go, girl . . . no, really, hey girl, don't go, please don't go . . ." They thought they were hilarious as they crooned. We just laughed at them. The four of us became best friends.

Kelly seemed to love high school. She had her old friends from St. Ann's and another group of new friends as well. However, the fights at home quickly returned due to some unfortunate fashion decisions. I soon learned that certain groups at Cornerwood would roll up the top of their plaid skirts to make them shorter, with the purpose of getting the attention of the boys in the brother school across the street. Kelly of course decided to roll hers up after being dropped off at school. Apparently, the shortening of skirts was an issue, due to violation of school policy, and the school sent a note home. The note was followed by a huge fight between Mom, Dad and Kelly.

Unfortunately, I was around for the fight. Dad seemed to think that trying to get attention from the boys meant she was a slut and told her so. At one point in the fight he grimaced at me. "Girls like your sister are sluts. Give it time: she'll be pregnant by the time she's sixteen, and nobody will want her. Don't be like your sister." Mom pursed her lips while she bobbed her head up and down in agreement with Dad.

I wasn't sure how or if I should respond. I didn't think Kelly was a slut, and I didn't think she'd get pregnant. I knew she was a little wild and broke the rules a lot more than I did, but I didn't think one thing meant the other. I couldn't look at Kelly as Mom and Dad said such horrible things. I told them I had homework and went to my room. After the yelling stopped, Kelly came into our room in tears. I glanced up from my homework and told her, "They're so wrong. They just don't get what it's like nowadays."

"I know. I hate them. I'm going to call Dad-Pete tomorrow and ask to live with him."

"Seriously? Last time you said it wouldn't work out and that you wouldn't have a bed or bedroom, for that matter."

"When I talked to him last month, after the cruise from hell, he said he was getting a two-bedroom."

"But what about school? Dad-Pete's so far away, it would take forever to get to and from school. Not to mention, he said he couldn't pay for it."

"I don't know. I just don't know how long I can stand living with them. Actually. I'm going to be sixteen in July. I'd only have to bus and BART until I get my license and a car. And I think there's tuition assistance at the school, so maybe I can get a scholarship."

"How are you going to get a car?"

"I'm sure Dad-Pete would buy me one. With all the money I'll be saving him on child support, I'm sure it won't even be a big deal."

"Oh."

It appeared to calm her down to have a plan. She started writing in her notebook, and I went back to doing my homework.

In contrast, Sam seemed to be doing okay. He kept to himself most of the time, playing video games in his room, did well in school and stayed out of trouble for the most part. There was the occasional talking back to Mom or Dad followed by being grounded, but he didn't seem to care when he got in trouble.

A few weeks later, at the beginning of November, it shouldn't have been such a shock that Anna got a fever and had to go back to the hospital. However, Mom seemed devastated and I didn't understand why. It happened so frequently, these unplanned trips to the hospital, that I thought she'd get used to it at some point. It wasn't until one day after school that I finally under-stood why it had bothered her so much. After we picked up Sam and were on the way to the hospital, I asked her, "Is Anna okay?"

"The doctors are optimistic."

"She's not in isolation, right?"

"No, she's not, but they want to keep her under observation for a while."

"Why?"

"They said sometimes when it appears that the cancer is gone, it can come back full force."

"Do they think it's back?"

"No, not yet." Mom began to tear up.

"Well, when can she come home? Is the fever gone?"

"The fever is down, and she is on antibiotics and some more meds. They want to keep her until the fever is gone, redo some testing and then decide it's safe for her to go home."

"Is that why you were so upset this time? You thought the cancer might be back?"

"That's part of it. I think what really got me was that I thought by Christmas we'd be done with all of this. Now there is no way that is going to happen. It looks like it will be another hospital Thanksgiving too."

Sam sat silently in the backseat staring out the window. When we got to the hospital, Anna was sitting in the chair next to the crib, "reading" to Grandma Jess. She climbed out of the chair when she saw us. She greeted us with a "Hi! Hi! Hi!" and stormed over to Sam and me for hugs, nearly knocking over the IV pole onto Mom. Luckily, Grandma Jess caught it just in time. Anna certainly was a force. We had gotten to the hospital early enough to go to the playroom and then have dinner in the cafeteria. Anna led us around the hospital, as if she owned the place.

As predicted, we spent another Thanksgiving in the hospital, since Anna was still under observation, with store-bought sides and precooked turkey. Grandma Jess and Aunt Ella joined us and brought yummy cookies and pie that made up for the sad dinner. Mom made us say what we were thankful for, before we could eat. Mom began. "I'm thankful for Anna, my children, my family and for getting the chance to know Tony, even if for just a little bit." The rest of us echoed Mom's sentiment in our speeches. However, I also added, "In addition to being thankful for all of the things mentioned, I am also thankful for my new friends." Mom curved her mouth upward as she patted my back. As we ate dinner, we chatted about school, chemo and when Anna would get out of the hospital. Thankfully, Anna was discharged the next week.

With Anna home and Christmas only a few weeks away, Mom got the idea to decorate the house to the max. We had a tree in the living room, a tree in the kitchen and a little tree under the stairs by all of Anna's toys. Each tree was decorated and lit up. We had lights on the fireplace mantel, on the fence outside and around the windows in the kitchen. The house was bright and cheerful.

After the last tree was decorated, Kelly and I went back into our room. I asked her, "Did you talk to Dad-Pete about moving in with him?"

"Yeah. I talked to him. He thought it wasn't the right time. He said it would be better if we waited until after the holidays."

"That sucks."

"Yep."

Based on her tone, I could tell Kelly wasn't happy about how the conversation had gone. I didn't know what else to say, so I didn't say anything.

Us kids couldn't wait for Christmas vacation to start. When it finally arrived, I asked Mom if Patty could come over and hang out. She agreed, but it wasn't an easy sell. Patty's Mom had agreed to drive one way but not both. I needed Mom to pick up Patty in Lafayette and do the forty-five-minute drive to our house. I attempted to guilt her. "You decided to move me to a school far away. Obviously all of my friends would live far away from us too. So if you never help with the drive, I'll never get to see any of my friends outside of school!"

I don't know if she felt guilty or just generous, but she finally agreed with a less-than-enthusiastic response. "Fine, Casey. I'll pick her up."

I didn't care why she had agreed. I was just excited to have a friend over.

When Patty came over, we decided to go on a bike ride to the athletic club my parents were members of, in the next town over. We had concocted a plan to tell the desk clerk her name was Sam so she could get in. We were surprised when it worked. We hid our laughter as we went back to the locker room. We played racquet ball and basketball and then biked home. The bike home felt much longer than the bike out. When we got back to the house, we laughed at how dumb it was for us to bike so far away to "get exercise" at the club. After dinner, Patty's mom came to pick her up. We talked on the phone almost every day over Christmas vacation.

Christmas was the same hectic routine as every year. Dad-Pete picked up Kelly, Sam and me on Christmas Eve. We enjoyed our crab cioppino, catching up with our cousins and playing with our eldest cousin's baby. It was a nice feeling that some things hadn't changed. Christmas Eve dinner at Grannie and Grandpop's was the one thing Kelly, Sam and I had in our lives that was constant.

When we got home Mom, Dad, and Anna were waiting by the tree in our living room for our Christmas Eve present. We opened our present, ate cookies and then went to bed. Christmas morning there were lots of presents and pancakes before heading out to the next celebration at Aunt Marney's. From Aunt Marney's we went to Grandma Jess's.

For New Year's Eve, Kelly went out with her friends after successfully arguing that she was almost sixteen and that everyone else got to go to the party. Dad went to bed early, but Mom, Sam, Anna and I watched TV and drank sparkling apple cider until the ball dropped in Times Square. We decided against any pacts, since last year's didn't come true and we didn't want to jinx it. When the ball dropped, Anna was asleep, and Mom and Sam were cheering in a hushed tone. It was 1989.

CHAPTER 24

NEW YEAR'S EVE was off the hook. I can't believe Mom let me go to the party. We stayed up all night. I was so buzzed, and Jamal was lookin' so fine. We totally hooked up, for like an hour. In the morning I thanked Sasha for another great party and gave her a hug before leaving. I walked back to our house feeling on top of the world. Except that I wasn't because I still lived in that house with those people.

When I got home, I put my stuff in my room and fell down on the bed, exhausted. A few minutes later Mom walked in and asked how the party was. It was like her goal in life was to pester me. I told her it was fine, but she kept pressing for details. I told her we basically sat around watching TV and did a countdown as a group and then fell asleep. She seemed to buy it and walked out of our room. After she left, I went back to sleep and didn't get up until noon.

After my nap, I went into Sam's room and told him I was going to move in with Dad-Pete. I explained to Sam that Dad-Pete had told me we could talk about it when the holidays were over. Sam got excited. "Do you think I could move in with him too?"

"You'd have to ask him. I plan to call him, like, tomorrow if you want to talk to him too."

"Yeah. I can't fucking stand it here."

"No kidding." I chuckled.

"Jasper's such an asshole. He thinks he owns all of us. He doesn't. He's not even our dad. And Mother? She just let's him get away with everything. I want out of here so bad. And that fucking preppy school she has me at? Jeezus."

"I thought you were okay at school?"

"I do what I have to, to not get in trouble, most of the time."

"Yeah, just keep your head down until we can get out of here."

Sam smirked. "No shit."

Dad-Pete was going to be so happy to not have to pay child support for two of us and of course to have us with him. I bet he would buy a house and then we could each have our own room. It was all going to be good, and we were finally going to get out of this hellhole.

The next day when Mom was out with Anna, I called Dad-Pete. Sam was with me so he could ask him to move in with him too. Dad-Pete acted surprised by the request. Both Sam and I explained the situation going on at the house. Dad-Pete told us maybe we should wait until Anna was done with chemo before we made any decisions. I didn't understand why that mattered. Sam and I were disappointed but agreed to wait. Deflated, Sam went back into his room to play video games, and I called Sasha to see if there were any more parties going on over break.

Right after I got off the phone with Sasha, Mom and Anna walked in the front door. I said hi to Anna and gave her a hug as she ran up to me. I asked how Anna's appointment went. "Good. Dr. Baker still thinks just one more round is all she needs. They actually want to start her last round of chemo next week."

"But it's Anna's birthday next week!"

"I know, that's what I told them. We have the big party at Tilden Park planned. Anna would be so disappointed."

"What did Dr. Baker say?"

"She said it was probably okay to delay the chemo a week. So the party's on!" Mom cheered.

"Oh, thank goodness. Anna loves going to see her pony at the park!"

"Yes, she does!"

Anna chimed in. "We get to ride pony? See pony?"

"Not today, Anna. For your birthday next week. How many are you going to be?" Anna held up three little fingers.

"That's right, Anna! You're so smart! You're going to be three!" Mom beamed.

Anna loved her pony at Tilden. Ever since the Make-A-Wish foundation got her access to a pony with riding lessons, she'd been obsessed. She never went anywhere without a My Little Pony in hand. She was totally adorable in her khaki riding pants, black boots, white shirt and black helmet. If you saw her, you'd have thought she was a professional rider, if they had three-year-old professional riders.

On the way to Tilden Park for Anna's birthday party, I gazed out the window at the hills and trees as we drove up the winding road to our picnic spot. All of us helped set up the plates, napkins, table cloths and food. Sam and I stuffed and hung up the colorful star piñata. Casey wanted to help, but she was too short to be of any real help. I finally told her she could help by telling us if the piñata was centered or not.

Guests started to arrive as we were finalizing the placement of the piñata. Grandma Jess and Dad's family were the first, followed by Grandma Mary and the rest of Mom's family. Grandma Mary, a slightly plump woman with short brown curly hair and blue eyes, was the first to comment on the fact that we were having a party at a park in the middle of January. Grandma Mary always seemed to be complaining about something. I was surprised she had even shown up since she'd hardly ever gone to the hospital to visit Anna. I told her and everyone else who asked that Anna had a pony at the park and that she had insisted on seeing her pony for her birthday. Most people appeared to understand. It was a little cold out, but with a jacket it wasn't too bad. People seemed to deal with it.

After food, cake and the piñata, most of the group went down to see Anna ride her pony. The ponies were set up on a circular track, attached like spokes on a wheel. Next to the ponies, bigger kids or adults could ride full-size horses that walked around a track. Sam went off and rode the big horses, as did some of our cousins. I stayed and watched Anna ride. She waved at her crowd of admirers each time she went around.

THE NEXT WEEK, Mom and Anna packed up to go in for Anna's last round of chemo. I'm not sure I believed it was going to be her last round. It had been almost two years since her diagnosis, and every time we thought she'd be okay something devastating would happen. Fevers. Infections. New Broviacs. Surgery. Tests. Chicken pox. Chicken pox again. It seemed endless. I had a hard time believing this was truly the end. As Mom was packing up I asked her, "So when will we know if she's cured and done with chemo?"

"After this round, they'll wait a little while and then do a full battery of tests to see if there are any traces of cancer left. If there are no traces of cancer, she will be considered to be in initial remission."

"Does remission mean cured?"

"No. It just means it's gone for now."

"For now?" I became quite concerned.

"She won't be considered to be in 'full remission' until after five years of being cancer-free. That is when we'll celebrate like it's 1999!" Mom laughed.

"Do they think it will come back?"

"They don't know. It's possible. Once she goes into 'initial remission,' she'll be tested every six months until the five-year mark. If they told us she was in 'initial' remission, it would be wonderful news."

I'm not sure I was as optimistic as Mom. It sounded like we could be optimistic in five years from now. Five more years of agonizing over whether or not Anna would make it. It was torture.

Mom finished packing, and we all said good-bye to her and Anna as they walked out the front door. It was difficult to imagine this would be the last time they would pack up and leave for the hospital. I wondered if I should start visiting more. Sam and Casey went all the time, not necessarily by choice, but more because Mom had to pick them up at school, so she'd leave the hospital to pick them up and head straight back. They were at the hospital almost every day that Anna was. If this was truly the end, they'd get their lives back. We'd all get our lives back. No more sad birthdays or holidays spent huddled around a small table in Anna's hospital room. No more being surrounded by sickness and death.

That next weekend Sam, Casey and I went to Dad-Pete's. On the way to his new apartment, Sam and I asked about us moving in again. "Sorry, guys, but I think we need to wait until your sister is cleared of cancer."

Sam's face twisted. "I still don't understand why that matters."

"Because I'm going to have to take your mom to court to stop child support and get custody. It would look bad if I was fighting her when she has a kid on chemo."

Sam glanced down. "Oh."

"How about you, Casey, do you want to live with me too?"

Casey stared out the window and spoke softly. "No, I just started making new friends and don't want to have to change schools again."

Dad-Pete didn't press the issue.

Later I explained to him that Casey and her friends were obsessed with the music group NKOTB, and that the group and her new friends were basically her whole life. I didn't think she'd ever give it up. He said it seemed strange. I told him it was strange. I swear Casey lived in her own fantasy world.

ANNA CAME home from her last round of chemo on a Saturday in March. She ran into the house with her arms in the air, shouting, "No more chemo! No more chemo!" All of us cheered. She kept repeating it until everyone got a hug and kiss. Casey grinned at Mom. "That's so funny that she would run in here and say that!"

Mom confessed with an impish grin, "Well, actually, I told her to say it, but isn't it adorable?"

It didn't matter that Mom had told her to say it, it was perfect. It was weird to think that now that she was finally going to be home, we wouldn't be living together anymore. I'd still visit of course. Breaking my thoughts, Casey jumped in with her usual round of twenty questions. "So when will she get tested for remission?"

"Next month we go in for CT scans, blood work and appointments with Dr. Trekker and Dr. Baker."

"Will they take out her Broviac?"

"Not until they are sure she doesn't need it anymore."

"When will that be?"

"Hopefully soon after all her tests come back and show the cancer is gone."

"So she'll have to have surgery again?"

"Yes, but it will be a simple surgery, but like any surgery there are still risks. However, if there is no more cancer, that is a wonderful thing! And at this point, taking out her Broviac is easy peasy."

"Oh. Cool. Anna Banana, we need to dance to celebrate! I've got just the thing!"

Anna giggled. "'Shake Your Love'! Dance!"

Casey went and got Anna's favorite cassette with "Shake Your Love" on it. She put the cassette in Anna's player, had Anna push the button and sang as they danced. Sam and Mom joined in, so I did too. They rewound and replayed the song so many times, I couldn't keep count.

After that Mom went on a church kick, insisting on going to church at least twice a week to pray for Anna's remission. She tried to make Sam, Casey and I go with her, but we usually refused. I said to her, "Is it not enough to go to Catholic school but to have to go to church twice a week too?" Casey gave the excuse that you didn't have to go to church to pray and that God was everywhere. She was always coming up with these crazy excuses. I swear she'd grow up to be a lawyer. The only day we were forced to go was Sunday. At least we got to sit in the child's room and play with Anna instead of paying attention to the sermon. Except for one week when Mom had gotten the priest to talk about Anna and ask that all the parishioners pray for her. It was so embarrassing.

It seemed to take forever for Anna's tests to be completed and for the results to be in. When Mom and Anna got ready to leave for the hospital that afternoon, to talk to Anna's doctors, Mom stared back at us. "Please pray they have good news." We agreed to as they walked out the front door.

CHAPTER 25

ON THE EVENING of April 6, 1989, Mom and Dad walked through the front door of the house, each holding one of Anna's little hands. Mom was shaking and had tears in her eyes. "She's clear. The cancer is gone! God has answered our prayers!"

Anna cheered. "No more chemo! No cancer!"

We laughed as Kelly, Sam and I each gave Anna a hug and kiss. Sam suggested we go out to dinner to celebrate the good news, but we quickly found out they had already gone out to eat because Anna was hungry. Dad said we could order pizza.

We gathered in the living room and sat on the couch while we waited for the pizza to arrive. Anna walked over to her toys and pulled out three ponies and then brought them over to Sam, Kelly and me. We each asked her how she felt to be cancer-free and didn't have to stay in the hospital anymore. I'm not sure she fully understood being cancer-free, but she definitely understood that she didn't have to go to the hospital anymore. She glanced at Mom. "No more hopp-ital!"

"Well, no more overnights in the hospital. We still will go for visits to the doctor and to get your Broviac out."

Anna answered sternly, "No more hopp-ital! No pokies!"

Mom tried to calm her down. "It will be like today. We just go and talk to the doctor. We won't sleep in the hospital anymore. Just visit."

Anna pointed at Mom. "Just talk. No pokies!"

Mom hesitated, knowing she couldn't promise her no more "pokies," Anna's word for injections, blood draws and anything that caused discomfort. Anna continued playing ponies with Kelly and Sam. I then asked, "When will she get her Broviac out?

"We scheduled an appointment for next week. So we have one more week of flushes and dressing changes, and then good-bye Broviac! I can't wait."

"Cool."

I went back to playing with Anna, Kelly, Sam and her colorful ponies. When the pizza arrived Kelly, Sam and I got up from the couch to go into the kitchen. Anna's eyes lit up. "Pizza? I want some!"

Kelly waved her over. "Come on then, let's get some pizza!" Anna ran into the kitchen after Kelly. Mom told me she would be surprised if she ate any and that it was likely she just wanted to be with the big kids. Anna ate only a few bites of pizza but stayed at the table with us until we finished our dinner.

THE NEXT WEEK, Mom and Anna went to the hospital to have Anna's Broviac removed. That morning, on the drive to school, Mom explained that it was a simple outpatient procedure but it still required Anna to go under general anesthesia. She said that they would be at the hospital most of the day and may be a little late picking us up from school. Sam and I said it was fine and that we were used to it by now. This seemed to annoy Mom, but it was the truth, so I ignored her attitude.

When I got to school, I ran into Patty, Sarah and Jasmine before class started. They were huddled in the hall staring at a magazine. Sarah glanced up at me from behind her big glasses. "Casey! New Kids are on the cover of BOP!"

"No way! Oh my gosh!" I forced my way into the huddle to see the pictures.

While we stood in the huddle, mesmerized by their awesomeness, Sarah continued to tell us that the article said they were touring that summer with Tiffany.

"Do they list the cities?"

"No, we'd have to go to the record store to ask when they'll be in the Bay Area."

Jasmine formed a half grin. "Actually, I have a friend whose dad's in the biz. I could ask to see if he knows anything!"

We caught the attention of surrounding students as we screeched with excitement. We were giddy the rest of the day with thoughts of Danny, Donnie, Joe, Jon and Jordan.

After school, as I stood by the Carter Middle School sign, my mind raced with thoughts of the NKOTB. Until now the only photos we had were from the album cover. It had to be one of the most exciting days I've had in a long time. I couldn't wait to hear from Jasmine on whether or not they would be coming to the Bay Area. While deep in thought about which one of the NKOTB was my favorite, Mom's car pulled up.

When I got in the car, I told Mom about the magazine and how maybe the NKOTB would be coming to the Bay Area and asked if we could go to the store and get a copy of BOP. Mom seemed annoyed. "No, we can't go to the store to buy some magazine. Anna needs to rest—she just had her Broviac removed!"

I glanced at Anna sleeping in her car seat. I felt sick to my stomach. "Right. I forgot. Sorry."

Mom continued to lecture that Anna's health was a lot more important than some silly magazine with pictures of a musical act all the way to Sam's school. As if I didn't know that? I was glad when Sam got in the car, knowing she'd have to stop lecturing to say hi and ask how school was. I quietly asked Sam to ask Mom how Anna's procedure went. He agreed. Mom explained the procedure had went well and that in ten days all of the bandages should be gone and Anna could start living a normal life, as could we.

THE NEXT DAY Anna was running around the house pretending to be a pony. She would go up to each of us, bumping her nose on our leg as if asking to be petted. Us kids thought it was hilarious, but Mom thought she was going to exhaust herself. Mom kept trying to get her to sit still and read books or watch a movie, but Anna had other ideas. She continued to pretend to be a pony and refused to eat anything but apples or carrots.

While Anna was a pony, the rest of us got to help Mom box up the medical supplies and do the rest of the household chores. Although it was Saturday, Mom told us it would be a good idea for all of us to go to church that night. Kelly objected. "Why? It's Saturday."

"Because we have to continue to pray for Anna. We don't want her cancer to come back!"

Sam shook his head. "Why can't we just go tomorrow?"

"It's not enough!" Mom was crazed.

Kelly raised her eyebrows. Sam shook his head. We went to church that night and the next morning.

I had often wondered what life would be like when Anna was off chemo. It was what we had always wanted; it was supposed to make everyone's life better. However, when the day arrived, it didn't exactly go as expected. When Anna was diagnosed and started chemo, we had to adjust to a new normal. A normal that included numerous hours spent in the hospital, including both birthdays and holidays, a sterile house, barely any supervision and taking care of ourselves. We had gotten used to that life. With Anna off chemo, we were redefining what our normal was again. Since Kelly, Sam and I had gotten used to our independence, we had a difficult time adjusting to being told what to do and constantly being questioned on what we were up to. There was a lot of bickering with Mom. By the end of the week, all three of us were grounded for talking back.

It was soon apparent that Kelly was not coming straight home from school like she had said and fought with Mom constantly. Whenever Dad was around, he'd join in on the fight and say his hurtful words. This just made her more angry and unhappy living at home with us. She had begun sneaking out at night again, even during school nights.

Sam started getting in trouble again too. He started fights at school and with Mom and Dad. It got so bad that they grounded him on his birthday and made him cancel plans to go to the movies with his friends. He was so mad, he punched a hole in his bedroom wall.

I quickly learned to keep to myself, spending most of the time in my room listening to music and talking to my friends on the phone. My only escape was at school, where I got to hang out with Patty, Sarah, and Jasmine.

We had all waited for the day Anna would be cancer-free, yet within one month it pushed us farther apart instead of pulling us together. I hoped it was temporary, but I knew that Kelly and Sam were secretly planning to move in with Dad-Pete. Although, according to Kelly, Dad-Pete had put her and Sam off again. He claimed it was better if they waited until the school year was over, which was still two months away. This just seemed to make things worse. Our house was always tense, and now Kelly and Sam were even more upset, since they had to wait until the summer to move out.

CHAPTER 26

A FEW WEEKS LATER, I was talking on the phone with Sarah, and I told her what was going on with Kelly and Sam. Sarah was always fascinated by my stories about Kelly and Sam, because she only had a little brother and didn't know what it was like to have older siblings. That day I told Sarah, "I found Kelly's notebook. I peeked to see what she writes about."

Sarah asked, "What does she write about?"

"Mostly boys, school and going out . . . But I found something kind of weird."

"Like what?"

"Well, she had a whole page written about different baby names. Why would she do that?"

"Wow! What if she is pregnant?! Or one of her friends is pregnant! Oh my God!" Sarah squealed.

"Oh. My. God. I hadn't even thought about that!"

"Are you going to ask her about it?"

"I don't know, should I? She'll know I went through her stuff and get totally mad. I guess I'll think about it."

The conversation soon changed back to NKOTB. Sarah

started going on about how if she married Joe, they would have two kids. She had already picked out the kids' names, and then she told me she was going to put an album together. It was going to be an album dedicated to the life of Sarah and Joe McIntyre and of course their two lovely children. We laughed and planned out what our life would be like if we were married to Joe.

After I got off the phone, I thought about what Sarah had said. Could Kelly be pregnant? It was possible that I had misinterpreted what was written. Before asking Kelly about it, I decided to go back into her notebook and read it again. When I did, it wasn't there anymore. There were just small shreds of paper on the spiral indicating she had torn it out. It didn't appear to have any other pages ripped out. I thought that was weird and wondered if she had realized I had gone through her stuff and wanted to hide any evidence that she might be pregnant? I decided not to say anything to Kelly or anyone else.

AT SCHOOL THE NEXT DAY, Sarah, Jasmine and Patty ran up to me, practically bouncing. Sarah tried to contain herself enough to speak. "Oh my God! They're going to be here June twenty-fourth! June twenty-fourth!"

"What? Here! Where at?"

"Great America Theme Park in Santa Clara. I already talked to my mom, and she's agreed to stand in line with us for tickets this weekend!"

"I'd have to ask my mom if I could go. Ahh! This is so exciting! New Kids here in the Bay Area!"

This was the best news possible. When I asked Mom about standing in line for tickets, she said she couldn't drive me but Sarah's mom agreed to buy my ticket and Mom would reimburse her (it would be an early birthday present). I was excited beyond comparison to anything up until that point in my life. I couldn't wait for school to be out and for June 24 to arrive.

Other than my exciting news about the upcoming concert, things weren't getting much better around the house. Kelly and Mom continued to fight all the time. Because they were always fighting, Kelly was usually sulking in our room over her latest grounding. I remembered when Mom was pregnant with Anna and she would have wild mood swings. I wondered if Kelly was having mood swings and that is why she couldn't get along at home.

At least Sam was lying low. He went back to spending most of the time in his room playing video games and stopped picking fights with teachers and kids at school.

Anna was a happy little girl at home. When the three of us would come home from school, she'd always run up to us and say, "Play ponies?" There was no way we could resist. When she'd tire of ponies, we'd listen to music or read books. When it was time for me to finish my homework, she would insist on helping. She'd sit at the dining table next to me, ready for her assignment. I would give her a piece of paper and a pencil so she could write for me. She'd always respond, "I help." She'd grin as she scribbled on the paper. Once she would finish a full page of scribbling, she'd hand me the paper and say, "All done." I continued to give her paper to scribble on until she tired of doing homework with me and went back to ponies. It was nice to have her home.

A FEW WEEKS LATER, right before school was out, Mom walked into my and Kelly's bedroom. I was about to fall asleep when I heard her sit on Kelly's bed and saw her tap Kelly on the shoulder to wake her up. "Kelly, I need to talk to you. I found this in the garbage." I had a feeling I knew what she wanted to talk about, so

I decided to pretend to be asleep. I did not want to get involved in that conversation. Kelly mumbled, "I'm sleeping. Can't we talk tomorrow?"

"No. We need to talk now."

"Fine."

"I found this in the garbage."

"You went through the garbage? And taped my letter back together?"

"Is it true?"

"Is what true?"

"Are you pregnant?"

Kelly started to cry. Between sobs, she said, "Yes." Kelly and Mom sat there crying for a few minutes before Mom went into about twenty questions: "Who is the father? When did this happen? What are you going to do?" It was difficult to hear over both of their crying.

What I picked up was that the father was some guy she met when visiting Dad-Pete and that they weren't in a relationship. Mom was pretty ticked off that it happened over at Dad-Pete's. Mom continued to tell Kelly that she loved her and would support whatever decision she made but to remember it is a child, more specifically her grandchild, and that she hoped she was going to take responsibility and keep the baby. This just made Kelly cry more. Finally, Kelly got Mom to leave by telling her she was exhausted and promised to talk more about it the next day.

The next morning Kelly didn't say anything on the ride to school, and Mom didn't bring up the baby. The whole car was quiet as we tried to block out the Sade songs coming out of the speakers. I decided not to tell anyone at school about the baby, especially since Kelly hadn't said she was going to keep it. Luckily, my friends were too preoccupied with the end of school and the upcoming NKOTB concert.

When we got home from school that day, Mom told me she needed to talk to Kelly privately in our room and asked that I keep an eye on Anna out in the living room. A few hours later, Mom came out with pink puffy eyes, which made her blue eyes seem to glow. I went in after Mom rounded the corner to the kitchen to see how Kelly was doing. I opened the door to our room to see Kelly lying down on her bed with her eyes closed. She opened them as I walked in. I said to her, "So. How's it going?"

"Not great. It's nothing. Don't worry about it." She moved onto her side, facing the window.

"I know what you were talking about."

She sat up and raised an eyebrow. "How do you know?"

"I heard last night. I was only pretending to be asleep."

"Oh." She let out a light laugh. "Well played."

"I try. So how are you feeling?"

"Okay. I guess."

"Are you going to keep it?"

"Yes. If I didn't, I think Mom would accuse me of murdering her grandchild."

"Seriously?"

"Yes, but that's not why I'm going to keep it. I'm going to have this baby. I'm going to love it and protect it and put it first above all else. I won't be like some parents I know."

"Do you know when you're due?"

"I think January or February."

"Wow! I'm going to be an aunt!" Kelly's face brightened.

I was happy to hear such a positive attitude about the baby. I didn't know anything about having babies, but it sounded like she had a good plan.

A little while later Mom called out to us that dinner was ready. We all sat around the kitchen table not saying much. Anna must have picked up that Kelly had been sad because before we started eating, she went up to Kelly and gave her a hug. I sat there wondering if Dad knew about Kelly's situation.

After dinner, Anna went into the living room to play with Sam, and I stayed behind to clear the dishes. While I was clearing, Dad said to Mom, "I told you so."

Mom glared at him. "Is that necessary?"

"I told you by the time she was sixteen, she'd be knocked up. Here we are. One month ahead of her sixteenth birthday!"

Mom's face reddened as she clenched her fists. "Jasper, just stop. She's my daughter, and she's carrying my grandchild. Lay off."

Kelly yelled at Dad, "Oh yeah. You're sooo great. You predicted this. Congratulations!" And then stormed back to our room. I quickly followed behind. The conversation didn't end as we left. I could still hear them shouting from our room. Kelly laid on her bed and cried. I sat on my bed, put my headphones on and did my math homework.

Tensions remained high in the house. Even the usual excitement around the last day of school was muted. From what I could tell, Mom and Dad weren't speaking. Kelly just seemed sad, and Sam was clueless. At least Anna was still a happy little girl.

It was weird to think that in a few years Kelly would have her very own toddler. I wondered what it was going to be like around the house with the new baby and Anna. Maybe Anna and the new baby would play together like siblings or become best friends. I thought that would be cool. We'd soon find out that wasn't going to happen.

A few days later, Mom and Kelly announced at dinner that Kelly was moving in with Dad-Pete.

I asked, "But I thought there wasn't room?"

Kelly grinned. "Dad-Pete finally got a two-bedroom apartment. He and his new girlfriend, Theresa, said they would help with the baby so I could still go to school."

I glanced over at Mom. "You're okay with this?"

"I had a long talk with your Dad-Pete, and we both think this is best for Kelly and the baby. This way she'll be able to continue her education."

I sat back in disbelief. "Oh."

After that Mom had to break it to Sam that there wouldn't be room for him at Dad-Pete's now that Kelly was going to have a baby. He didn't take the news well. He mouthed off something about things not being fair and stormed off to play video games. I didn't know what to say or how to react. I just acted like everything was okay. Maybe I thought she'd be back? By the end of the week, Kelly had packed her things and moved in with Dad-Pete. Anna and I stood in the doorway of the house and waved as she drove off with him.

It was weird not having Kelly around anymore. For starters, I finally had my own room for the first time in my life. I listened to music all the time and put NKOTB posters on the walls. As much as I liked having my own room, it was strange without Kelly, and I was getting fed up with all the changes. I think the only thing that kept me sane was knowing that I had the NKOTB concert to look forward to.

When June 24 arrived, Sarah's mom agreed to pick me up and drive me to the concert with her, Sarah, Jasmine and Patty. At the concert, we screamed and cheered until we had no voices left. While we walked through the crowds back to the car, the four of us agreed that it was the best night of our lives.

When Kelly's birthday rolled around, she was still living with Dad-Pete and didn't want to come over to our house to celebrate. Mom, Sam, Anna and I called her and sang to her over the phone. It felt strange that she was no longer with us; we had never spent a birthday apart. At the time I didn't realize it, but I had to start getting used to it.

My thirteenth birthday was a month later, and she didn't come over for my family dinner celebration. I even invited her to my birthday party with my friends, but she said she didn't feel up to it. It was strange that she wasn't around, but at the same time I felt lucky that Mom let me go out for pizza and to a movie with my friends. The last few years nobody had friend birthday parties. Times had changed. Sam was even signed up for football that summer, and I did cheerleading. We were kind of a normal family again, except for the fact that Kelly wasn't there.

THE SUMMER SEEMED to go by too quickly, but at the same time the start of a new school year brought excitement into our house. Sam and I were both happy to be in our last year of middle school. Top dogs at school! Next year we would be in high school, and per our teachers' reminders, we had to get ready for it now. Even at the beginning of the year, there was buzz around who was going to what high school. Typically there were two high schools the kids from Carter would split off to. I had no idea where I would go, since I was out of district. Any speculation we had was just that. Mom told us she wasn't sure yet where we would go and explained that we had plenty of time to figure it out.

A few weeks into the school year, we began to get notifications for the eighth-grade graduation dance, ceremony and impending activities. Despite graduation still eight months away, all anyone could talk about was what they were going to wear. Jasmine said her mom had already set a date for dress shopping, and Sarah's mom was organizing a group event, for which I was invited, to shop at the Jessica McClintock outlet in San Francisco.

When Mom picked us up from school, I told her all about it. She seemed puzzled. "All of this for an eighth-grade graduation?"

"Um yeah. It's a big deal. Can I go?"

"I don't know. Maybe we should wait until it gets closer."

"Why?"

"I don't know. You just never know what the future holds."

I thought that was an odd comment. Not know what the future holds? What did that mean? Did she think graduations and dresses would all of a sudden go away?

When she picked us up at school a few weeks later, it became pretty clear what Mom had meant. When I walked up to the car, I noticed the back of the station wagon was full of suitcases; I got in the car and asked why the back was all packed up. She told me she'd explain after we picked up Sam.

When Sam got in the car, he also noticed the back was full of our belongings. He asked, "What's with all the stuff?"

"I'm divorcing Dad. We have left him. We're going to stay at a hotel for a little while."

My mouth dropped open. "What?! What hotel are we going to? Why can't we stay at the house and he leave?"

Mom told us, "I called to tell him to pack up his things and leave. We need to give him a few days, and then we can go back home."

I glanced at Sam from the front seat. His eyes were wide as he shook his head in disbelief.

Later that night at the hotel, we were surprised at the knock on our door from the police. Somehow Dad had tracked us down and had requested a citizen's arrest of Mom. I didn't understand what a citizen's arrest was or why she was being arrested. All I knew as Sam, Anna and I huddled at the door of the hotel room was that Mom was being cuffed and read her rights. She stood in the parking lot yelling at Dad and the police. Dad yelled back. We couldn't hear from the room what was going on, but eventually the police let Mom go and made Dad leave the hotel parking lot. Mom walked back to us and explained the police had advised us to find a different hotel and to not use a credit card when she checked in. We packed up our stuff, left the hotel and drove off.

AT THE NEW HOTEL, Mom tried to convince us that it could be fun to stay in a hotel, like a vacation. I think she was trying to be positive, but nobody was feeling like we were on vacation. I sat on the edge of the hotel bed and stared at her. "Where's all of this coming from? Why did you leave Dad?"

"It was a long time coming. We've had problems for a long time. I just couldn't do it anymore."

I asked, "What do you mean?"

"Well, there is some adult stuff I don't want to get into but for one, I found out he was using again."

Sam laughed bitterly. "Did he ever stop? C'mon! Think about it: he's never around. Always 'running errands'—did you believe that?"

Mom explained, "He told me he was clean. I believed him. I was so busy with Anna, I didn't have the capacity to realize he was lying to me."

She gave a half grin. "I think we'll be better off. I think this will be good for us. We deserve a good life, a happy life. One without liars, drug addicts and abusers. We will be happy again, okay?"

We acted like it was possible, but I'm not sure either Sam or I believed it. We ate our takeout, did homework and went to sleep early, since it was a school night.

At school, I made the mistake of telling Patty about what had happened at the hotel and with the police. Before I knew it, some stupid boy had overheard and decided to announce it to the class. "Hey, everyone, Casey's mom got arrested!"

I shouted. "She did not! You don't know what you're talking about!"

Patty told me to ignore the jerk and encouraged me to sit down and get ready for class to start. I sat at my desk, humiliated.

After a few days in the hotel Mom told us it was time to go back to the house. She had assured us that Dad had moved out, the locks were changed and that we should be safe. When we got back to the house, it looked the same as it always did. I guessed that Dad just took his clothes and nothing else.

LATER THAT WEEK, Mom took Anna in to get her first six-month testing done at the hospital. She left the house telling me to pray that the cancer had stayed away. I said I would.

Home alone, I heard a knock on the door. I squinted through the peephole and saw Dad on the other side of the door. I was a little surprised and wasn't sure what to do. I opened the door. He grinned. "Hi, Casey."

"Hi."

"I just left a few things. It's okay, you can let me in. I'll just be a few minutes."

I felt uneasy about it but wasn't sure what to do. I wasn't exactly in a position to not let him in. "Umm. Okay."

While he walked up the stairs I wondered if I had made a mistake by letting him in. All of a sudden I heard a creaking noise. At first I wasn't sure what it was. I thought about it for a second. I had heard it a million times. What was it?

Within a few minutes he was walking back down the stairs, without anything in his hands. He said good-bye to me and let himself out. I felt a sick feeling in my stomach. At that moment, I realized what the creaking noise was. It was Mom's jewelry box. I felt so stupid for letting him in. I felt like I had betrayed Mom. I went into my room, laid on my bed and cried until I fell asleep.

I woke to the sound of knocking on my bedroom door. I got up and found that on the other side of the door was Anna. "Hi, Casey! Sleepy?"

"Yes, I was sleeping. How are you? How was the hospital?"

Anna pointed at her arm. "Pokey done. Ponies?"

She continued talking, but I wasn't exactly sure what she had said. I just followed her out into the living room.

When Mom walked up, I told her what had happened. She ran upstairs to check the jewelry box. Sure enough, Dad had taken everything she had, except for her wedding ring, diamond earrings and the necklace she was wearing. I was surprised that Mom wasn't mad at me. She actually assured me that it wasn't my fault and that I had done the right thing.

CHAPTER 27

THE NEXT WEEK we were happy to hear that Anna was six months cancer-free. That was about all the positive news we had. In the same conversation, Mom told us we needed to talk about our expenses and that we needed to cut back. "The only money I have is child support for you and Sam from your Dad and about fifteen thousand dollars cash that I hid in your old hamster cage."

I gasped. "You hid fifteen thousand dollars cash in my dead hamster's cage?"

"Yes. I figured no one would look there."

I laughed. "No, I don't think anyone would look there!"

"Exactly. Also, I'm going to have to apply for welfare, or Aid to Families with Dependent Children. I thought you should know. It's nothing to be ashamed of. It's only temporary until we sell the house and receive a settlement from the divorce."

I was shocked. "We're selling the house?"

Mom explained, "I don't have a choice. We can't afford to keep it."

Sam asked, "Where are we going to live?"

"I don't know yet. It is going to depend on what I can afford."

Stunned, I sat there staring at Mom and then Sam and then Anna. I thought to myself, six months ago we heard the news Anna was cancer-free. It was supposed to mean that everything would be great, better than before. Now Kelly was pregnant and gone. Dad was gone. We were selling our house and going to live somewhere else?

WE GOT EXCITED about the holidays approaching despite our new circumstances. We always had a good time visiting with our cousins and extended family. Unfortunately, Thanksgiving at Aunt Marney's ended up quite disappointing, since most of our family took it as an opportunity to gossip about Mom and Dad's divorce, Kelly's pregnancy and what would happen to all of us. It wasn't fun. However, Sam and I were excited for Christmas Eve. It was our once-a-year constant.

Dad-Pete picked us up as usual. What wasn't usual was that Kelly wasn't with us. Before going over to Grannie and Grandpop's, we stopped by Dad-Pete's apartment to pick up his girlfriend, Theresa, and Kelly. It was the first time we'd seen Kelly, since she moved in with Dad-Pete. She was dressed in a festive red lace dress that fit her now rather large belly. During the drive I asked her about school and how she was feeling. She said going to school was too hard this year and she would start up again after the baby was born. She said she felt good and couldn't wait to meet the baby.

When we got to Grannie and Grandpop's, we said our normal hellos and Merry Christmases. We ate our favorite dinner, crab cioppino, and then sat around chitchatting. This year's gossip was a similar theme to two years ago, when our cousin Kathryn had just had a baby at seventeen, except now the gossip was about Kelly. It was apparently my year to be lectured to. "Don't let that be you!" Grannie said. I quickly tired of all the gossip and put-downs. They never talked about how brave Kathryn or Kelly were to have their babies. I was happy when it was time to go home, back to Mom and Anna.

When we got back home, Mom and Anna were sitting by the tree eating cookies. Both Sam and I walked up to them and gave Anna a hug. We sat down and started eating the Christmas cookies Mom had made. Mom looked apprehensive as she told us, "So you guys know this is a tough year. You each only have one gift. It's up to you if you want to open it tonight or wait for tomorrow."

Sam glanced at the tree. "What's that big pile, then?"

Mom fidgeted. "Those are for Anna. She's too little to understand, but I know you guys do."

Sam and I decided to open our present that night.

I thought to myself, what is it that she thought we understood? That there is no Santa Claus or that there is only enough money to buy Anna presents? I didn't understand what it was that we supposedly understood that Anna didn't. I thought it was the opposite actually. We understood that Anna got the same huge pile of presents while we got hardly anything. Anna was so little, I didn't think she'd even remember not having a bunch of presents and we would.

The next morning, instead of the normal chaos of four kids opening piles of gifts, Sam and I sat and watched Anna open her presents. After breakfast we headed to Aunt Marney's for Christmas. It was similar to Thanksgiving, and we were relieved when it was time to leave. That evening Dad, or Jasper as we were now calling him, came by to pick up Anna to bring her over to Grandma Jess's, or what we were now calling her, Anna's Grandma Jess. Sam and I sat dejected as we waved to Anna as she left. We hadn't understood until that moment that when Mom and Jasper got divorced that Grandma Jess and Aunt Ella wouldn't be our family anymore.

On New Year's Eve, Mom, Anna, Sam and I sat around the TV and watched the ball drop, drinking our sparkling apple cider. We each crossed our fingers and hoped for a better year. I thought to myself, 1990 couldn't possibly be worse than 1989.

ON THE RIDE home from school, shortly after Christmas break had ended, Mom broke the news to us about the house. She lowered the volume on the radio. "I have good news, guys. The house sold! Not only that, I figured out the perfect place for us to move to, out on the delta where I grew up!"

I shook my head. "On Bethel Island? Are you kidding? You know I hate it there! I'm not moving there."

"Well, then you really aren't going to like my next set of news. I already rented us a house, right on the water. We move there next month!"

I began to shake. "This is good news? I have to leave all of my friends and my school, and this is good news?"

"I told you we had to sell the house. We can't afford it! We would stay if I could afford it, but we just can't!"

"We don't have to move over an hour away to some godforsaken place!"

Mom said, "I think it will be good for us."

I yelled, "Maybe for you. Certainly not for us. You're just being selfish!"

I rode the rest of the way home in silence as she lectured us about embracing change and that we needed to stick together as a family. Sam didn't say a word as he sat in the back with his head down. As soon as we got home, I ran to my bedroom and slammed the door. I called Sarah to tell her the bad news. We both cried and promised to write letters and talk on the phone every day.

A FEW WEEKS LATER, while we were packing up the house, we got a phone call from Kelly that she was in labor and was already at the hospital with Dad and Theresa. Mom told her we'd be there right away. Mom told me, "Pack a bag for Anna and you guys. Get snacks, books . . . whatever you think you'll need while waiting for the baby to arrive."

I grinned at Anna. "Okay, c'mon, Anna, let's pick out some books!"

"And ponies!"

I laughed. "Yes, Anna, ponies too."

When we got to the hospital, we were directed to Labor and Delivery. Sam, Anna and I sat in the waiting room while Mom went into the delivery room with Kelly.

In the waiting room was Kelly's friend, Sasha, Dad, previously known as Dad-Pete, and Theresa. We made nervous small talk about school and the weather. I mostly played with and took care of Anna.

Several hours later Mom came out to announce that the baby had arrived. She had a wide grin. "It's a girl! Her name is Angelina, and she's a big healthy baby! Nine pounds, one ounce and twenty-one inches long!"

We cheered and hugged. Dad asked, "How is Kelly doing?"

"She's doing well. We can visit. A few at a time is probably best."

I couldn't believe it. I was a thirteen-year-old aunt. Even funnier was that Anna was a four-year-old aunt!

When I walked into Kelly's room, she was lying in the bed holding baby Angelina. Angelina was beautiful with olive skin, dark hair and dark eyes. I walked toward her and said, "Hi. How are you?"

"Hey. I'm okay. Sore but okay."

"She's so beautiful!"

She thanked me as I walked up to the bed and touched Angelina's cheek and spoke softly to her. "Hi, Angelina, It's me, Auntie Casey. Welcome to our crazy family!" Kelly and I laughed.

"So what's it like to be a mom?"

She glanced up at me with tears in her eyes. "When I held her for the first time, I finally knew what love is."

Just then Mom, Dad, Anna and Sam walked back in. I smirked at Mom and Dad. "Hey, it's the grandparents!" Sam laughed and walked over to Kelly and Angelina. I studied the room and realized I wasn't sure of the last time all of us, Mom, Dad, Kelly, Sam and me, were in the same room.

———————

WE GOT BACK to the house around two o'clock in the morning after the exciting arrival of Angelina. All of us were exhausted and went straight to bed. The next day we were back to packing up the house and getting ready for the move. I only had one week left at Carter with all of my friends and spent most of my time moping around thinking that I wasn't sure what I'd do without being able to see my friends anymore; they were the only support I had. Sam said he didn't care about leaving St. Ann's but I wasn't sure I believed him.

On my last day at Carter, my friends got me balloons and cards saying they would miss me. We hugged, cried, took lots of pictures and promised to keep in touch. Before Mom picked me up I made sure I got a picture of my "We'll miss you" balloon in front of my sign, which was the Carter Middle School sign that I had started referring to as mine, since I spent so much time there waiting to be picked up.

The new house was a small two-story with peeling gray paint. The inside was even less impressive. The upstairs had a small kitchen, living room and two bedrooms on either side of the single bathroom. The downstairs was a big open room with a dirty, yet functioning bathroom. My days of having my own room were over, as I got to share a room with Anna across the hall from Mom. Sam stayed in the lower level of the house, which he thought was pretty cool, since it had its own entrance.

We started school that Monday on a chilly January day, at Franklin Junior High in Oakley. It was quite different from Carter or St. Ann's. Most of the kids were ESL, English as a second language, poor and involved with gangs.

On the first day of school, I walked across the quad toward the classrooms to whistles and shouts asking for my phone number. I tried to ignore them and keep my head down but one group of boys followed me across campus. I finally turned around and told them I didn't have a phone yet; they left me alone for a while after that.

Later in the day I walked into my new math class and saw a familiar face, Sam's. Yep, there we were in the same class. The kids were rowdy and wanted to know why we were in the same class. Sam laughed. "We're in the same class because she's a nerd and skipped a grade."

One of the boys stared at me. "Dang. You smart, huh?" I didn't feel it was necessary to go into detail how or why I skipped kindergarten. Partly because the details were a little fuzzy to me, since Mom seemed to change the story each time I asked.

I replied to the kid, "It's a long story, and it's seriously not a big deal."

The teacher with floppy, straight brown hair seemed to be able to sense the crowd getting unruly. "Okay, class, settle down. Let's welcome Sam and Casey and then let's do some algebra!"

The class groaned and sat down. I sat at my desk, annoyed. I had actually skipped a grade, but that wasn't why we were in the same grade; Sam clearly just didn't want anyone to know that he was held back, which I could understand. I just didn't appreciate the nerd reference he added and felt it was unnecessary. Either way, I certainly wasn't going to tell anyone his secret.

When the day was finally over, Sam and I took the bus home. When we got home, Mom and Anna were waiting to hear all about our first day. I grimaced. "It was the worst. I don't wanna talk about it."

Mom's mouth contorted. "Ohhh. Well, Sam, how was your first day?"

"Fine."

We had dinner in our sad little house and went to our rooms. I called Sarah from the phone in my room to tell her how awful my new school was. After I got off the phone with her, I did my homework and then cried myself to sleep.

BEFORE SCHOOL each day and at lunch, I'd hang out in the bathroom to avoid harassment from the boys. After a few weeks I met new friends, Paula and Minnie. I was happy to have someone to eat lunch with. Paula was a tall girl with blond hair and a big personality. Minnie was as her name implied. She was also blond but quite petite at four foot eight inches. Paula lived pretty close to our house and often invited me over to her house to hang out. She lived with her dad, who was friendly and often invited me to stay for dinner. Paula and Minnie made the days go by a little quicker. I still talked to Sarah almost every day and we had plans to attend another NKOTB concert in the fall. We were super excited and couldn't wait. It was the one thing I had to look forward to.

While Sam and I were adjusting to our new school, Mom was beginning to adjust to having her first job since high school. She was a waitress at the local diner. Her friend, MaryBeth who lived on the island, watched Anna while I was in school, and then I'd watch her on the weekends while Mom worked. It was a lot of change for all of us.

Sam and I couldn't wait for our eighth-grade graduation and then for summer vacation to start, until some realities set in. Soon we found out that we couldn't afford to go to the eighth-grade dance or the eighth-grade field trip to Great America with the rest of our class. We could barely afford the cap and gown we were required to wear for the ceremony. Paula must have told her dad that I couldn't go to the dance and Great America with her and Minnie, because right before graduation, Paula's dad called Mom and offered to pay for Sam and me to attend all the festivities. When she told me, I was happy and grateful but at the same time felt so ashamed. We were so poor that we now had to accept charity to go to a school dance.

Summer couldn't arrive soon enough. When it finally did, I spent most of the days babysitting Anna and talking on the phone to Sarah and Jasmine. Sometimes Paula and Minnie would come to visit and hang out with Anna and me. I had no idea what Sam was up to. He only came upstairs for food.

That summer, Mom met a man at the diner that she began dating. He was a single dad named Tom and had three little kids. He had brown hair, a funny mustache and a bit of a belly. I thought he was an okay enough guy but didn't understand why Mom thought he was so great. We only met his kids a few times, since they lived out of state and only visited during the summer. One time Tom brought over the kids, and we all went out on his boat; it was fun and it got us out of the house. Sam said he didn't want to hang out with the "Brady bunch," as he called us, so he stayed back doing whatever it was he did.

Mom seemed happy until it was time for Anna's dreaded one-year testing at the hospital. On the drive to the hospital, Mom insisted that we pray the entire way, which was about an hour and a half, that Anna's cancer wasn't back.

WE WALKED up to the information desk at Children's Hospital, and a surge of memories hit me all at once. The first memory was of our first visit, the day before Anna's surgery nearly three and a half years before; I remembered being nervous like it was the first day of school. Then I suddenly flashed to the moment, about a year into chemo, when I realized the hospital had become our second home. Now here we were a year after we found out the cancer was gone, having Anna tested to see if it was back.

I sat in the waiting room with Sam while Anna and Mom were with the doctors. I asked Sam, "Doesn't it feel weird to be back here?"

"Yep, but it doesn't exactly bring back fond memories."

"Nope. Anna doesn't even look the same anymore. She doesn't look like she did before or during chemo."

Sam gazed at the ceiling. "You're right. She looks totally different with her long dark hair and chubby cheeks. Now she's like every other bratty kid. No trace of chemo."

We both laughed. I then thought back to how we couldn't wait for her to be off chemo so that our lives could go back to normal. Instead our lives had flipped and twisted. Mom and Dad got divorced. Kelly was now a mother and no longer lived with us. We moved away from our home, and Sam and I had to start all over at a new school. Mom worked outside the home and had a new boyfriend. Everything was different.

When Anna and Mom walked through the door, I asked Anna how it went. Anna replied, "Okay, done now."

I saw that Mom was fidgety and tense, so I asked, "All okay?"

"There were no problems. Being back here, it just all comes back. I have the same worry I had the last time she was tested. I fear each time she gets tested they're going to say it's back. I'm not sure this terror will ever go away."

"Yeah, it's weird being back here."

Sam shook his head. "Can we go already?"

Anna put her hand on her hip. "Yes, let's go. Want out."

Mom led the way as we walked out of the room and down to the elevator to exit the hospital.

The next week, we were relieved to get the news that Anna was still cancer-free.

CHAPTER 28

IN THE FALL OF 1990, Sam and I took the bus to our first day of high school at Delta High School in Oakley. When we got home from school, Mom asked how our first day was. I blinked and opened my eyes wide. "It was fantastic! I love it here!"

Mom grinned apprehensively. "Really?"

I shook my head. "No, it totally sucked, just like Franklin."

"Sam?"

"I think Casey summed it up nicely."

Mom didn't seem pleased; neither Sam nor I cared. We were miserable. However, we didn't know things were about to get a whole lot worse.

A few weeks later over dinner Mom shared with us some pretty big news. Her face was lit up. "So, I have some news!"

I got excited. "We're moving?!"

Her face seemed to melt. "No, that's not the news. I'm pregnant. You are going to have a new little brother or sister!"

I sat there stunned. At first I thought maybe she was joking. How could this possibly be good news? I glanced at Sam, whose face had turned so red, I thought his head was going to explode. He didn't say a word. She went on to explain that of course, Tom was the father. However, Tom decided that he had enough children and didn't plan to be around.

Sam was so mad that Mom was bringing another kid into the house, they began fighting all the time. A few weeks after the announcement, Sam and Mom got into a big fight, which ended when Sam pushed our pregnant Mom up against the wall. Mom screamed at him to get out of the house and then called the police. When the cops arrived, Sam was downstairs. Mom explained to the police what had happened; they suggested she call our Dad and have Sam stay there for a while. She called Dad as the officers waited. The only part of the conversation I heard was, "You either take him or he's going to jail." Dad picked him up later that night.

Just when I thought things couldn't possibly get worse, it did. The divorce settlement Mom had been counting on didn't come through on account of the fact that Jasper had disappeared. He didn't show up for any of the divorce proceedings and had liquidated the jewelry store and all of his assets. Mom didn't get a dime. This put us in a bit of a financial pickle. We were unable to pay rent, and we got evicted from our crappy little house.

We moved in with Mom's friend, MaryBeth who lived on the island, for a few weeks while she figured things out. I slept on the couch while she and Anna took the spare room. At night, lying on the couch I thought, Wow, less than a year ago we had a beautiful house, friends, parents and all of our siblings together. Now it was just Mom, Anna and me. Miserable, broke and homeless. Things couldn't get worse, right? Right?!

Thankfully, we had, in fact, hit rock bottom. After school, Mom sat me down at the dining table in her friend's kitchen. "I have a plan."

I smirked. "Yeah. What's the plan?"

"I think it's best for you, and us, if we move to Lafayette. You'll get to be near your friends and be in a good school. The academics here are atrocious! Also, I plan to enroll in the accounting program at St. Mary's."

"Are you serious? We're moving back?!"

Mom grinned. "Yep!"

I couldn't believe it. I was stunned, but in a good way. Mom continued to explain that she would enroll in the accounting program at night and I would watch Anna. She further explained that this was important for our future. If she could get the accounting certificate, then she'd be able to get a good job and we'd never end up in our current situation again.

That weekend, in late November, we moved to Lafayette. We could only afford to rent a single room in a house, but I didn't care, we were back! The house itself was impressive. It was a big gray two-story house surrounded by giant trees. The lower level had separate entrances, which made it easy for our landlord, a creepy single guy with a big dog, to rent out nearly all the rooms in the house. Mom, Anna and I shared a bedroom with a private entrance until a few weeks after we moved in and the landlord took pity on us and offered to rent us a second room cheap. Anna and I again shared a room, and Mom had a room that she would share with the baby, when it arrived.

I started at Camarino High School, in Moraga, despite it being a twenty-minute drive. Mom had agreed to let me go there instead of Salano in Lafayette, which was only a five-minute drive, because Sarah and Jasmine were there. Things were improving in a major way. I was actually happy again.

Shortly after we moved to Lafayette, we started to see Kelly and Angelina more. Kelly would come by and visit, or she'd come by and drop off Angelina for us to babysit. Now that Kelly had the baby, she was taking continuation classes to work toward her high school diploma. Things were going well for her, and she seemed happy too.

Despite the rest of us recovering and thriving, Sam's situation seemed to get worse. Shortly after moving back in with Dad,

Sam got busted for drugs and was now serving a one-year sentence in a boys' ranch, which was essentially a juvenile detention facility. I would have loved to have gone up to that judge and said, "Hey! Do you have any idea what our lives have been like the last few years? Give'm a break! Time served, dude!" It didn't seem like there was a crime he could possibly commit, with the exception of maybe rape or murder, that he hadn't already done time for.

Mom seemed heartbroken over Sam's incarceration despite their explosive fight. It didn't help that it happened right before Anna's one-and-a-half-year testing at the hospital. She was a nervous wreck, as usual, but got through it. By the end of 1990, we were celebrating the new upturn in our lives and that Anna remained cancer-free.

We rang in the year 1991 drinking sparkling cider and watching the ball drop on TV. I was hopeful that 1991 would be a great year. Despite my having to watch Anna all the time so that Mom could go to school and study, things were going well. I didn't start worrying again until Mom pointed out that once the baby was here, I was going to have to watch it too. It hit me that soon I was going to have to babysit two kids with every minute of my free time. None of it seemed fair. Mom explained, during one of our recurring fights, that we were family, and family helps out.

A few months later when Cara was born, it was quite different from when Anna was born. For starters, we were in a hospital, and in the delivery room it was just Mom and me with the doctor and nurses. By default, I was Mom's birthing coach. The doctor even asked if I wanted to cut the umbilical cord. I said, "Why not," took the scissors from his hand and cut. I grimaced as blood splattered all over my white blouse.

Once she was freed from the umbilical cord, the doctor handed Cara over to the nurse, who washed her off. When she finished, she handed Cara to Mom. Mom kissed Cara on the top of her head, and then I said to her, "You know, she kinda looks like an alien."

Mom chuckled. "I think she gets that from Tom." We both laughed.

A few minutes later, Mom let me hold Cara. While holding her, I gazed down at her big brown eyes, squishy pink face and oversize forehead. Despite her alien looks, I instantly fell in love with her. Later, Mom's friend Stacy from the accounting program, who had driven us to the hospital when Mom went into labor, brought Anna by to see Cara. Anna and I stood together, hand in hand, gazing at our new baby sister.

Mom was determined to finish the accounting program as soon as humanly possible, so she went back to school, during the evenings, when Cara was just six weeks old. This meant that I got to be a full-time nanny to a six-week-old and a five-year-old, except for when I was in school myself. Cara was a pretty good baby, and Anna seemed to calm down a little after Cara was born. I liked to think that the three of us worked together as a team with a single goal: survival.

When Cara fussed, Anna would help fetch diapers, bottles, toys or anything to make her stop crying. When nothing else worked, I'd rock Cara from side to side and sing her New Kids on the Block songs. Anna would either sit next to us and sing along or play quietly in the room.

With a newborn and school, driving me out to Camarino was getting to be too much for Mom. For the second time my freshman year of high school, I transferred to a new school. The drive to Salano was only five minutes, not to mention across the street from what would be Anna's school in the fall. I already knew most of the kids at Salano from when I was at Carter, so it wasn't too terrible. I got to reunite with Patty and all the other friends I had left behind.

That summer, Kelly turned eighteen and moved into her own apartment with Angelina. She was working at a retail shop, going to school and overall doing well. When she wasn't working, she would come by the house in Lafayette, and we'd have fun catching up and watching Anna, Angelina and Cara play together.

Since I was on babysitting duty all summer, Sarah and Jasmine would come out and hang out with Anna, Cara and me. We had fun trying to get Anna to sing NKOTB songs, and everyone loved holding Cara. It wasn't long before Anna and Cara were part of our crew. For my fifteenth birthday, the whole family, including Mom, Anna, Cara, Kelly, Angelina, Sarah, Jasmine and Patty, went out to dinner to celebrate. To outsiders, we must have seemed like an unlikely bunch.

In the fall of 1991, Anna started kindergarten across the street from my high school. It was soon apparent that she was far behind the other kids. Anna had never gone to preschool, and most of her early years were spent in the hospital. The school notified Mom that she would need to go into special resource classes. Mom was thankful that the school had such resources available, as many schools didn't.

For me, sophomore year seemed to go off without a hitch. It was nice to return to the same school. I had my friends to hang out and eat lunch with. I was never harassed or bullied. A lot of my teachers understood my situation at home, which was that I was the primary caretaker for my sisters after school and on the weekends. Many of my teachers would ask how I was doing with everything as well as inquire about my sisters.

Despite living in a stranger's house with new roommates coming and going, we started to get used to it and we had settled in. It wasn't until Sam had gotten out of the ranch that our harmony seemed to be disrupted again. Mom invited Sam to come live with us, renting another room in the big house.

When Sam moved in, he also started at Salano with me. Kids I had known for years asked if we were twins, as if he was my secret twin just now to be revealed. Sam instantly gravitated toward the only bad kids in the school. Most of the kids were nerdy athletes, and nearly all were college bound. Not Sam's friends. Four houses down from us, which happened to be the worst house on the street, was where one of the kid's lived. What were the odds? It wasn't long before Sam was getting into trouble again.

In the early spring of 1992, Sam got expelled from Salano High School for starting a fight with another kid and moved back in with Dad. Mom was disappointed that she and Sam couldn't get along and he was getting in trouble again but told us we needed to move ahead and not let anything stop us from achieving success.

A few months later, Mom graduated from the accounting certificate program; Kelly, Angelina, Anna, Cara and I attended the ceremony. Soon after graduation, Mom had gotten a job at a prestigious accounting firm and we could finally afford a place of our own. We told our creepy landlord, "See ya!" and that summer we moved into a two-bedroom apartment. I shared a room with Anna and Cara, while Mom had her own room. We still didn't have much money, like we couldn't afford a phone or TV, but at least we didn't have to live with strangers anymore. Since Anna, Cara and I were a survival team, we made it work.

Despite our successes, later that summer, Sam got into more serious trouble. He and a friend had allegedly participated in an armed robbery. Sam's alleged role was the robber. We heard about the incident from the police, who couldn't locate him. One day, Kelly, Angelina and I were over at Dad's visiting when we saw The Five O'Clock News flash sketches of Sam and his friend on the TV. That's a real family moment for you. When the police finally caught them, Sam and his friend were both charged and convicted of felonies and sentenced to juvenile hall, not to be released prior to their eighteenth birthdays. Mom and Dad both said they were lucky to be charged as minors and didn't say another word about it.

In the fall of 1992, I started my junior year of high school. Our new morning routine was reminiscent of when Kelly, Sam and I were together. After the three of us kids got ready in the morning, we'd drop off Cara at day care, then Anna at school and then lastly I'd be dropped off across the street at my high school.

That year Mom finally let me get a part-time job at the local mall, since Anna had after school care and Cara was in daycare. I'd take the bus after school to go to work. I liked working and having some money of my own. It allowed me to pay for things like going out with my friends, clothes, a TV and a phone. Don't get me wrong: I still babysat a lot but not nearly as much as before. Now when I babysat it was more fun because I had some money and the kids were a little older. We could get pizza for dinner and hang out at the mall with my friends. Anna loved to shop, and Cara loved being pushed around in the stroller.

Cara quickly became a bit of a trickster in her young age. Knowing that I was sensitive about people thinking that I was a teenage mother, whenever someone would ask if she was my baby, I would start to explain, "No, she's my sister . . ."

But then she'd point at me and say, "Mom," followed by an evil grin.

After the person would flash a strange expression and walk away, Cara would point and laugh. "I said, You Mom." And then laugh some more. It was hard to get mad, since she was so darn cute. She had outgrown her alien baby beginnings and was now an adorable chubby-cheeked, brown-eyed, strawberry blonde toddler.

In the spring of 1993, Sam turned eighteen and was released from juvenile hall and moved back in with Dad.

A few months later all of us, Mom, Dad, Kelly, Sam, Anna, Cara and Angelina, attended and celebrated Kelly's high school graduation. She was a year late, but considering she had a three-year-old and a job, it was not only an accomplishment, it was impressive and a testament to her will and determination.

That same summer I turned seventeen and got my driver's license. I didn't have a car, but I still liked the idea that I could drive sometimes. Little did I know that getting my license meant that starting in the fall, I would take over carpool duty. Mom was able to take BART to work, so I drove Cara to day care, dropped Anna off at school and then went to my senior year of high school.

Despite babysitting and carpool duty, senior year was great. I had money from my job, so I got to participate in all the senior activities without needing a donation from a friend's parent who felt sorry for me. We were seniors with our whole lives ahead of us, and I had my plan to start at Mount Diablo Community College, the local junior college in Pleasant Hill, in the fall with some of my best friends. It was exciting.

In the spring of 1994, I graduated from Salano High School. After staying up all night at Grad Night, Patty, Kate and I left for a camping trip to Lake Tahoe. It hadn't occurred to us that maybe it wasn't a great plan, considering none of us had ever camped before. Around the campfire we dined on McDonald's and laughed about the time Patty and I had biked down to the athletic club back in seventh grade. When our tent fell down in the middle of the night, we laughed until we cried.

In the fall of 1994, I started at Mount Diablo Community College, still living at home and on carpool duty. I had to explain to some of my professors that I had to leave in the middle of class to pick up my sister from school and then return. They didn't seem happy about it but allowed it at the same time.

It was a big year for Anna too. When she started third grade, she had graduated from the resource program and was in regular classes full-time. In addition to graduating from resource, it was time for Anna to go back to Children's Hospital for her five-year testing. All of us went to the hospital with her. I stayed in the waiting room with Cara while Mom went in with Anna.

I sat there and thought about the last five years. It seemed like a dream, or a nightmare, depending on the memory. All we had endured, yet here we were today. Mom had a good job, Kelly was a high school graduate, I was in college, Anna was a thriving third grader and we had another sister! Cara didn't even know about Anna's cancer or what it was like to live with a baby on chemo. I gazed at Cara playing with her doll and smiled to myself.

My heart sank when Mom and Anna walked through the door. Even though it had been more than five years since Anna finished chemo, Mom still had the same panic-stricken look on her face as the first time they tested her for cancer. I asked Mom how she was feeling. She said, "I will never get used to this. I don't think I'll ever stop worrying."

"How likely is it to come back after five years?"

"Not likely, but possible. We'll never really be in the clear."

I glanced over at Anna. My goodness, she was almost nine years old. She seemed to be a different child from that chemo kid running the halls with her IV pole. I asked Anna how it went. "It was fine. I got a pokey, and I'm ready to get out of here. Mom said we could go to the mall and get some new clips."

Mom laughed. "To the mall!"

I laughed, picked up Cara and followed Mom and Anna out the door.

The next week we got the news that Anna was five years cancer-free. She was in full remission.

EPILOGUE

THIS PAST YEAR, Anna celebrated her thirtieth birthday. Being Anna, she got to choose whatever it was she wanted to do. She said she wanted a tea party, and then she said she wanted to go on a trip, and then she said she wanted to go to Disneyland. What were we to do? The only thing we could. Mom, Anna, Cara and I flew down to Anaheim for high tea at the Disneyland Hotel. In addition to going on the rides, having high tea and drinking cocktails, we spent the weekend reminiscing on thirty years of Anna and all we had gone through. It was hard to believe that all of it actually happened.

Anna didn't have an easy path, even after beating cancer. The years of harsh chemotherapy drugs caused additional medical issues ranging from benign tumors to her needing major reconstructive surgery of her jaw, which caused her to miss an entire semester of sophomore year of high school. Despite her medical issues, she excelled at school and always had friends. I think having beat cancer gave her a different perspective on life.

After she graduated high school and started college, she decided to take a break to pursue her aesthetician's license. Mom was not thrilled about this, as she had always stressed the importance of a college degree. Anna's response to Mom's objection was, "This is what I love to do—doesn't it make sense I follow my passion?" I fully agreed with her. I told her, "Hey, you are young, you can always go back." Which is exactly what she did. After getting her aesthetician's license and trying out that career, she decided it wasn't what she wanted to do after all. A few years later she graduated with a bachelor of science in business communications. She went on to have a successful career in sales, buy a condo and get married.

At her wedding, our whole family, Jasper, Agatha, Kelly, Sam and I, were reunited for the first time since Mom and Jasper's divorce twenty-five years earlier. We saw one another again when Anna gave birth to her first child and he had his first and second birthdays. I used to think that our family revolved around Anna and the rest of us were just "the other forgotten kids." I realized that I got it wrong. It wasn't that our family revolved around Anna, it was that Anna brought all of us together. We flocked to her. From the day she was born, all of us gathered around Mom and the midwife, waiting for her arrival. She brought us together. She made us a family.

Watching her now, I still see glimpses of that chemo kid leading us down the hall, pushing her IV pole and stopping at every person she would meet, saying, "Hi! Hi! Hi!" Simply put, she's still a diva. In addition to loving sparkles and being center stage, she's beautiful, funny, intelligent and outgoing. Since she became a mother her warm and loving nature shines brightly. Her son is a little-boy version of her in both looks and personality. At two years old, he likes to pick out his clothes and loves shoes. He's loving, smart, self-assured and a bit sassy. We all pretend we don't know where he got that from. Anna currently lives in the Bay Area with her family and is a successful vlogger and DIY expert.

CARA WAS the lucky one of the bunch. Anna's cancer was before she was born, and she was too young to remember the hard times. Not to say growing up without her father wasn't difficult, because it was. Tom never did come around. However, when Cara was in high school, she got the opportunity to meet Tom's other children. Not long after having a relationship with her other siblings did she get to meet the rest of her father's family. She is grateful to get to know them despite her father still only playing a small role in her life. Our stepfather filled in at father-daughter dances and other similar events over the years, which I know was special for her.

Anna, Cara and I still spend a lot of time together and are close, despite our significant age differences. I was sitting at a work lunch several years ago and one of my coworkers told us that people should have their children close together in age, otherwise they'll have nothing in common and won't have a relationship when they're older. I said, "Actually. I'm fourteen years older than my baby sister, and we are very close and see each other all the time."

Despite being the only kid in my high school who had the responsibility of helping raise my two younger siblings, I'm not sure I would change that experience if I could. The bond between Anna, Cara and me, aka the survival team, is something I will always cherish. Sometimes we just sit and laugh until we cry about some of the craziness that we went through. Others would find it sad, but we laugh because we know we have come so far.

Last year, Cara graduated with a bachelor of arts in theater and is currently pursuing her dream of becoming a comedic actress. Considering she was pranking me at the age of two, this should not have come as a surprise to anyone. Cara lives in North Hollywood.

IF IT WASN'T obvious by Kelly's drive to receive her high school diploma while working and taking care of a three-year-old, she has gone on to do many great things. By the time Kelly turned thirty-eight, she had four children, ages twenty-one, twelve, ten and six, as well as a one-year-old grandchild. That same year, while working and taking care of her three youngest children, she graduated with a bachelor of arts in business administration.

The road she took wasn't an easy one. Most women in her situation would have given up or settled for something less. She has commented that she pushed forward to make a better life for herself and her children. Knowing that a life without education wasn't going to provide for her and her family, she charged ahead despite the long hours, emotional and financial costs—not to mention the people who told her she couldn't possibly get a college degree while working and taking care of three kids. Kelly is pretty active in the community and volunteers in many organizations. I'm always telling her to relax and have some fun; I'm not sure she knows how.

All of her children are truly wonderful, and that is my unbiased opinion. I always want to steal them, but I don't, mostly because I know I'd get caught. Her oldest, Angelina, is one of the most lovely and warmhearted people I've ever known. She's a loving mother and an aspiring vlogger and fashionista. Her second oldest, a brilliant young lady, is about to graduate high school. Her current dilemma is which top-ranked university to attend; the poor girl, there are just too many choices when you're a multitalented straight-A student. Kelly's third child is her spitting image in both looks and personality. Whip smart and full of attitude! Her youngest is a sweet and smart young man who loves magic. I've seen his tricks; he's pretty good.

Whenever my friends are at one of our family gatherings, the first thing they say—this is from multiple occasions from multiple friends—is, "Wow! Kelly has some beautiful children." It's true, on the inside and out. Kelly currently lives in the Bay

Area with her three youngest children and works in the biotech industry.

THE FAMILY HAS BEEN in and out of contact with Sam for the last twenty-five years. He had a rough time growing up and has a lot of anger toward our parents and by proxy our entire family. I don't judge nor pretend to not know why he has the anger he does. Some of the most painful childhood memories I have were of how he was treated.

He shocked the heck out of everyone about fifteen years ago when he and his girlfriend announced they were expecting a baby. It was around this time that he started to come around the family again. When things didn't work out with the girlfriend, he distanced himself from the family again.

When I say he distanced himself from the family, I don't mean his son. He is the most loving and involved father; it's shocking. He certainly didn't have a role model of how to be a great dad. I like to think he treats his son like he would have liked to have been treated. His son is now a fifteen-year-old star baseball player and honor roll student. Not to mention, the kid is a sweetheart. Since we don't see Sam often, we don't get to see his son either. Years can pass before we see Sam Jr. in person, but whenever we do, he's a sweet, funny, polite and intelligent young man. Sam is a proud father, as he should be. Thank goodness for social media! With social media, I always get to see what Sam and Sam Jr. are up to. Sam currently lives in the Bay Area and is a full-time college student.

SHORTLY AFTER WE received news of Anna's five-year remission, we were able to locate Jasper. The details are a little fuzzy concerning his whereabouts, but it is believed he was serving a prison sentence related to drugs. Although Jasper continued to struggle with his own demons, his priorities always seemed to include Anna. He was able to start visitation with her around her ninth birthday; once visitation began it never stopped. He wasn't like my dad, who said he'd pick us up and just not show up. Jasper wasn't a holidays-only father. From the time he came back into Anna's life, he gave her everything and anything he could.

After hearing of the struggles Anna and the family went through after he disappeared, he has expressed regret and a lot of remorse. A few years ago, Jasper wrote a letter to me with a formal apology and the acknowledgment of the hurt he put us through. I appreciated the letter, but I didn't respond. Maybe one day I'll send him a thank-you letter or a copy of this book so that he knows that I am not angry or hurt anymore. I like to think the struggles and pain we live through make us who we are. I am who I am partly because of him, and for that I am grateful.

It makes me happy to know that after a lifelong struggle with a heroin addiction, he has been clean for more than five years and plays a significant role in Anna's life. We see him at all of Anna's events, like her college graduation and the birth of her son. He is always polite and asks how we are doing. Jasper never remarried or had any other children. He currently lives in the Bay Area and works as a property manager.

AGATHA, our matriarch, wasn't perfect. As nobody is. As children, we forget that our parents aren't super humans who know all the right things to do. Parents are children like ourselves who ended up having children when they got a little older. We often joke that Mom didn't teach us how to cook or change a tire, but she definitely taught us how to have fun.

Although definitely true, it wasn't all she taught us. By

divorcing Jasper, she showed us that we didn't have to settle for a life of abuse and unhappiness. She showed us that being poor and on welfare was temporary. She showed us that through education we could make a better life for ourselves. She showed us that you never give up until you reach your dreams. She showed us how to be strong. She showed us how to be survivors. The important point here is that she didn't tell us these things; she showed us.

Prior to Agatha's children, not a single member of her family held a college degree, nor stressed the importance of obtaining higher education. Yet, since I can remember, she pushed us to do well in school and drilled into us the importance of going to college. Every day, I'm not exaggerating, it was every day, she dropped us off at school and said, "Have a truly academic day!" It has become a family saying, and we often joke about it among ourselves and the next generation. It shouldn't have surprised anyone that the first four-year degree obtained by a member of the family would be by one of Agatha's children. Of Agatha's five children, four have obtained a four-year college degree and one advanced degree.

It was a lifelong dream of Agatha's to obtain a four-year college degree. As kids, she would tell us that she had plans to go to college but then got pregnant with Kelly instead. Throughout our childhood and adulthood she had taken classes but never transferred from community college or obtained a degree. She often joked that she had been going to college for forty years. We don't joke anymore—well, not about that.

Last year, Agatha obtained her associate of arts degree and has since transferred to the University of California at Berkeley. She is currently a senior, set to graduate with a bachelor of arts in English. She often jokes that she is a senior who is a senior . . . in college. She has already started getting the order forms and information for commencement. The new joke is that she is going to refuse to graduate. She says, "What, are they trying to get rid of me? I've only been here a little over a year! I love it and don't want to leave. Just let'm try to get rid of me. I'll tell'm to go talk to the community college—it took them forty years to get rid of me!" This is followed by hearty laugher from her and everyone around her.

On one of our weekly runs, Mom told me that she wanted to write a book about her family from the Great Depression. She told me that my grandfather had told her that for a whole year all they ate was peaches. I told her I doubted that was accurate but that if she was going to write a book it shouldn't be about her family eating peaches. I told her she should write the story of her life; it's much more interesting and inspiring. She seemed surprised. I think sometimes it is difficult for us to understand the impact we make on the world around us.

Agatha continued to work in her career as an accountant and ultimately retired at the age of fifty-eight from a government position. Currently she is remarried and living in a home, that she owns, and is working in the private sector in addition to being a full-time college student. If work, married life and school isn't keeping her busy, she enjoys spending her time with her family that now includes five children, seven grandchildren, one great-grandchild, two Chihuahuas and a Shih Tzu. Agatha lives in the Bay Area and is an accountant and full-time university student.

WHEN I THINK BACK to what my family has overcome, I feel a tremendous amount of pride. Everything life threw at us we beat. Whether it was cancer, poverty, abuse, lack of education or living three to a room in a creepy dude's house, we beat it. Actually, we didn't just beat it, we killed it. Each of us has overcome momentous challenges and has come out better than before, better than anyone could have imagined.

In my own life, I like to think that all of my experiences

shaped who I am today. Anna's cancer and the time we spent in the hospital shaped my future significantly. When I entered college, my goal was to become a pediatric oncologist. After I transferred to a four-year university in the Bay Area, I volunteered at Children's Hospital in Oakland during my junior and senior years and worked in the very playroom I frequented as a kid. Although I opted against medical school along the way, I decided I still wanted to be in the health-care field so that I could make a difference in patients' lives. After obtaining a bachelor of science in chemistry and later a master of business administration, I worked in the biotech industry for many years and was quite successful.

Yet, there was still something missing. I wasn't happy. I came home one day and said no "Hello, how are you" to my husband but instead, "Everything sucks! My job sucks! This place sucks! Everything sucks! Statistically I should be on welfare or working at some dead-end job at the mall. I didn't work my ass off and beat every statistic to have a life that sucks!"

After my rant, I thought back to a few months earlier when Cara had decided to move to Hollywood to continue the pursuit of her dreams. She told me she was nervous about it because she'd been in the Bay Area her whole life surrounded by her family and friends and was afraid it wouldn't work out. I told her, "You're young! Follow your dreams! What's the worst that can happen?" I realized maybe I ought to start taking my own advice.

A few months later I quit my high-paying corporate job to pursue my dream of becoming a full-time writer. After all, what is the worst that could happen? I've already gone through some of the most traumatic experiences a person can go through and came out ahead. I've gotten to the point in my life that I know there isn't anything I can't overcome. I know that I am too strong to be broken. After all, I came from a family of survivors, and it's pretty obvious, we *can't* be broken.

PLEASE LEAVE A REVIEW!

Thank you for reading *We Can't Be Broken*! I hope you enjoyed reading it as much as I loved writing it. If you did, I would greatly appreciate if you could post a short review.

Reviews are crucial for any author and can make a huge difference in visibility of current and future works. Reviews allow us to continue doing what we love, *writing stories.* Not to mention, I would be forever grateful!

To leave a review, please go to the Amazon page for *We Can't Be Broken* and scroll down to the bottom of the Amazon page to the review section. It will read, "Share your thoughts with other customers," with a button below that reads, "Write a customer review." Click the "Write a customer review" button and write away!

Thank you!

COMING SOON BY H.K. CHRISTIE

Picking up seven years after the end of *We Can't Be Broken*, a novel inspired by true events - *Where I'm Supposed To Be* follows Casey through her late twenties as she navigates marriage, career, and defining who she is and what she really wants from life.

When Casey and husband, Jason, decide to add a new addition to their home, a feisty Shih-Tzu named Roxie, a glimmer of hope resonates for the first time in their young marriage.

Months into life with Roxie, Casey and Jason's marriage is on the rocks and they're confronted with Jason's surprising diagnosis. Not soon after, Casey's deepest fears come to fruition leading her to question herself, her choices, and all she thought she knew.

Greeted with the reality that life will never be the same, she wonders what's next?

RELEASE DATE: AUGUST 24, 2018

JOIN MY NEWSLETTER CLUB

Join my newsletter club to be the first to hear about upcoming novels, new releases, giveaways, promotions, and more!

It's completely free to sign up and you'll never be spammed by me, you can opt out easily at any time.

Sign up today by going to
www.authorhkchristie.com

ABOUT THE AUTHOR

H.K. Christie is the author of *We Can't Be Broken*, a novel inspired by her own family's battle with childhood cancer. She found her passion for writing when she embarked on a one-woman habit breaking experiment. Although she didn't break her habit she did rediscover a love of writing and has been at it ever since.

She is a native and current resident of the San Francisco Bay Area and a two time graduate of Saint Mary's College of California. Before becoming a writer, she worked in the Biotech industry in various roles ranging from scientist to project manager. She currently lives in the Bay Area and is working on her next set of novels, a series of stories about the adult lives of Casey and Anna.

www.authorhkchristie.com

ACKNOWLEDGMENTS

This is a work of fiction. However, it was inspired by my own family's battle with neuroblastoma and what seemed like, at the time, never ending struggles. Like Casey, my younger sister was diagnosed with neuroblastoma at the age of sixteen months old. Our family faced many hard years during and after her cancer, but in the end we survived. Not only did we survive, we are stronger than ever. This book is dedicated to my family.

While writing this story I learned many things. Most notably: writing is hard. Second: writing *a book* is hard. Third: without the support of your friends and family you're doomed.

I'd like to thank all of my family and friends who have supported me on this project.

I'd like to thank my critique partners, Jon Olsen and Juliann Brown. I think someone once said, "your book will never be worse than your first draft." Jon and Juliann were troopers. These two agreed to read this book at it's worst and helped me shape it into a better story. Without the two of you, I'm not sure my story would have made *any* sense. Not only do I thank you for your invaluable feedback but also for your continued love and support.

I'd like to thank my beta readers: Jon Olsen, Juliann Brown, Serina Santoleri-Costanza, Barbara Carson, Jennifer Jarrett, Dusty Fox, Suzanne Stadler, Kaitlyn Cornell and Monique Lazzarini. I gave these wonderful people only two weeks to read the book and provide full comments as well as complete a questionnaire. To my surprise, they all did it! This awesome bunch of people provided me with extremely thoughtful and detailed feedback. Betas, I appreciate your time and effort more than I can put into words, but I'll try since I'm a writer now. All of you have made me a better writer and I am eternally grateful. How's that?

I'd like to thank Tricia Callahan for the detailed comments and explanations that accompanied her copyedit. They were extremely helpful for this new writer. I thank you and look forward to working with you on future projects.

I'd like to thank Michael Rehder who designed the beautiful cover. Mike, I appreciate your patience in guiding me through the process and helping me find the best concept for the story. I absolutely love it!

Last but not least, I'd like to thank the wonderful nurses and doctors at Children's Hospital in Oakland, California. Without your heart, expertise and care, I'm not sure this story would have had a happy ending. In addition, a special thank you to Dr. James Betts, my sister's surgeon and our family's hero, who not only saved my sister's life but countless others throughout out his career.

Made in the USA
San Bernardino, CA
16 August 2018